A Splash

of

Substance

by Elizabeth Maddrey

Other Books by Elizabeth Maddrey

Arcadia Valley Romance – Baxter Family Bakery Series

Loaves & Wishes (in *Romance Grows in Arcadia Valley*)

Muffins & Moonbeams

Cookies & Candlelight (September 2017)

*Donuts & Daydreams (*March 2018)

The 'Operation Romance' Series

Operation Mistletoe

Operation Valentine

Operation Fireworks

Operation Back-to-School

The 'Taste of Romance' Series

A Splash of Substance

A Pinch of Promise

A Dash of Daring

A Handful of Hope

A Tidbit of Trust (Summer 2017)

The 'Grant Us Grace' Series

Joint Venture

Wisdom to Know

Courage to Change

Serenity to Accept

The 'Remnants' Series:

Faith Departed

Hope Deferred

Love Defined

Stand alone novellas

Kinsale Kisses: An Irish Romance

For the most recent listing of all my books, please visit my website.

For Tim

Just because you're you.

She could do this. Paige Jackson smoothed a hand over the neat bun at the nape of her neck and threw back her shoulders. She let out a breath, flicked a ball of lint off her black A-line skirt, and clutched her portfolio to her chest. The contract was all but hers, she just had to make a good impression on the guy in charge. *What's his name?* Her mind went blank. *Oh no.*

The moisture evaporated from her mouth as grasshoppers started up a conga line in her stomach.

"Can I help you?" The woman at the desk had to be in her sixties. Steel-grey hair cut close to her head that somehow still managed a whiff of femininity was her most welcoming asset.

"Um. Yes. I'm Paige Jackson, the owner of Taste and See Catering. I have an appointment…"

"I'll let him know you're here. Have a seat." A glint of something—it couldn't be humor, could it?—flashed in the woman's ice-blue eyes before she picked up the phone.

Paige hugged her leather folder and turned to study the expensively framed pictures on the wall. All featured the Senator with some dignitary or other politically important person. But her eyes were drawn to the tall, handsome man, probably in his late twenties, who stood in the background of most of the photographs. What was it about the stylishly spiked brown hair and dark eyes that made him stand out? Or was it the confidence that sparked off him?

"Ms. Jackson?"

Paige turned at the rich baritone, her breath catching in her throat. The photos didn't do his height, or his confidence, justice. With his height and build, if he hadn't played football growing up, his high school had missed out on a killer receiver. Unless he was uncoordinated. Or slow. She swallowed the saliva that had pooled in her mouth and extended a hand. "Hi. Paige, please."

"Jackson." He took her hand in his firm grip.

"Paige is fine, really."

His lips curved into the ghost of a smile, causing the barest promise of a dimple in his left cheek. "And I'm Jackson. Jackson Trent. Why don't you follow me back to my office and we'll look over your proposal?"

"Of course." Now she remembered his name. Though the woman who called had simply said Mr. Trent, Paige had gone online to look up the Senator's staff. Hadn't her roommate even made a joke about the Jackson thing? She followed Jackson down a long hallway lined with offices. Any wall space was covered with patriotic art or more photos of the Senator at events.

"Here we are." Jackson gestured for her to precede him into the small space. Had it been a supply closet before he jammed a desk into it? "Excuse the mess."

There wasn't room for a mess. Papers littered the desk, but it was more the debris of someone with too much to do and too little space. She sat in the guest chair and drew the menu plans out of her portfolio. "These are the menu options I worked up. The call for proposals wasn't specific about the type of meal you were hoping to have, so I worked up two plated menus and two buffet-style."

Jackson nodded, snatched the papers from her hand, and leaned against his desk. "It wasn't specific because the Senator hasn't decided yet. I think she's hoping to see a menu that tempts her and choose based on that."

"Ah." Paige licked her lips. "I was somewhat surprised that the hotel you listed was willing for you to bring in an outside caterer. Don't they generally cater things in-house?"

"They do. And they put in a proposal as well. But the Senator doesn't want the same-old hotel dinner fundraiser that every politician in D.C. puts on. The hotel isn't a firm venue, either. We're exploring some options that might be outdoors. Would that be a problem?"

"Not necessarily." Paige subtly wiped her sweaty palms along the side of her legs. "Though it does raise some questions about the kitchen. If I need to bring everything prepared, with no on-site kitchen space, a buffet is really my preference. Transporting chafing dishes and food to the venue is simpler than trying to plate somewhere without a kitchen. With a buffet, it's a simple matter of keeping things warmed appropriately and making sure nothing runs out."

"All right, we'll keep that in mind." He pursed his lips as his eyes roved over her suggested menus. "These definitely aren't the typical fare I'm used to seeing for events. Do people really eat beef tongue?"

She tensed to keep her shoulders from slumping. He hadn't read any of the information about her company and its principles, had he? "They do. It's an incredibly tender meat when it's done right and half the time, people don't realize what it is. One of the goals of Taste and See Catering is to maximize our stewardship of the Earth in our cooking. When I purchase beef, I buy a share of a cow and use all the cuts that come from that share. For an event of this size, even avoiding any of the inferior cuts, I'll end up with the tongue. It makes a great appetizer."

"What size cow is going to give you a hundred steaks?"

Paige sighed. "There isn't one. Even in the plated option, you'll notice that individual steaks—or chicken breasts or whatever—isn't an option. That's simply not in line with how my business runs."

Jackson scratched his chin as he looked at her. He gave a brief nod. "Clearly I need to re-read your initial proposal more carefully."

She gave a tight smile. "If it ends up changing your mind, I understand. Not everyone is comfortable with making an effort to live gently."

"I'll be in touch by the end of the week." Jackson motioned toward the door. "Let me show you out."

Paige banged her fists on the steering wheel. What a waste of time. She'd spent practically every evening for nearly a month on her proposal for the Senator, and that didn't take into consideration the week she'd spent praying about submitting an offer in the first place. Or the three hours her favorite instructor from culinary school had spent with her on a video call. It was a vicious cycle. She needed a high-profile event like this to get more clients. And she needed more clients if she was going to stay in business. Catering companies filled more pages in the phone book than she cared to count, and that didn't include smaller businesses like her own that hadn't bothered with the book and had just setup shop online.

The handful of personal chef clients she kept happy provided only a little more than she needed to pay her half of the rent and utilities. Some days, filling the car with gas to get to her appointments was an iffy proposition. She *needed* this event. And it was very possible—probable even—that it had just tumbled out of her grasp.

Her phone chimed with an incoming text.

Call as soon as you're done and tell me how it went.

Paige sighed and hit the call button. Slipping her Bluetooth headset over her ear, she started the car and backed out of the twenty-dollar parking spot she'd managed to snag in a lot near the Senate office buildings. She could've parked at Union Station for less, but that would have meant walking in shoes that were better suited for sitting. Even if they were professional and went with her suit she wasn't hiking around D.C. in the things if she could help it. At the end of the day, the extra six dollars for this parking space wasn't going to matter one way or another if she had to close.

"You're done already?" Clara, Paige's former instructor turned mentor and friend, sucked a breath through her teeth. "It either went incredibly well or... not so much."

"Ding ding. We have a winner with option number two." Paige frowned at a slow-moving truck and slammed her foot on the accelerator, dashing in front of it and squeaking through a light that she'd term orangey-red. Provided a cop hadn't seen her. Or those blasted cameras they had all over the place in DC.

"Why would they have you come in with menus if they weren't going with you? That doesn't make a whole lot of sense. Tell me what happened."

Paige recounted the conversation with Jackson. "It's not that I didn't get the event, necessarily. He just has to go back and actually read my proposal. Seems to me, despite any protestations to the contrary, the senator doesn't actually want to stray too far from the typical fundraising meal where everyone gets their own slab of cow and no one thinks about the waste that goes into preparing the meal."

"Hmmm. Did you consider... let's say 'setting aside'... the strength of your convictions just this once? In the name of getting business? You can't save the world with your catering company if you go belly up."

Paige slapped the steering wheel. She wasn't going to be the crazy person laying on her horn, but good grief, would it kill the other drivers to pay attention to the lights and go when they turned green? It was hard enough to dodge the tourists that crowded the streets like clueless cattle, totally oblivious to the little things like cars needing to drive there. "I'm already selling out plenty, thank you, by even bidding on this event. I mean really, politics? What was I thinking?"

"You were thinking that you need a chance to network with people who have parties and routinely use caterers. Those people, at least in Washington DC, are most likely going to have something to do with politics. Unless you're ready to take your father up on his offer, this is good business, not selling out. It's one event... "

"That I may not even get now." Paige cranked the wheel hard to the left, cutting off a commuter van, and sped onto the Interstate.

"Perhaps. But if you *do* get the event, it's only one. One event done in a more traditional manner isn't going to condemn you to the ranks of people who don't care about the planet. And if you're able to make contacts, well, then you actually have a business to build your platform on."

Maybe Clara was right, but it still didn't sit well. A typical cow could provide maybe twenty New York strips. A fundraising event like this, even if it was "only" a hundred people, meant five, possibly six, cows And what happened to the rest of the beef? Did it get used? There was no way to know when you bought that way. Presumably it got sold, but when she dealt with the Higgenbotham Farm, Paige knew they were only slaughtering what would be used. In its entirety. She had no way to store five cows worth of other beef cuts just to get a hundred steaks. Besides, if she started out serving in a non-sustainable way, wouldn't new clients expect that same type of thing?

"I don't know, Clara. Having spent so much time reading up on sustainability, I can't go back now. I mean, sure, I'm not exactly living the dream like the girls at Green Acres Farm in Idaho, but I'm doing the best I can with where I am. How much back-pedaling am I supposed to do just to get my business going?"

"That's something only you can answer. Just make sure you're not letting pride run the show."

Pride? "What do you mean? I'm not… "

"Paige. I love you. You know that. You were one of my best and favorite students. It's why I took you under my wing after you graduated. But this sustainability thing—it's not that I don't believe it has merits—you've just taken it to an extreme. It's good to have principles. It's good to want to change the world. But you need to be less rigid, more willing to bend when it's warranted. Just think about it."

Paige swung the car across two lanes and squeezed onto the exit ramp with a heavy sigh. "All right. I'll think about it. Thanks, Clara."

"Let me know as soon as you hear something."

"Will do." Paige ended the call and skidded into the parking lot of her apartment complex. 'Rigid' and 'proud'. Two new words to add to the ever-growing list of adjectives that explained why she was twenty-six, unmarried, and had no prospects on the horizon.

ELIZABETH MADDREY

2

Jackson groaned. Why had he accepted responsibility for this fundraiser again? Oh, that's right, because Lisa had wrangled him into it. Wasn't there some sort of statute of limitations on having to be nice to the girl you'd broken up with? Surely this would make them even. If it didn't... well he might have to start polishing up his resume. Wanting to spare her feelings is what had gotten him in trouble in the first place when she'd asked him out. But her dropping the L-word on their second date was too much and he'd had to end things. Now it was as if she roamed the office looking for ways to make his life miserable.

"How did the meeting with the caterer go?" Senator Beatrice Carson smiled from the doorway.

"We might have to reopen the bids. Or look seriously at the hotel package."

Frowning, Beatrice sat across from him and crossed her legs. "Why's that? I liked what she had to say in the proposal. Plus, a woman-owned business is something I'm excited about supporting."

"I know. I understand that. But maybe there's another local woman-owned business we could use? Taste and See, that's Paige's— Ms. Jackson's—company, is all about sustainability. Did you know that?"

Beatrice nodded, a tiny line forming between her eyebrows. "And?"

Jackson lined up the edges of the file folders on his desk. Why did it feel like he was taking—and failing—a test? "And that means we can't do something where everyone gets the same cut of meat. Because apparently she buys beef by the cow."

A grin split Beatrice's face as she leaned forward. "That's exactly what we need, don't you see? It'll shake up the fundraiser perfectly. None of the matchy-matchy plates with the same chicken divan you had last week. Let me see the menus she prepared."

She was excited about this? Jackson flipped open the presentation folder Paige had left and offered the pages. "Two are for a buffet setup, which seemed to be her preference. But there are two for plated dinners as well."

The Senator tapped her finger against the edge of the pages as she skimmed them. She flipped through a second time then pulled one page free and handed it to Jackson. "This one. Give her a call and let her know. I might want to make a few tweaks once we nail down the theme and venue, but this has all the right elements."

Jackson swallowed a sigh. "Yes, ma'am."

"I know you only took this on as a favor for Lisa. I don't know if you heard, but she'll be leaving us at the end of the month. I'm glad this isn't something she'll have to transition." Beatrice smiled and left the tiny office.

Lisa was leaving? So much for the nascent thought that he'd dump this back on her desk. At least she'd be out of the office and unable to make any more demands on his ill-placed sense of guilt for ending their relationship before it had a chance to start. *Find and focus on the silver lining.* Plus, working with Paige would be easy on his eyes. Not that he'd been looking. Much. He sighed and flipped through the papers to find her contact information and picked up the phone.

Jackson dropped his football helmet on top of the rest of his gear inside the garage and pushed open the door, walking into a wall of aromatic spices that filled the kitchen. He lifted a hand in greeting to his roommate Zach.

"Smells good. What is it?"

Zach shrugged. "I played around with a recipe for Tandoori chicken that I got from one of the other teachers at school. She brought it in for her lunch a few weeks ago. It's one of the few bright spots of my summer-school experience so far. The teacher's lounge smelled great for a week. Thought we might enjoy it."

"I'm game. Ben home yet?"

Zach shook his head. "Nope. Not sure when he'll be here. We can wait, or not, up to you."

"I need a shower. Practice was good, but we have a few new guys on the team who are just obnoxious enough that I wasn't ready to deal with the ragging I'd get for using the shower stall instead of the open area. So I just pulled on my clothes and came home."

Zach laughed. "That's what you get for playing semi-pro football, man. Maybe it's time to let the dream die."

Jackson jogged through the living room and down the hall to his bedroom. Since he'd worked out the rental details with their landlord, Jackson had claimed the master bedroom, with the en suite. Every time he walked by the hall bathroom Ben and Zach shared, he blessed his forethought. They kept the common areas clean enough, and everyone took turns with dinner and shopping, but the two of them wouldn't be able to keep a bathroom clean if they had a magic wand. If they let it go much longer, they were going to have to start charging the shower curtain rent. He shuddered and spun the handle to hot.

Stepping under the spray, he groaned. Heaven. Zach's comment rang in his ears. Is that what everyone thought? That he was on the team to hold on to his glory days? He just loved the game, playing more so than watching, though he'd spend time in front of the TV with friends and a ball game given the chance. He wasn't charging around the field hoping to make it big in sports. Not anymore. When he hadn't been able to take the college scholarship because he needed to pick a school closer to family, he'd let the dream go. He wouldn't have made the pros anyway. He had good hands and was fast, but there were far better players out there. Now he played because he loved it. But maybe it was time to think about quitting.

With Lisa out of the office and the Senator trying to slim down her budget, he was liable to get a ton more work dumped on him. That wasn't necessarily a bad thing, provided they weren't all fundraisers. He sighed, shut off the water, and fumbled for his towel. Fundraisers meant caterers. Caterers needed to answer their phones.

Jackson tugged on pajama pants and a t-shirt, paused to toss his towel over the shower rod, and ambled back to the kitchen. "Any word?"

"Ben's five minutes out. You wanna set the table? Then we can eat as soon as he gets here."

Jackson grabbed plates and forks and set them on the 1950s-style chrome and formica table they'd found on the curb a few houses down just after moving in. It wasn't in perfect shape, but it meant they didn't have to balance plates on their laps in the living room. Given Ben's inherent clumsiness, that was a good thing.

"Hey, sorry I'm late. I know it's roommate dinner night. Got caught up at work. They're hoping to start a new fundraising drive, but the ideas we've had have all been shot down by the head of the charity for being too similar to what other agencies are doing." Ben dropped his laptop bag on the floor and pulled out a chair at the table. "I just don't see how we're going to come up with a completely original idea. But I guess we'll keep throwing out suggestions until something sticks."

Zach brought two steaming serving bowls in from the kitchen and set them on the table before sitting. "Maybe Jackson can offer some ideas, seeing as how he's helping the Senator with her fundraising these days."

Ben scooped rice onto his plate and pushed the bowl toward Jackson. "You're working a fundraiser? How'd I miss that?"

"You were on a date. Lisa dropped it on me last week, though the RFP went out two or three months ago."

"Dude. Why didn't you say no? You two have been over for what, a year? She's gotta stop making you her patsy." Ben shook his head and spooned chicken over the rice. "When'd you learn to cook Indian food, Zach?"

Zach's eyebrows shot up. "When'd you learn to recognize it? Jackson had no idea what it was."

"Hey. I would've figured it out. Probably. Anyway, the Lisa thing is moot, since she's leaving. Of course, that means I'm stuck dealing with the caterer who can't manage to answer her phone when I'm calling to tell her she got the job."

Zach frowned. "I thought she already got the job… wasn't she coming in today to start going over menu ideas?"

Jackson replayed the conversations with Paige and the Senator for his roommates as he shoveled spicy chicken into his mouth. "So, not only do I have to do this crazy event, I have to deal with a caterer who scores pretty heavily on the weird-idea scale."

"Wait a minute. What's wrong with thinking about where your food is coming from and making sure that the animals we eat are being used responsibly? I mean, it's not as if I'm going to jump onto the 'meat is murder' bandwagon anytime soon, but God did put us here as stewards." Ben reached for the rice, adding another heaping scoop to his plate.

"Maybe you can deal with her for me. You'd probably have a lot to talk about." Jackson drained his water glass. "Look, I'm not saying there's anything wrong with it if that's what you want to do personally. But as a caterer, shouldn't your focus be on providing the food that your clients want?"

Zach shrugged. "Seems to me if the Senator chose her, then that's exactly what she's doing."

"Whatever." Jackson pushed back from the table and shot a glare at his roommates. "I have to go research seasonal food so I can talk to this woman intelligently on Monday. Assuming she picks up her phone."

Paige shuffled to the door, cinching her bathrobe tight. Who was pounding on their door this early on a Saturday? And why hadn't Whitney answered it? Where was Whitney? She peered through the peep hole and grinned, twisting the deadbolt and pulling open the door.

"Daddy! This is a surprise. Come on in. Why aren't you at the restaurant?"

Lawrence Jackson chuckled and shook a white paper bag. "I brought bear claws. I've got a new sous chef who's proven himself pretty well so far, thought I'd see if he could handle getting all the lunch prep started without me so I could have a pastry with my baby girl. I tried to call, but it just goes to voicemail."

"Yeah, my battery died and I can't find my charger. It'll turn up. When did you have time to make bear claws?" Paige scooped dark-roast coffee grounds into a reusable pod, dropped it into the coffee machine, checked that that water reservoir was full, set a mug under the spout, and hit brew.

Lowering his substantial bulk into one of the dark wooden chairs at her kitchen table, Lawrence shook his head. "I didn't. Gave up pastry making when I moved away from serving breakfast. There's too much competition, and no one wants to sit down and eat in the morning anymore. So, I found a bakery that does a passable job and visit them entirely too often for your mother's taste."

With a chuckle, Paige took the mug out from under the spout on the machine, filled and dropped in a new pod, put a clean mug in place, and hit brew again. "She's still on you to diet, I take it?"

"Mmm." Lawrence gave an eloquent shrug. "But who trusts a skinny cook? Anyway, even having moved the restaurant to ethical, organic, and sustainable fare hasn't required that I stop using butter. The butter just tastes better now."

Paige sat, blowing across the top of her coffee, and reached for one of the "toes" of the bear claw. "These are good. A little too much almond extract though."

"You see? I told them that. They very nearly asked me not to come back again. But I think I'm their best customer, so they couldn't very well do that."

"Daddy. How many of these are you eating?" He wasn't obese, not really, but even a frame as large as his had limits to the weight it should be carting around. He was pushing them.

"Now you sound like your mother." He sighed and shook his head, his face the picture of sorrow. "Fine. If it'll make you both happy, I'll limit my visits to Saturdays. If the new sous works out, at least."

"And if he doesn't?"

"Maybe by then my daughter will have come to her senses and be ready to join the family restaurant instead of this crazy catering business idea she concocted."

Paige closed her eyes. There it was. Though she'd left the door open, so it was probably her fault. Still, it would have been nice to have one conversation where it didn't take that turn. "It's not crazy, Daddy. It's every bit as viable an opportunity as your restaurant. People are starting to see the need to live more gently, and they want companies who understand and embrace those values."

He shook his head and filched a toe from Paige's pastry. "Choosing to eat at a restaurant that serves local, seasonal food is one thing. This is a smart decision and something people can do without it intruding on their comfortable lives. They can come eat at my place and then stop at the grocery store on the way home and never feel a twinge of guilt, because they did their part. But a caterer? If you're hiring a caterer, you're not thinking about the plight of the small farmer or how chickens are treated. You just want to feed a multitude as cheaply as possible."

"Not everyone is like that." Paige's shoulders slumped. She could say the words, but they still sounded hollow. If the contract with the Senator came through maybe that would be evidence that this wasn't a naïve undertaking. On the other hand that didn't seem likely. And her personal chef clients weren't enough to provide a living, they barely paid the bills.

"Ah, Paige. I didn't come to pick a fight. I just want what's best for you, and for my restaurant. And in my heart, those are the same thing. People say running a restaurant is risky, and they're right, but it's much riskier to start a catering business from scratch. Why not focus on doing good where you can rather than tilting at windmills?"

"I don't see it that way, Daddy. This is living out my convictions, not finding a way to keep the guilt from plaguing me in the middle of the night. Maybe I don't take it as far as some people— I love my car, I love to drive, and it's necessary around here since the public transportation isn't so fabulous. I only have a tiny garden plot across the street, so I still end up having to buy food that travels, though I aim to keep it in-state. I'm doing what I can in a way that makes sense, and that's so much more than people who say all the right words but all they manage to do is eat at your restaurant every now and then and buy bananas that have an 'organic' sticker on them even though they were flown in from South America."

Lawrence held up his hands. "All right. All right. Just remember the offer stands, for now at least. But I'll also say your mother is starting to talk about me retiring so we can do all the travel we've been putting off for years. Sooner or later, I'm going to have to pass the restaurant on to someone else, even if it isn't you."

Paige looked up from her computer when the front door opened. "Hey there."

Whitney winced and pushed the door shut, clicking the deadbolt and holding up a hand. "I can explain."

"I'm not your mother, I'm your roommate. You don't owe me an explanation. I was just saying hello." Paige turned her attention back to the meal planning worksheet she was putting together for a potential new personal chef client. She tried to respond to all web inquiries within twenty-four hours, but this client's food allergies made it a challenge. She'd have to modify nearly every one of her recipes in one way or another. Did she even want a client like that?

"Here's the thing." Whitney perched on the arm of the sofa and leaned forward, her hands on her knees.

Nothing good ever started that way. Paige slid off the glasses she needed for computer work and met her roommate's gaze. "Okay?"

"You remember Elliot, right?"

"The guy you met at your work Christmas party and have been dating, off and on, since then? That Elliot?" They'd been off more than on, but that didn't seem to matter to either of them. Sometimes it seemed like they enjoyed fighting with one another more than just hanging out. Whatever. Not her relationship. "What about him?"

"We're engaged!" Whitney squealed and stuck out her left hand, wriggling her ring finger so that the enormous rock on it caught the light.

"Wow. Congratulations?" She couldn't keep the hint of a question out of her voice. They'd been "done for good" just two weeks ago.

Whitney pouted. "You're not happy for us?"

"I am. He seemed like a nice guy the few times I met him. You said he's a Christian… "

"But?"

Paige sighed. "But it's fast. Aside from the fact that you never wanted to speak to him again less than a month ago, you've only known each other what, six months?"

"Seven." Whitney frowned. "Don't you think sometimes you just know when it's right?"

Well, sure. But how could that possibly be the case for a couple who fought like big horned sheep in the spring? "I guess. Sorry, I'm preoccupied with catering stuff. I really am happy for you. Let me know when you set a date."

"Oh, we already did. Labor Day weekend."

Paige blinked. "Next year? Or in two months?"

"It's ten weeks. That's plenty of time. We're not planning on doing anything extravagant, just a simple ceremony and then a get-together in the church hall. You can do that for us, right?"

"I... well, probably, yeah, but it'll depend on what you want. We can talk about that later—have you checked with the church?" There was no possible way it was available that weekend with this short notice. But Paige wasn't going to be the one to say it.

"I figured I'd call on Monday and reserve things. After all, it's not like that's a popular weekend for people to get married. They're too busy planning picnics and getting ready for school to start." Whitney stood. "We're going to start looking for a condo or townhouse for after we're married. But I'll probably move in as soon as we close on it. Elliot can't get out of his lease until December, so we'll have to keep paying that, but since I'm not on the lease here I didn't figure it mattered when I moved out."

Paige's mouth fell open. Didn't matter? How could it not matter? She couldn't afford the rent on her own, that's why she'd advertised at churches in the area for a roommate in the first place. Whitney had been the only taker, so she'd put up with her. But this was ridiculous. "It does matter. And you do actually have a lease. With me. Remember the documents you signed when you moved in? Those are legally binding. You have to give me six months notice, or until I find a replacement."

Whitney wrinkled her forehead and frowned. "You aren't seriously going to hold me to that, are you? I thought it was just a formality."

"The rent has to get paid, Whitney, whether you're married or not. Six months. I'll start advertising now, but that also means you

19

have to be ready to move out if I find someone sooner than Labor Day."

"You can't do this to me. Just because you're single and bitter doesn't mean you get to take that out on me because I found a husband." Whitney stormed down the hall and slammed her bedroom door. Music with a thumping beat shattered the silence of the apartment.

Paige dropped her head back and stared at the ceiling. Could her life get any worse?

Jackson set the phone back in its cradle and rubbed the back of his neck. He should go check the fax machine before someone else got to it. Technically, he shouldn't be getting the handful of bids that he was waiting for. The Senator wanted Paige Jackson and Taste and See Catering. He shook his head. Maybe if the Senator saw ideas from environmentally friendly restaurants she'd change her mind. A restaurant, at least, should be willing to provide the same thing to all the guests. Unlike Paige. She seemed nice enough as a person, but really, beef tongue? All because she had some grand desire to save the world one cow at a time?

"Got a minute?" The Senator stood in his doorway, a stack of papers in her hand.

His stomach plummeted. *Don't panic. She always walks around with something in her hand. It isn't necessarily related to the fundraiser.* "Of course. What's up?"

Beatrice tossed the papers on his desk, deep frown lines etched around her mouth. "Just wondering what these are. I thought we agreed to go with, oh what was the name? It was cute. Taste and See."

He fought to keep his shoulders from slumping like a little boy caught with his hand in the candy jar after his mother told him no. He cleared his throat. "Right. But she hasn't answered her phone and I've tried to call her three times now, so I thought… "

"You thought you'd just do what you wanted instead of what I asked you to do?"

"No. That's not…"

Beatrice planted her hands on his desk and leaned forward so her face was only inches from his. "Figure out a way to get in touch with Taste and See and set things up. The dinner is only eight weeks away and we needed to have invitations in the mail last week. As it is, they're just getting to the printer because I only made the final decision on location this morning."

"But—"

"Jackson. I admire your initiative and appreciate that you think you're looking out for me somehow. But I've made a decision and I expect you to follow orders. Am I clear?"

"She's not even registered to vote."

Confusion flickered across the Senator's face before she shook her head. "That just means she didn't vote for my opponent. I asked if I was clear?"

Jackson sagged back in his chair and nodded. "Yes, ma'am."

"Good. And I've settled on Mount Vernon, out on the back lawn, facing the river. Janine's taking care of those details. She'll also handle mailing the invitations as soon as they're in. Should be tomorrow afternoon at the latest. So you just have to focus on the rest of the event. *Like the food.* Get it handled, Jackson."

"Yes, Senator."

Her lips curved. "You can be annoyed with me, that's fine. Just don't let it hinder getting the job done, all right?"

He nodded.

"Good man. And for the record, Jackson, I do understand your concerns. But there's something there… I think it's going to be the right decision in the long run. I know you can handle it."

Jackson waited until the Senator left before he sighed. So close. He'd been so close. He pushed the faxes aside and flipped open the Taste and See proposal. Double-checking each number as he dialed, he tried the infuriating woman for the fourth time.

Pulling his tie out of his collar, Jackson checked the dashboard clock of his car. How had he managed to get here twenty minutes early? He'd been banking on traffic to keep him on track. It figured that the one day he actually allowed enough time for it, there wasn't any traffic to speak of. He looked over at the pile of folders on the passenger seat. Did the Senator really expect him to take all of that into a dinner meeting? Surely the tablecloth swatches could wait for a meeting in the office? Whatever. He'd do as instructed. Regardless of her annoying tendencies, Lisa had been great at handling these events, and if the Senator said Lisa always gave this info to the caterer, then he would too.

Jackson grabbed the stack and kicked open the car door. He'd go and get a table, then when Paige got there he'd have home-court advantage. Or something. He clicked the lock button on his key fob and crossed the main level of the parking garage, stepping out through the creaking metal door onto the busy street in Clarendon. He scanned the signs lining the storefronts. Aha. An old-style wooden sign speared out over the sidewalk. Four cornucopias, each clearly representing a different season's harvest, surrounded informal gold lettering spelling out the restaurant's name. With a quick look for oncoming traffic over his shoulder, he jogged diagonally across the street and tugged open the restaurant door.

"Welcome to Season's Bounty. Table for one?" The hostess, dressed all in black, her hair pulled back in a sleek pony tail, flashed him a starched smile.

"I'm expecting one more. I'm a bit early, but if I could go ahead and get a table?"

"Of course. Can I get the name of your guest?"

"Paige Jackson."

"Oh, Paige." The hostess' polite smile stretched into a genuine grin. "She's already here, at the Chef's Table in the back. Follow me."

Jackson trailed the hostess through the dimly lit, rustically-styled restaurant. There was a low hum of conversation blending in with subtle classical music and the clink of flatware on china. They did a brisk business, that was certain. Pony-tail-girl pushed open a swinging door and the understated, quiet restaurant was replaced by a cacophony of shouts, bangs, and clangs as three chefs worked on the line, calling out to one another as they danced an intricate ballet with hot pans and sharp knives. It was a wonder no one ended up injured. A four-person banquette was tucked into the corner at the end of the kitchen by the swinging doors. Paige sat on one side, chatting with a man across the table from her.

"Paige, your guest is here." The hostess bobbed her head to the other man. "Mr. Jackson."

"Hi, Jackson. I'd like you to meet my father, Lawrence Jackson. He's the owner and executive chef here at Season's Bounty. Since he also specializes in sustainable, ethical foods, I thought you'd enjoy getting a taste of what I hope to provide for your event."

Lawrence rose to his feet and Jackson extended his hand. "Jackson Trent. It's a pleasure to meet you, Mr. Jackson."

Lawrence pursed his lips. "Jackson is your first name?"

He nodded. "Makes remembering Paige's last name easy."

"Ha. Yes, I imagine so. I'll leave you to your dinner. Paige already ordered your tasting menu. What can I get you to drink?"

She'd ordered already? So much for home-field advantage. Though in her father's restaurant, getting to the table first wasn't going to do help anyway. "Just water is fine."

"Get him the sparkling water, Daddy. So many people don't realize Virginia has a mineral spring with a local bottling plant that makes sparkling water that would easily rival all those French companies if they were interested in globalization. Thankfully they're not."

Lawrence arched a brow at Jackson, eyes twinkling as he glanced at his daughter.

"That sounds great. Thanks." Jackson smiled and slid into the seat across from Paige. "You didn't mention this was your father's restaurant when I suggested it."

She chuckled. "I couldn't quite figure out how to do that without it being weird. Plus it's perfect, really. I'm the one who convinced him to make most of the changes in his menu and operating methodologies. Several of the recipes he uses are mine, too.

So, in addition to getting a feel for sustainable cuisine like you suggested, you'll actually get to try several of the specific items on my sample menus."

Lawrence returned with two skinny rectangular plates balanced on his arm and a green bottle of sparkling water. "Here's the first course. I'll let Paige do the descriptions—one of the line cooks is having an off day and I need to jump in for a bit before we annoy the guests out front."

"No problem, Daddy. If you holler when the next courses are ready, I can come and get them."

"You don't mind?" Lawrence leaned over and pecked her hair. "Thank you. Bon appétit."

"Well, go ahead." Paige gestured to the plate in front of Jackson. Selecting a fork from the array in front of her, she scooped one of the three bite-sized portions into her mouth.

Jackson glanced down at the plate. Thin slices of meat were artfully arrayed on small circles of...something. Steeling himself, he mirrored Paige, his eyebrows lifting as the flavors exploded in his mouth. "This is incredible."

Paige grinned. "I told you beef tongue, done right, was something that would fit in the swankiest of events."

Jackson swallowed. That was tongue? Cow tongue? He waited, half expecting his stomach to revolt at the revelation, but there was nothing besides the lingering flavor combination urging him to try another morsel. "All right. You win that one. This is fantastic and I can't imagine anyone not enjoying it. I'm looking forward to the rest of the meal."

Each dish that followed was a fascinating twist on the familiar, and unique enough that Jackson was surprised by how good it tasted. But then, he'd had fairly low expectations. And even though the chef had plated their portions, the food would easily work as a buffet item. If Paige could deliver on the food as well as this restaurant, the fundraiser was sure to be a success. At least as far as eating went. He couldn't control how readily people opened their wallets. Still, full and satisfied bellies never hurt.

"So, what do you think?" Paige leaned in, her hands clasped on the table.

He broke into a grin. She looked so earnest and hopeful with those wide, amber eyes. "It was fantastic. Definitely not the typical banquet fare. Upscale without feeling snooty or staid. I'm impressed."

She sat back, eyebrows raised. "So… I got it?"

"You did." No point in mentioning that she'd landed the contract before they'd even met today. The Senator was adamant and once Beatrice made up her mind, you didn't change it. They didn't call her 'Bulldozer Bea' behind her back for nothing. Of course, that was a large part of what made her a success in the Senate. Still, having tasted the food and after talking with Paige, he'd revise his opinion of her philosophy. It was interesting... *she* was interesting. He slid the pile of folders across the table. "This is more information you'll need for planning, along with the initial deposit as indicated in the contract. It also has venue information, tablecloth swatches and that kind of thing. I'm not entirely sure why you, as the caterer, care, but I'm told you do."

"Bonus points to whoever told you that. I'm providing the china, right?"

He nodded.

"So this," Paige tapped the folders, "helps make sure that it all goes together cohesively. I don't want to rent dishes that I think are pretty but that end up clashing with the overall décor of the event. Haven't you run one of these things before?"

"No. This is the first one." And hopefully the last.

"Ah. So are you in charge of the whole thing? Menu specifics and so forth?"

Jackson drew his eyebrows together. Where was she going with this? "Yeah. Well, the Senator has final say on everything, but she's relatively hands-off unless there's a problem. Why?"

"Just making sure I knew who to contact. With only eight weeks, I need to get in touch with my suppliers and see what they have that will last that long and what they'll have fresh, that kind of thing so I can ensure I can get everything for my proposed menu, or make substitutions where needed. Since it's July fourth this weekend, I've got a lot on my plate this week, but I should be able to get you a firm menu by the middle of next week. Will that work?"

"Sounds good. The Senator is out of town all next week, so if you need to wait until the thirteenth, that's fine as well. But I do need you to sign the contract before I go. There's a copy for each of us."

Paige's tongue darted between her lips. "I shouldn't need any extra time, and if you're going to need to make changes, sooner is better than later. Can you reach her while she's gone?"

He laughed as she flipped the top folder open and began to scan the contract. Even when the Senator was out of the office she might as well be in it. "Oh yeah. I don't think she understands the meaning of the word 'vacation.'"

"Not so different from the food service industry I guess." Paige flipped to the second page of the contract, her head bobbing slightly as she worked her way down the page. "This looks pretty standard."

Jackson offered the pen he always kept in his shirt pocket. She grabbed it and scrawled across the bottom of the document then flipped another two pages and signed the copy as well. She handed him the original contract and his pen. "All set."

Jackson checked his watch. "Great, thanks. I should scoot. My email and phone numbers are all in there if you need to get in touch."

Paige stood and extended her hand. "That's perfect. And thanks. When I finally found my phone charger and saw the missed calls I was worried I'd missed my chance. You have no idea how much I wanted this job."

He captured her hand in his. Electricity shot up his arm and across his chest. *What was that?* "We'll see how you feel after you've worked with the Senator for a few weeks."

Paige peeked out the circular window in the kitchen door and watched Jackson wind his way through the restaurant and out the front door. She let out the squeal that had been building in her throat and danced back to the table. They chose her! Now she just had to do such an incredible job with it that the deep pockets attending would all take her business card and use Taste and See for their personal events. People who paid whatever-it-was the Senator charged for a dinner at, where was it going to be? She sank onto the bench of the banquette, flipped open the folder and coughed. Mount Vernon? She was catering an event on the lawn of Mount Vernon? Oh yeah, she was definitely going to get her business off the ground.

"Your meeting went well?" Lawrence wedged himself into the booth across from her.

"Very well. Two months ago, Clara let me know about a request for proposals for a political fundraiser. She had to do a little fast-talking to get me to submit something, but in the end, the potential to find high-end clients was worth more than a little selling out. So I put the packet together. Last week I went in, thinking I'd gotten the job, but Jackson—the guy who was here tonight—hadn't really read the information about how I operate."

"He was looking for more traditional banquet fare, not something sustainable?"

"Basically. So when I left, I figured any chance at the contract was gone. Then there was the whole phone charger debacle this weekend when he was trying to get in touch that probably almost cost me the job again. But he called today and said the Senator was excited about what I had to offer. So I invited him here so he could see that doing things the smart way doesn't mean you're stuck with casseroles of mixed cow parts."

Lawrence chuckled. "I'll have to consider adding that to the menu. Sounds tasty."

"You know what I mean. Anyway, the dishes I had you put together were close to what I proposed, particularly the tongue appetizer. And he loved them." Paige patted the stack of folders. "I'm officially catering Senator Beatrice Carson's mid-summer fundraiser. At Mount Vernon, Daddy. Can you believe it?"

"Congratulations. I hadn't realized the bid came out so long ago."

Paige tipped her head to the side. "What do you mean?"

"I got an email late last week asking if I was interested in submitting a proposal. So we put something together and faxed it in this morning. If I'd known you had already applied I wouldn't have bothered." He offered a gentle smile and reached across the table to lay his hand on top of hers. "As much as I want you for the restaurant, I also want you to be happy. To succeed. I know I'm not always good at saying this, but you make me proud."

Her dad's words did little to soothe her boiling blood. Jackson had put out a call for more bids? Did he target sustainable restaurants? He probably had, the backstabbing jerk. Did the Senator ask him to? If so, why the change of heart? It didn't matter. It couldn't. She had the signed contract. *Focus on the important part.*

"Paige?"

She shook her head. "Don't worry about it, Dad. I know you think my catering idea is destined for failure. Maybe you're right. I don't know. But I know I have to try. I'm not ready to be just another cook on the line."

"You wouldn't be… " Lawrence stopped and dragged his sleeve across his face. "Never mind. You'll be great. And if you need any help for the event, let me know."

"Thanks." Paige gathered the folders as she stood. "I need to get home. I have a big day of prep for the weekend tomorrow. Oh…

if you hear of any single gals needing a place to live, can you point them my way? It seems that Whitney's getting married on Labor Day. I put up a notice at church yesterday, but spread the word, would you?"

"Of course. Paige... you're not angry with me?"

Her heart thawed a few degrees. It wasn't her dad's fault Jackson Trent was a jerk. *A gorgeous jerk. But still a jerk.* She kissed the top of his head. "'Course not. Say hi to Mom for me, okay?"

"Whit? Are you home?" Paige kicked the door closed, craning her ears for any noise her roommate might make. Silence. Blissful silence. Ever since Whitney announced her engagement and her intention to move out, the time she was home was spent stomping around and dropping veiled—and not so veiled—comments about how true friends wouldn't hold someone to a contract when they were getting married. That was part of the problem though. It wasn't as if they were friends. They got along fine, mostly because they stayed out of each other's way. But Whitney had answered an ad for a roommate that she'd put on church bulletin boards in the area, thinking that would help narrow down applicants to believers. They hadn't known each other before then. And Paige was going to be doing a more thorough interview of any new applicants. It'd be nice not to dread finding her roommate was home at the end of the day.

Paige turned the deadbolt and ambled into the kitchen. She filled a large glass with water and carried it back to her bedroom. She wanted to spend time looking through the files Jackson had left with her. There wasn't going to be a ton of time the rest of the week. Her idea to offer July Fourth picnic baskets had, admittedly, been stolen from a book she read, but it had gone over well with her personal chef clients. She'd also received a few orders from referrals of one sort or another. Her fingers were crossed that those new clients were viewing the picnic as an audition and that that they might lead to future business. Regardless, she had gallons of potato salad and fried chicken, among other things, filling up her week.

Whitney knocked on Paige's bedroom door and poked her head in. "Hey, figured I'd find you in here. Can you come out to the living room? I have someone I want you to meet."

Paige frowned at the work spread out around her on the bed. "I'm not really... "

"It'll only take a minute."

Biting her tongue, Paige wiggled off the bed and trailed after her roommate. What now?

"Okay. So since I'll be moving out soon—you've got to see the little townhouse we looked at this weekend, I think it's going to be perfect—but anyway, I was talking to some friends and they mentioned that Fern was looking for a place and I knew it was just the answer to prayer I'd been looking for. Fern's a vegan." Whitney grinned and gestured to the waif-like woman perched on the edge of the sofa, her patchwork broomstick skirt pooling around her.

"Um, okay. Hi, Fern. Whitney, can I speak to you in the kitchen a moment?" Breathing deeply, Paige stomped into the kitchen. She turned and glared at Whitney, arms crossed. "What are you doing?"

"I'm finding you a roommate so I can move into the townhouse we're going to buy. Duh."

"Yeah, no. Why do you think a vegan is going to get along with me? I like meat. I cook and serve meat to clients for a living. Sure, I also cook and serve vegetables, but being vegan doesn't mean she has any interest in recycling or kitchen composting. For all I know, she eats only processed foods and is going to balk at putting her egg shells in the container on the counter rather than the trash."

"Oh, she doesn't eat eggs. So... "

Paige covered her face with her hands and peeked out between her fingers. "What have you promised her, Whit?"

"Just that I'd introduce you. And, well, that maybe she could hang out here for a few weeks and just see how it goes. I'm in and out a lot, you know that. So really, it'll just be like you have one roommate, not two. She'll sleep on the floor in my room, you'll hardly even notice she's here."

Paige closed her eyes and leaned against the counter. Though she hadn't specifically had nightmares about the roommate situation, this was close to the worst she could imagine. "You don't get it, do you?"

"What? I'm trying to help. Elliot and I can't afford to be paying rent on two places plus a mortgage when we get married. I know if I find you a replacement that you won't care where the rent is coming from, so that's one obstacle down. Then we just have to figure out what to do about Elliot's lease and we're set."

"That's the thing, I *do* care. I'm not settling for some random person that you find on the street. The contract is with you and it has you paying rent through the end of the year. Period. If you want to have other people staying with you in your room that's your business, but if they so much as leave a hairbrush in the common areas of the apartment, there are going to be problems. *If* I can find a replacement roommate who meets *my* requirements, then I'll *consider* letting you out of your contract. But after this? I'm not even positive I'll do that." Paige pushed past Whitney, storming into the living room.

Fern stood and held up her hands. "She said you'd be cool, but… have you ever considered meditation? It might help, I can recommend some CDs."

"Look, Fern, I'm sure you're a fine person, but Whitney's not the one who gets to make roommate decisions here. So if you need to crash with her for tonight, that's fine if she's okay with it, but I can already tell we're not a good fit for any sort of long term arrangement and I'm trying to avoid another roommate mistake." Her gaze flicked up and met Whitney's. "It was nice to meet you."

Back in her room, Paige lay on her bed, staring at the ceiling. She wasn't trying to be obnoxious, but honestly, what was Whitney thinking? Okay, Whit was obviously thinking about the money, but still. How hard was it to honor the commitments you made? At this point, maybe she'd be better off trying to make the rent on her own rather than finding a new roommate. Living with other people never managed to be anything but a disaster. What was wrong with her?

She sat up and frowned at the folders. Speaking of honoring commitments. Though maybe she had to give him a few points for choosing her when all was said and done. But really, wasn't it illegal to solicit new bids after the date had closed? It wasn't an official government bid, so maybe not. But it seemed underhanded. She slid the contract out of the first folder and read it more carefully. At least there were stiff penalties if they cancelled on her. She winced. Those penalties went both ways. Not that she was going to cancel. This was her ticket. She just had to keep her eye on the prize.

6

"How was your date?" Zach paused the game he was playing on the living room TV and waggled his eyebrows.

Jackson shook his head. "Not a date. Dinner meeting. But the food was good, so that's a relief. Since the Senator's determined to use the woman, despite my protests and misgivings."

"Huh-uh. I looked her up online. She's hot. Dinner with a hot woman equals date. Or have you become such a political robot that you're immune to normal things like chemistry?"

"Who's hot?" Ben padded into the living room in his boxers, rubbing a towel over his wet hair.

"Jackson here had dinner with a hot caterer... hang on." Zach exited the game and re-ran the search on Taste and See Catering. He clicked on the "About" page and zoomed in so Paige's face filled the screen.

Ben let out a low whistle. "Wow. She is hot. You had dinner with her? How'd that happen?"

"You two are morons. It was a business thing. The Senator's booked her for the fundraiser at the end of August. I needed a signed contract and she wanted me to taste some of the dishes she had on her proposed menu. That's it."

Zach and Ben exchanged a glance.

"What?" Jackson crossed his arms. Sometimes splitting the rent wasn't worth the price of having roommates.

Zach gestured to the screen. "If you had dinner with her and didn't come home with her number, you've officially crossed into 'single for life' territory."

The corners of Jackson's mouth twitched. "As it happens, I have her phone number. And she has all of mine."

"Ah, but you said you're working the fundraiser and she's catering. So I'm not sure phone numbers count." Ben perched on the arm of the couch. "Do you have any definite plans for future contact?"

"Yes." After all, Paige would be calling him in the next week with a final menu. So there were definite plans. Probably not what either of them had in mind, but they should be more specific. And after their commentary during his brief time dating Lisa, he really didn't need them on his case already.

Zach frowned. "For social purposes? Or work purposes?"

"Ah, good question." Ben leaned forward. "Well?"

"Don't the two of you have better things to do?"

"That's a 'no' on the social purposes, I'm thinking, Zach." Ben grabbed the second controller for the game console.

"Yep. Jackson whiffed his chances again. It's sad."

"You two are pathetic." Jackson stuffed his hands in his pockets and walked down the hall. It was tempting to grab a third controller and join in the gore-fest, but they were likely to keep poking at him about Paige and he wasn't ready for that. Why did it bother him so much? Was it because of the sparks when they'd shaken hands? Or was it just because she was a puzzle? How could someone who didn't vote—wasn't even *registered* to vote—be so gung-ho about a political hot topic that she based her whole business on it? Clearly she didn't see it as a political topic, but didn't she realize that it was one? If she cared so much about... how had she phrased it? Living gently, that was it. If she cared so much about living gently, why wouldn't she take every opportunity to vote for people who agreed with her point of view?

She was definitely an enigma. A beautiful, fascinating one, but a mystery to be solved nonetheless. As much as he disagreed with the Senator's decision to go with her as their caterer, there was something about her. He was looking forward to figuring out what that was.

"Aren't you ready yet, Jackson?" Zach's voice carried down the hall.

"Yeah, yeah, I'm coming." Jackson frowned. Why was he doing this? It was already creeping past ninety and it was barely ten in the morning. And the humidity... he'd need to make sure they had a lot of water with them so they didn't end up dehydrated. What had possessed him to leave the comfort of air conditioning?

"Come on, man." Ben poked his head into Jackson's room. "We're on the hook for bringing the hotdogs. You don't want the whole group to starve, do you?"

"I said I was coming. Do you have the cooler?"

"Packed with ice and the two cases of bottled water you insisted we buy last week. We'll all be floating by the end of the day."

Jackson slapped Ben on the back. "But we won't be in the hospital with heat stroke."

"That's a bonus. Grab your football. We've got plenty of time to kill. I imagine you can sucker some people into running around chasing the thing with you. Heck, I might even join in. Give you some competition."

"Right, that'll be the day. When did you last do anything more active than walk to the kitchen for a snack?" Shaking his head, Jackson tucked his football under his arm and brushed past his roommate.

"Harsh, man. Harsh." Ben kicked the bottom of Jackson's foot as he stepped forward, sending the foot farther than he'd anticipated. Jackson stumbled, barely catching himself on the wall.

"Oh, now you're on, man. You're on. Did you forget I know what I'm doing and you don't? The last time you chased a football you had flags tied around your waist." Jackson stopped, letting Ben ram into him from behind. He chuckled.

Ben laughed. "We'll see. Now come on, if we're actually going to get a decent spot to see the fireworks we need to get there soon."

The drive into DC in Jackson's jeep was filled with banter. His roommates were always good for a laugh, that was for sure. Maybe getting out of the house wasn't such a bad idea, though the mixture of people in the large single's group at their church was unique. He hadn't managed to click with anyone other than Ben and Zach, and he'd been attending faithfully for nearly two years. What was it about the transition from college students to single working adults that shifted the class into a dating club instead of a chance to make friends and study God's word? Sure, it would've been preferable to meet his wife while in college, but it hadn't happened. So Jackson would simply trust that God would bring her around when the time was right. Paige's face floated into his mind's eye. Maybe in the meantime he'd see if he couldn't stretch their relationship to include non-work-related things.

"All right, boys, keep your eyes open for a parking spot. It's already looking packed." Jackson steered the jeep down a narrow street by the Iwo Jima monument. It was lined on both sides with cars, and families were spreading out on the hill looking across the Potomac River toward the National Mall.

"Is that one? Up there?" Zach's finger shot past Jackson's nose aiming for what looked like a break in the cars toward the bottom of the hill.

Jackson sped up. It was a spot. Sort of. "Hop out and get the stuff out of the back. I'm not sure the lift gate will open once I wedge myself in there. But we're going to give it a try."

Zach and Ben jumped out of the car and grabbed the cooler and duffle bags from the back. When they were clear, Jackson took a deep breath and squeezed the car into the tiny space. Parallel parking was for the birds, but if you worked downtown it was a skill you had to learn. Thankfully, he'd had enough practice that this spot hadn't been too bad, though getting out might prove more challenging if the people in front of him weren't already gone.

"Nice." Zach raised his hand for a high five. Jackson slapped it and reached for one of the duffel bags.

They found several groups of young adults from church in a prime location just before the hill started to really slope. Zach and Ben wandered off with the hotdogs and balcony-sized hibachi. Jackson spread out a blanket and dropped the football on it. He tucked his hands in the pockets of his shorts and looked around. He recognized several faces, but so far there wasn't anyone he was particularly interested in talking to. With his job, more often than not people wanted to talk politics. It wasn't that he didn't enjoy doing that, but it got old trying to have a meaningful conversation with people whose information came entirely from the headline of a post someone shared on social media. That wasn't exactly informed citizenship.

He sighed. He would've been better off at home. In the air conditioning. Sweat was already trickling down his back and all he'd done was stand around. Sweating on the football field was one thing, but this was ridiculous. If the Founding Fathers had had any sense, they would've signed the Declaration of Independence in April when the weather was almost always nice.

"Jackson?"

He turned and the corners of his lips curved up when his gaze landed on Paige, looking cool in a star-studded red tank top and navy blue cotton shorts. "Hey, Paige. What are you doing here?"

"Delivering picnic orders. Just dropped off the last one. I was getting ready to brave the traffic home when I thought I saw you. Figured I'd come say hello."

"What would it take to convince you stay? There'll be plenty of food." Jackson winced. "Probably not gourmet though. Just some dogs and whatever anyone brings. Maybe that's not your thing."

She grinned. "I do actually eat hotdogs on occasion. And if I don't have to cook them myself, that's even better. You're sure there's enough?"

He nodded. "There's a group of us from church. Everyone probably brought enough to feed an army."

"You're sure I'm not intruding?"

"Absolutely. I really only know my roommates and they're off mingling." He cleared his throat. "I was just thinking that I should've stayed home where it was cool and watched the fireworks on TV. Big groups like this aren't really my thing."

She shot him a quizzical look. "As a Senator's aide? Doesn't that make your job hard?"

He shrugged. "When it's a work event I'm in my element. I have a job to do."

"Ah. I guess I get that." Paige shaded her eyes with a hand and looked across the lawn. "Think that pile of deck umbrellas belongs to your group?"

Jackson followed her gaze. Zach and Ben were standing next to the umbrellas, chatting with several of the women from church and a handful of other guys. "Probably. Want me to see if we can snag one?"

Paige followed him with her eyes as he jogged the short distance to where the other group of people stood by a pile of umbrellas. She lifted her hand in a wave when everyone turned and squinted at her. Just great. What was he saying? Did they understand that this really was a huge coincidence? She'd had no idea Jackson would be out here. If anyone was following someone, it was him following her. Had she told him she'd be delivering picnics most of the day? Whatever. This was ridiculous. She was making more out of this than necessary. He probably only pointed her out to be polite. And to get the umbrella. She should just go and let him hang out with his friends.

Jackson came back brandishing an umbrella. "Some shade, m'lady."

In spite of herself, Paige chuckled as he stabbed the striped monstrosity into the ground and popped it open.

"Did you want a drink? I should've asked before I headed over there. They've got coolers full of everything imaginable. Well, everything non-alcoholic. Church function."

"I don't drink anyway, so it's fine. I... are you sure I'm not interrupting your day? You came with friends, don't you want to hang with them?" She edged away from him, glancing over her shoulder toward the road where she'd left her car.

His eyes shifted to hers as he frowned. "I'm sure. My plan was to make the best of it and enjoy some fireworks. You being here makes that first part considerably more pleasant. Unless I'm interrupting your day by hijacking you?"

Heat that had nothing to do with the pounding sun or sweltering humidity spread through her. Paige cleared her throat.

"Okay. I didn't have any plans beyond avoiding my roommate. So this helps, actually."

"Glad to be of service." Jackson winked and slipped under the umbrella to settle on the blanket. "Pull up a square in the shade and stay awhile. Busy week?"

Paige sat cross-legged on the blanket, angled so she was facing Jackson but still in the shade provided by the umbrella. "You have no idea. I got a handful of last-minute picnic orders, plus my usual personal chef clients and I was scrambling to find the time I needed in a commercial kitchen. I ended up having to ask my dad to use the restaurant, which means I owe him now."

"Wait. You don't have your own kitchen? How does that work for catering jobs?"

Her shoulders slumped. She should've kept her mouth shut. Then again, kitchen rental had been in the cost proposal she'd included with her bid, so surely if he'd had questions about it he should've said something then. "Most of the time I rent one of the classrooms at the culinary school I attended. It's in Arlington and there's almost always plenty of time when it's not in use. When something crops up, I head to the restaurant before they open or after they're finished for the night. Since Dad's only open for lunch and dinner, I can get a few good hours in if I get up early. Most of my personal chef clients want me to cook in their homes, so that's not a problem."

"That must keep you busy, running from place to place and lugging food around."

Paige nodded. "If I can get just a bit more steady business I'll be able to afford to get my own place and have the kitchen certified as a commercial space. That's the goal, at least. The Senator's event is, hopefully, a big step toward making that happen."

"Make sure you bring cards or some other small promo material to put out around the buffet. You'll be listed in the program, but it's always nice to have something separate for people to take home. Unless they're new to the political scene, most people chuck the programs on the way to the car." Jackson leaned back, propping himself on his elbows. "Why are you avoiding your roommate?"

Paige blew out a breath. Why had she mentioned Whitney? "Ugh. 'Cause she's newly engaged, they're planning to get married Labor Day weekend, and she thinks she can foist anyone off on me as a new roommate to get out of honoring her lease. It's just a mess and I'm sick of the drama. I've already sent one poor girl packing— literally—which just made Whit even angrier. She thinks I'm doing this to keep her from getting married because, in her words, I'm single and bitter."

Jackson's eyebrows shot up. "She sounds like a peach."

"Eh. She's not a bad person. And really, until recently, she'd been a great roommate. She stayed out of my way, I stayed out of hers. It was almost like living alone with extra help toward the rent."

"But she doesn't see the problem with trying to weasel out of her lease?"

Paige shrugged. "I don't think she's thinking about anything other than the fact that she's in love and getting married. If she had a clue, I don't think she'd be talking to me about catering their reception."

"She isn't."

"She is." Jackson's mouth dropped open and Paige laughed. "Yeah, that's pretty much how I feel every time she brings it up. I finally gave her a contract and price sheet to shut her up. And I found a signed contract with deposit attached to it sitting in my inbox the next day. So that didn't go quite the way I'd planned."

Jackson shook his head. "That ought to be interesting. Will you be able to handle a wedding reception and the fundraiser? I mean, I know the wedding is after, you said Labor Day, but... "

"Yeah, I know. Should be okay. I'm going to hold onto the deposit for a bit. I can't honestly believe they're going to go through with it this quickly. I keep waiting for sanity to prevail."

"Does that happen when people are in love?"

If she hadn't caught the bitterness in his words, the air quotes he put around "in love" would have triggered the gut-deep uh-oh on their own. "Not a big believer in love, I take it?"

Jackson blew out a breath. "It's not that. I just don't think people understand what love really is. Not generally, at least. If they did, I don't think we'd be seeing the divorce rate we have—both in and out of the church. Somewhere along the line, it's like people decided love was the squishy feeling you get in your stomach when someone cute winks at you. So then, when the squishing stops, the automatic assumption is that you aren't in love anymore. And if you're not in love anymore, well then, why bother sticking around? That whole 'til death do us part' bit is overrated anyway. Right?"

Where was she supposed to go with that? Obviously there was hurt there. Did she want to prod and find out why? The squishy stomach syndrome he described was an accurate description of her own insides whenever she was around him. But since that was all of three times now, she'd chalked that up to a strong attraction and a long dating hiatus, not love. Still, she wanted to know more about him and what made him tick.

"You're quiet." Jackson rested his fingers on her arm for a brief second. "I freaked you out, didn't I? I'm told I have too many soapboxes. Sorry."

"No, it's okay. Probably a hazard of working in politics. Lots of strong opinions and no fear about expressing them."

His eyebrows arched up. "I hadn't thought of it that way, but maybe it fits. Or maybe I went into politics because of it. Either works. Again, I'm sorry."

"Should I not ask what's behind it?" She pulled her lower lip between her teeth and avoided meeting his eyes, turning instead so she looked out toward the already crowded National Mall. Everywhere visible was a sea of people settling in for the day before the evening program began. It'd be another packed night of fireworks. If they lived through the sweltering afternoon to get there.

"Maybe another time. It's not really Fourth of July conversation."

She snickered. "What exactly *is* Fourth of July conversation?"

"Oh, I don't know. What's your favorite firecracker, that kind of thing."

"That's an easy one. I like sparklers. The white ones."

"Sparklers? They're kind of girly aren't they?"

Paige lifted her hands. "And?"

"All right. Fair enough. I like the loud, manly ones that rattle windows for miles."

One after another, fireworks shot into the sky, exploding into showers of red, white, and blue stars. Thunderous booms shook the ground and drowned out the orchestra playing on the radio nearby. Paige grabbed his arm and Jackson suppressed a grin. That was one reason he'd always enjoyed the noisy ones. She didn't pull away as the sparkles in the sky crackled into nothingness and groups across the lawn broke into spontaneous applause.

"Why do people clap for fireworks? I've never understood that. The people who did them are too far away to appreciate it." Jackson leaned back on his elbows.

Paige clasped her hands together, a pretty blush spreading across her cheeks. "I don't know. Maybe it's just a way to show appreciation of something beautiful rather than saying thanks to the guys who lit the fuses."

"I guess. Still seems silly." Jackson stood and offered his hand to Paige to help her to her feet. "How are you getting home?"

"My car's down the hill a little way." She pointed. "I'll just sit in the traffic like everyone else. At least from here it's not so bad, just a right turn and a zip by the Pentagon and I'll be on the Interstate. What about you?"

"Same. Can I walk you to your car?"

"Shouldn't we help clean up?"

Jackson glanced over his shoulder. His roommates had given him space—maybe too much space—once they realized Paige was going to stay. Now they were busy helping the single's pastor and his wife collect soda cans and paper plates from the grass. He caught Zach's eye and jerked his head toward Paige. Zach gave him a thumbs up. "Nah. They'll be okay. I'll grab our blanket and meet them at the car when they're done."

Tiny lines formed between Paige's brows and the corners of her mouth tipped down, but she nodded. "All right. Thanks."

Jackson scooped up the blanket and stuffed it in his duffel bag along with the football and a Frisbee he recognized from their house. He slung the bag over one shoulder and cocked his elbow toward Paige. "M'lady?"

With a laugh, Paige threaded her arm through his. "I'm this way. The same direction everyone seems to be going."

In the brief time since the conclusion of the fireworks, what seemed like the entire population of the hill around the Iwo Jima Memorial had begun to surge toward the two-lane street that separated the monument from Arlington Cemetery. Cars were already stacked up down the hill, waiting for a break in the traffic that would allow them to turn right. Drivers in other vehicles lay on their horns as they attempted to wiggle out of their boxed-in parking spots. "No hurry, I guess."

"Nope. But this has still got to be better than the people trying to shoehorn themselves onto the Metro. I did that one year." Paige shuddered. "Never again."

"I ride at rush hour, I know what you mean. Some days it takes everything I can muster to pretend I'm not getting groped from every direction during the entire ride. And of course, living at the penultimate stop of the Orange line means it's a long ride."

She smiled and tugged his arm, leading him between two cars whose bumpers were practically touching. His leg caught on the corner of one license plate and he flinched. That was going to leave a mark. His jeep came into view and he dug his keys out of his pocket.

"I'm right up here." Paige pointed to the car in front of his. She craned her neck as they walked past the back bumper. "Man, whoever parked that jeep is gutsy. Think they hit my car when they were squishing into the space?"

Heat rushed up Jackson's neck. He cleared his throat and clicked the unlock button on his fob. The jeep's lights flashed.

"Pretty sure I didn't." Jackson grabbed the handle to the back door and tossed in the duffel before hurrying to Paige's door. He grabbed it by the frame as she sat in the driver's seat. "I'm glad you ran into me this afternoon. I had a nice time."

The corners of her mouth lifted. "Me too. Thanks for inviting me to stick around. I'll be in touch this week with more details about the menu for the Senator. I really do need to get my ordering done soon if things are going to go smoothly."

How did she switch so quickly to business-mode? He nodded, watching her movements as she snapped her seatbelt in place and put the key in the ignition. "Okay. Maybe we could meet for dinner again?"

Those little lines between her eyebrows formed again. Jackson fought the urge to rub his thumb over them, see if he could smooth them away. "Why?"

What did she mean, 'why'? He swallowed, weight dragging his stomach to his knees as beads of sweat popped out on his neck. "I thought maybe... you know, never mind."

"Jackson, wait." Paige angled her head to the side. "You didn't mean a working dinner, did you?"

The acid in his stomach sloshed into waves that would rival the best surfing sites in the world. His mouth was a desert. "No."

She offered a lopsided smile. "I think I'd like that."

"Friday?" He tucked his hands in the pockets of his shorts to hide their trembling.

"Perfect. We can figure out details later. You've got my number?"

He nodded.

Paige pulled the door shut and rolled down her window, poking her head out with another smile. "Thanks again for today. It was fun."

Jackson grinned as she wormed her way into traffic, her tail-lights disappearing into the long line of cars leaving the area.

"Yo, Lover Boy. Think maybe you could drive us home at some point tonight?"

"So, how was your day?" Zach's sing-song almost drowned out Ben's snort of laughter from the back seat.

Heat swamped Jackson and it had nothing to do with the fact that the thermometer still hovered in the upper eighties. "Good. You?"

"Dude. We left you alone, now we want details. Spill." Ben punched his shoulder.

"Hey. No hitting the driver."

"Like we're even moving. Come on, man. She's even better looking than her website photo."

Jackson frowned. Paige was pretty, no question, but there was so much more to her than that. Their conversation had ranged all over the map during the course of the day. The woman was smart and sassy and… perfect. And even if he didn't find her attractive, he'd want to be her friend. But there was no way he was telling that to his idiot roommates. That'd be like admitting to the football team that he didn't shower in the locker room because he was self-conscious. You just didn't open yourself up for that. "We had a good time. She's excited about catering the Senator's event."

"Tell me you didn't talk about work all afternoon. Please, *please* tell me that." Zach covered his eyes.

"We didn't talk about work all afternoon. Just here and there. It was good."

"Sheesh. It's like pulling teeth. Maybe you need to hit him again, Ben."

"Now that we *are* actually moving, I'll hold off. But you're right, it's like he's never dated before. And yet, we both know that's not true. We got every detail of his snore-inducing dates with Lisa, whether we wanted them or not."

"Hmm." Zach turned so he could see Ben better. "You're right. Which means one of two things. Either Jackson has realized that this girl is completely out of his league but isn't quite ready to admit it or he's smitten."

Jackson flinched. "Smitten? What kind of word is that? Nobody with a Y-chromosome uses the word 'smitten' unless they're mocking it. Smitten. Whatever."

Ben snickered. "What was it Shakespeare said? Methinks he doth protest too much."

"I do believe you're right. Which leads to the next question. Have you asked her out yet?"

Jackson sighed. He obviously wasn't getting off the hook. "Friday. We're having dinner on Friday. What about the two of you? It looked like there were a handful of interested and eligible young women hanging around this afternoon."

Zach grinned. "I might have a few new numbers programmed into my cell. What about you, Ben?"

"One or two, yeah."

"Maybe the two of you ought to compare notes, make sure you're not both calling the same young lady."

Jackson caught Ben's puzzled look in the rearview mirror and stifled a chuckle as both roommates pulled out their cell phones. It wouldn't be a permanent distraction, but it gave him a few more minutes to savor the memory of his afternoon with Paige before they dragged out all the details and dissected them. It had gone well. And she'd agreed to dinner—even though it seemed as if she wasn't going to at first. So she had to be at least a little interested, didn't she?

9

Paige hummed to herself as she got ready for church. She had a date this week. With Jackson Trent. He of the dark chocolate eyes and adorable dimple in his left cheek. *Get a grip, Paige. It's just a date.* It wasn't as if she'd never been on dates. They just usually weren't with guys who were as good looking as Jackson. Did he have an ulterior motive? Her humming trailed off. He'd said it wasn't work-related. Was he just being kind? She pulled her lower lip between her teeth. Maybe she should cancel.

Drained of her energy, Paige dragged a brush through her hair and clipped it back into a ponytail at the base of her neck. She didn't want to cancel. But she also didn't want to be the butt of some kind of joke. She swiped gloss across her lips and forced the corners of her mouth upward. The smile reflected in the mirror was genuine enough to pass all but the keenest observer's attention.

Pulling open her door, she nearly walked into Whitney. "Morning. What are you doing up?"

Whitney shrugged. "You were making so much noise with your humming this morning I figured I might as well get out of bed. Off to church, I see?"

"Yep. You going?"

Whitney scoffed. "Not to your church. I still don't understand why you go to that tiny little place full of old people when there's a perfectly good big church a block away. One with a bustling singles group, at that. Even someone like you could probably get a date if you went there."

Paige bristled. The people at her church were loving, welcoming, and wise. She loved that she was one of the few young people there, and most of the folks her age were married and starting families. Maybe it limited her dating pool, but it also kept her off the single's merry-go-round that she'd observed in other churches. Of course, not everyone was like that but just look at the folks from Jackson's church who were hanging around yesterday. Trading numbers. Batting eyelashes. Maybe that worked for some people, but she'd rather be single if that was what she had to do. She'd tried it, briefly, in college and had just ended up feeling foolish.

"All right. Well, I need to run so I'm not late."

"I need to talk to you." Whitney followed Paige down the hall. "You've got to let me out of this lease. Elliot and I found a place. We need to put in an offer and I need to be able to show that I can help with my part of the mortgage. I can't do that if I'm still paying rent here."

Paige poured coffee into her travel mug. "I'm not sure how you wanting to move in with your fiancé before you're married is my problem. I can't make the rent here on my own, which is why I got a roommate—that's you—in the first place. And why I have a legal, binding lease for said roommate. I'm doing all I can to find a replacement, but it's going to take time, and until then, you're going to need to honor your financial obligations."

"We're not moving in together. Sheesh give me some credit. I'll live there until we're married. Elliot will stay in his apartment. But me moving in beforehand gives us a chance to decorate and get set up. And since we can't afford a honeymoon, it gives us a place to go once we're married. Don't you even care that we could lose the house because of this?" Whitney stomped her foot, following Paige toward the front door.

Paige gathered her purse and Bible. "I do care, Whitney. And I'm sorry about it. But it doesn't change anything."

She pulled the door closed on Whitney's objections and hurried to her car.

"I'm so glad you could join us for lunch, Sweetheart." Paige's mom reached over and squeezed her hand.

"I never miss when Dad's trying out a new recipe, you know that." Paige grinned and looked around the empty restaurant. "Though it's still weird to be in here when it's closed. Why isn't he doing this at home like he usually would?"

"Because I've been saying he never takes me out to eat at a restaurant." Renee's laugh was a delicate tinkle. "That's why he won't let us sit in the kitchen either. He said wanted me to have the full experience. Frankly, I'm surprised he didn't hire the wait staff for the day to bring the plates out."

"Oh, Mom. That's sweet." Paige scooted her chair back. "I'm going to go see if he needs some help."

She pushed through the swinging doors into the kitchen. Lawrence was ladling a thick stew of some sort into wide, shallow bowls.

"That smells fantastic. Need any help?"

"Mmm. You can help me carry out the soup if you like. Let me just—" He reached behind him and grabbed a small white bowl. Taking a pinch of the green slivers it contained, he made a neat pile in the middle of each bowl. "There. The chicken won't be ready for another fifteen minutes. You take yours and I'll grab mine and your mother's."

Paige reached for the bowl and leaned over it, inhaling deeply. Bacon and something deep and earthy. "Did you find a new supplier for mushrooms?"

Lawrence grinned and held open the door into the dining room. "A year ago, I spoke with the Higgenbothams."

"The cattle farm?"

"The very same. They have an abundant supply of the primary requirement for mushroom growth, after all. Turns out, Mr. Higgenbotham's daughter was looking for something to do to supplement her income now that they have the twins. They set up a few logs to test the theory. These are from the first crop."

"What is it, dear? It smells heavenly." Renee dipped her spoon into the rich concoction.

Lawrence sat and reached for his wife's hand. "It's cream of mushroom with bacon and leek. Should we say the blessing?"

Pink stole across Renee's cheeks and she dropped her spoon into the soup. "Of course, Dear."

Paige bowed her head as her father said a quick prayer. The heady scent of bacon and leek wove through the air around them. As soon as he said "amen," she dipped her spoon into the soup. Flavors exploded on her tongue. "This is incredible. Is she going to expand her business?"

"She's talking about it. But for now, she has enough for me and for anyone I send her way. I will, of course, always send you her way. As long as you don't clean her out. The logs need to rest for several months before being re-fruited. So far, it seems like she has a rotation schedule worked out and will always have something in stock. Plus, she's adding a few more racks of logs, but those will take a year to be ready for fruiting. So for now, she's a small operation."

"Still. Having someone growing mushrooms locally— organically?"

Lawrence nodded.

"Incredible. Good for you, Dad."

Renee scraped the last bits of soup from her bowl. "I'm not sure I understood all of that, but if it brings about mushrooms with that much flavor, I'm all for it. That was superb, Law."

Paige stifled a smile at her mother's endearment for her dad. He'd always hated the possible nicknames for Lawrence, and so her mother had settled on Law. He must be okay with it. He never said anything, anyway. But there was always the slightest twitch of his eyelids. Was he trying to avoid rolling his eyes? "Need help with what's next, Dad?"

"I've got it. Just be a second." Lawrence stacked their bowls and carried them into the kitchen.

"Dad says you've been after him to start traveling soon?"

Renee frowned. "If he doesn't want to, he should say something. Honestly. Why would he try to get you to talk to me about it? Am I that difficult?"

"No. He didn't. I—that came out wrong. Sorry. He was just saying that the two of you were looking forward to having the time to do that when he retired. He didn't ask me to do anything. I was just trying to make conversation." Paige loved her mother, but lately it had been increasingly difficult to talk to her. Why was anyone's guess.

"Hmm. We do have a long list of places we want to see first-hand. Places we never managed to get when we were younger." Renee sighed. "You always think you have all the time in the world and then, poof, you're old. I'm not sure traveling at our age is the smart thing to do, but it's now or never. I just wish I'd had that attitude when I was your age."

"But you did. You and Dad started the restaurant. That was a huge risk and you embraced it. Do you regret it?"

"I guess not. It's just that I look around this place and I wonder what it means that this is all we have to show for the last twenty years of our lives. This isn't even the initial vision that your father and I shared, it's more your vision now. And you don't want it."

Paige sagged into her chair. "It's not that I don't want it, Mom. But you and Dad chased your dream and that's what I want to do, too."

"Here we are." Grinning, Lawrence came through the kitchen doors and, with a flourish, set a platter holding a whole chicken surrounded by a jumble of vegetables in the center of the table. "Chicken a la Renee."

"Looks great, Dad." Paige forced a smile, her cheeks hot and tight.

Lawrence stared at her, then at Renee and shook his head. "What happened?"

"Nothing. Don't worry about it, okay?"

Lawrence moved around the table and squeezed her shoulders before resuming his place at the table. "I added a few surprises that I'd really like your opinion on before this goes live on the menu."

Paige chewed on her lip. Spices wafted through the air and saliva pooled in her mouth.

"Renee, would you like to carve? I know you've always enjoyed that." Lawrence offered his wife the handle of a long knife.

Hopefully she won't stick it in me. Was she letting her parents down with the catering company? Had her dad really only switched to sustainable fare because of her? Sure, she'd introduced him to the ideas, but she hadn't pushed him to make changes. She didn't force her convictions on others. Much.

"White or dark, Paige?" Renee's eyebrows lifted, knife poised over the bird on the platter.

"Dark please. Will you serve the chicken whole, Dad, or pieced for the customers?"

Lawrence's entire face lit. "Ah. I thought I'd make it part of a special family style menu section. The chicken will probably be carved table-side since I'm not sure patrons will be able to handle that part of the process. You know how everyone complains about carving the bird at Thanksgiving. And then choices of three or four sides, depending on how many are in the party. I figure one chicken and sides should handle up to six diners. I'll list it for four to six. The soup, or a salad, as a starter."

"Dessert?"

He shook his head. "Not as many people are ordering dessert these days. Here, I think, in particular. The folks coming in are commenting on the healthy aspects of our food. Dessert sales have dropped. I'm considering slimming that menu down, actually, to maybe one or two signature desserts."

Paige nodded. That was definitely one of the downfalls of promoting the organic and sustainable aspects of their business models. It attracted the health nuts. Not that there was anything wrong with healthy eating, but it was hard to explain that organic, locally made butter was a viable and valid addition to food preparation. And so delicious. In fact, since she got her milk through a share in several cows, she was able to get a portion of the milk she used raw, which made fantastic butter. Not everyone wanted raw milk though, so the bulk of what she bought was sent through a local processor who did small batches for hobby dairies. And either way, raw or processed, she could sleep at night knowing that the milk she got wasn't from cows that were hormonally forced to produce month after month but instead were following the more natural pattern of breeding and producing young. Many of those offspring eventually turned into the beef she ordered for clients since the dairy and livestock farmers were neighbors and friends.

"This is wonderful, Law. And the vegetables are perfect as well." Renee beamed at her husband. "I can't imagine this not being successful. Who doesn't like to go out to eat as a family? And sharing a meal, the same meal, makes it more fun."

"We'll see. The staff is on the fence about it. They seem to think people go out to eat specifically so everyone can get what they want and not have to share. What do you think, Paige?"

Paige chewed for several heartbeats. She could see both sides, honestly. "I'm not sure, but it's definitely worth a trial run. I think it's a great idea."

Lawrence nodded. "Tell me what you two were discussing while I was getting the chicken."

Paige's heart hammered in her chest. "It's nothing, Dad. It's fine."

"It isn't fine." Renee set her fork down on her plate with a clink. "She mentioned our dream to travel when you retire and I simply reminded her that one reason we're not off chasing that dream today is because you're not ready to throw away twenty-plus years of hard work. You built a legacy that you hoped to pass down to your daughter. And now she wants nothing to do with it."

"I don't—"

Lawrence raised his hand. Paige snapped her mouth shut. "There's more to it than that, Renee. Yes, I'd like to retire, but there's no reason I can't start stepping back. I think Hector, the new sous, is going to work out fine. There's no reason he can't be promoted to head chef in, say, a year. Then I can scale back and we can take longer trips. It's not as if we wouldn't still be in the area between trips if I didn't have the restaurant to worry about. Just because we want to travel doesn't mean we're going to sell the house and move."

Deep creases lined Renee's forehead as her lips turned down. "It's not the same. You know as well as I do that if you're not completely done with the restaurant, any trip we take will be full of calls and email to make sure everything is all right. And heaven forbid something go wrong. We'll be on the first flight home. No. There's no point in trying to go somewhere until you're free of these ties."

Lawrence covered Renee's hand with his. "There's no need to be extreme. Don't forget that God's got a plan, too. So we need to see what He's going to do. Besides, I'm not ready to retire tomorrow, even if you're ready for that. I like the idea of easing out of things. Closing on Sunday was a big first step, and now that the initial furor has died down, we're actually seeing a slightly higher overall bottom line. With one fewer day of work. So relax."

"I'm sorry wanting to branch out on my own is impacting your retirement plans. I'm apparently failing everyone these days. Maybe you and Whitney can start a club about how my catering business is ruining your lives." Tears stung her eyes and Paige blinked furiously as she stood. "I'm going to run. The garden isn't going to weed itself. It was good, Dad. Let me know how it works when you put it on the menu. I'll call later this week, Mom."

She snagged her purse off the back of her chair. Swallowing did nothing to ease the burning in her throat. Barely able to see through the blur of tears, she hurried from the restaurant.

10

Jackson lay back in the hammock and pushed with his foot to start it swinging. Even with the early-July heat, the shaded patio behind the house was a pleasant respite from the noise inside as Ben and Zach shouted at the aliens they were shooting in whatever game they were playing together. Sometimes it was fun to watch, and join in on the smack talk, but after lunch with his sister, her husband, and their four kids, he needed to recharge. A lawnmower coughed to life and its droning hum filled the air. He stared through the canopy of leaves at the patches of bright blue sky. What was Paige doing this afternoon?

He'd spent the morning at church scanning the crowd for her. She didn't go to his church, they'd discussed that while they waited for the fireworks. But something in him had half-expected her to give it a try. Stupid, really. Why would she switch, even for one day, from the place she felt at home? She'd gone on and on about her church and how much she loved it. There was certainly a draw to the smaller congregation, his church could get overwhelming. But he learned so much and was challenged every week by Pastor Brown… there was no replacing that. Would she be willing to give it a try if they got serious?

If we get serious? Jackson shook his head. Talk about the cart before the horse. They hadn't even been on a date yet. Not really. Their dinner at Season's Bounty had been work-related, and randomly bumping into one another at the fireworks didn't count. Did it? Maybe it did when you spent more than ten hours talking. He'd certainly learned a lot about her over the course of the afternoon, and all of it made him want to know more.

ELIZABETH MADDREY

Before he could talk himself out of it, he punched in her number on his cell, his heart racing as it rang.

"Hello?"

"Hi Paige. It's Jackson. Busy?"

"I should be, but you happened to catch me while I was procrastinating. What's up?"

Jackson gave another push with his foot to get the hammock swinging again. "I spent the afternoon with my sister and her family. It's a crazy, loud experience. Fun, but it leaves you drained. So I was hanging out on the patio, thought of you, and figured I'd give you a call. How was your day?"

Silence stretched across the line and his stomach knotted. Had he been too forward?

Paige sighed. "I've had better days, honestly. Between a fight with my roommate to start off the day, being late to church, and lunch with my parents that left me feeling like I'm letting them down, I was ready for a nap. But the garden plot that comes with the apartment doesn't care for itself, so I went over to do a little bit of maintenance and found that the gardeners on either side have each planted in my space and they took exception to my harvesting what they consider their produce. Of course, I hadn't realized they weren't my plants until they started in on me. Honestly, they were in my plot, right next to the same things that are mine... I just figured they'd gotten big."

"Uh-oh."

"Oh, we came to an agreement of sorts. I get to keep what I harvested and they're moving the plants back onto their plots. I'll be processing the tomatoes, peppers, peas, and zucchini I gathered this afternoon the rest of today and probably tomorrow. Anyway, I reinforced the stakes and strings around my space, but I think I'm going to need to fence it with some chicken wire or something. Who does that though? It's not as if they're small gardens and my borders were clearly marked, so they had to know what they were doing. If they really felt like they needed more space, there are always a few

62

fallow spots they could use, they'd just have to walk a little farther to get to them. I just don't understand why they'd plant in an area that's clearly being tended."

Jackson fought a chuckle. It wasn't funny, at least not to her obviously, but it was unusual to hear someone up in arms about a garden. "When you say processing, what do you mean?"

"Do you ever buy produce?"

"Well... Zach's more into cooking than me or Ben, but I've been known to buy an apple on occasion. Maybe a head of lettuce."

"Typical. All right, vegetables don't stay fresh forever, right? So if you want to have vegetables year-round, you have two options. The first is the one most people employ, which is to buy them at the grocery store. But when the local growing season is over, that food is, at best, shipped from somewhere else in the U.S. and, at worst, brought up from South America or somewhere else in the other hemisphere. The second option is to preserve your garden excess. So I make chutneys and pickles and tomato sauces and can them. Then I can use them throughout the fall and winter to supplement what I'm able to get locally from people with greenhouses."

What was wrong with the produce from South America? She'd probably tell him if he asked but... was that really the conversation he wanted to have right now?

"So you can them. As in put stuff in jars and do whatever it is that pioneer women did to make them stay fresh?"

Paige laughed. "I'm not sure pioneer women were doing it, but yes. It's a fairly easy process to learn. I'll let you help sometime, if you want."

"I'm game but... I'm not what you'd call handy in the kitchen. When it's my night to cook, we usually order in."

"Good to know."

The sliding door from the living room opened and the sounds of battle spilled over the patio. Zach hollered over it. "Hey man, we're ordering pizza. You want in?"

"Yeah, be right there." Jackson swung his legs down and sat up. "I'll let you get to it. I need to go make sure Ben and Zach don't put olives on the pizza we're ordering."

"Thanks for the call."

"Absolutely. Still on for Friday, right?"

"Not an olive fan. Don't cook. Your black marks are piling up. But, yeah. And I'll probably be in touch before that about the fundraiser. Go rescue your pizza."

Grinning, Jackson hung up and jogged into the house.

"Psst. Trent."

Jackson turned and glanced at his watch. He had another fifteen minutes before he had to be at the Senator's committee meeting. She'd be calling in, but she always liked to have a physical presence in the room, someone who could read the other faces and fill her in. So many nuances were lost on a phone call. Not that politicians gave a ton away with their body language, but you learned to read it. "Greg?"

"Hey, man. Heard I'd find you here."

Jackson's gaze traveled to the visitor badge clipped to Greg's lapel. "I didn't think they let the press just wander freely these days."

"Shh. I'm not here as press today, just visiting one of the admins who I'm trying to talk into dinner. She is, as you'd imagine, skeptical and taking quite a bit of persuasion."

"Yeah. We're discouraged from dating reporters. That tends to end up working out poorly."

Greg shrugged and tucked his hands in his pockets. "Speaking of that... "

Jackson frowned. He hadn't heard of any new scandals lately and he tried to keep his ear to the ground, if only so he could keep Beatrice in the loop. Though she usually knew all the details he had, and more, long before he got to her.

Greg leaned in. "You still working for Senator Carson?"

"Yeah?"

Looking over his shoulder, Greg's voice dropped to a whisper. "I'm not on the story, but Mercer says she's got something big cooking about your Senator, misuse of campaign funds or the like. They're planning to break it next week."

"There's no story there. Senator Carson has the best ethics of anyone in Washington."

Greg snorted out a laugh. "Like that's saying anything." He held up his hands. "Look man, I saw you and thought I'd give you a heads up. Maybe it'll turn out to be nothing, but you know how this town is."

"Yeah. I do. Appreciate it." Jackson dug a business card out of his pocket and scribbled his personal cell number on the back. "Look, if you hear anything specific, give me a call? I really don't think this is going to go anywhere, but it's always better to know what's going on before it's printed."

"I can do that, but you'll owe me."

Jackson sighed. "Which admin?"

Greg perked up. "Carol Ann, with Congressman Winters."

"I know her, she's a sweetheart. Look, I'll put in a good word, but you treat her wrong, you'll have half the guys in the building after you. She's like our little sister."

"Noted. Thanks." Greg clapped Jackson on the back and tucked the business card in his shirt pocket, patting it. "I'll be in touch."

"What did he say, exactly?" Senator Carson's voice was taut. Jackson imagined she was clenching her teeth. For every ounce of genteel, Southern woman, Beatrice had an equal ounce of steel. It didn't pay to get on her bad side. She'd been in Washington long enough to know which closets to open and when.

Jackson closed his eyes and pressed two fingers against the bridge of his nose. "I believe his exact words were 'misuse of campaign funds or the like.' What's going on?"

"I thought we'd handled this." The Senator's sigh rattled in his ear. "I was trying to salvage what I could of that...*woman's* career. But if she wants to play it this way, we'll play it this way. For now, don't worry about it. I'll handle it."

"But, the story—?"

"I've got this, Jackson. Since you gave me a head's up, we should be fine. Just keep doing what you're doing and let me know if you hear more."

This was the part of politics he hated. But it was part of the job. As long as nothing unethical was going on... and he trusted the Senator. "All right."

His reservations must have been evident because Beatrice added, "Just stay away from Lisa 'til I get back."

11

"Sorry to keep you waiting, Paige. Come on back." Jackson nodded toward the hallway leading to his office.

Paige swallowed as she rose and followed him. His charcoal suit had to be custom tailored. It emphasized his broad shoulders and lean frame. The pop of color provided by the teal and grey tie was subtle, but eye-catching. Had he really meant for the dinner on Friday to be a date?

"Have a seat. I'm so glad you called. Even if an email would've been fine for the menu, it's great to see you again."

A giggle escaped and she clamped her lips on it. *Could you sound any more like a brainless idiot?* "Thanks. Can I ask you something?"

His eyebrows arched and he folded his hands on his desk. "Of course."

"Did you really... is Friday a date? Like a date-date?" Her heart dropped into her stomach. There. It was out. And she could stop wondering. That was better either way, right?

One corner of his mouth quirked into a smile, the dimple in his cheek deepening. "I was hoping so. Is that all right?"

She nodded, her tongue darting between her dry lips. "Yeah. Of course. That's great. Um, okay, so I brought the menu—"

There was a sharp rap on the door before it swung in to reveal a tall, slender blonde in a pencil-skirted suit that left no doubt about her hourglass figure. Paige tugged her blouse down over what she always jokingly referred to as her caterer's bump. Her friends all swore she was the only person who noticed it, but in the presence of a woman who could give Barbie a run for the flat-stomach award... she really needed to figure out where to put exercise into her daily routine.

"Yes, Lisa? I'm in a meeting."

Lisa's eyes raked over Paige before flicking up toward the ceiling. "Whatever. Visits from friends don't count, and really, I should tell the Senator. I need you to come and look over some things in my office. Now."

Jackson shook his head. "Sorry, I'm swamped. This is the Chef and Owner of Taste and See Catering. She's handling the next fundraiser. So, as you see, it is actually a business meeting. Why don't you just send the Senator an email about whatever it is you don't understand?"

"Whatever." Lisa spun on her heel and left, slamming the door behind her.

Paige winced. "If you need to—"

"I don't. Just… ignore her. I'm sorry you even had to be introduced. She's leaving on Friday, so there's only two more days of her attitude infecting the place. I'm just trying to keep my head down 'til she's finished clearing out her desk. Where were we? The menu, right?"

"Right. Unless you, or the Senator I guess, have any major objections, this is what I'd like to do. I've tentatively reached out to my suppliers to make sure they'll have what I need in the right quantities and it looks like we should be set. And on the positive side, I can do it all through Virginia-based farms. I thought I might have to tap a few Pennsylvania sources, but we have just enough lead time that the Gormans are going to put in a few extra plants for me."

"Wow. You do a lot of business with them, I guess?"

"Yeah." And Paige had promised to prepare Thanksgiving dinner for them and run it out the night before so all they had to do was tuck it in the oven. It wasn't a big trade. She spent much of the week before Thanksgiving doing just that for other clients. It was the drive that would be the pain, particularly since Mrs. Gorman had insisted they couldn't possibly take it before Wednesday. Or meet her half-way for the hand-off. If there was another small farm that had the same impeccable standards in organic growing, Paige would switch in a heartbeat if it meant never dealing with Mrs. Gorman again. Though she'd miss Mr. Gorman. He was a dear.

Jackson studied her for a moment before nodding and returning his gaze to the menu. "This looks fine. It's not much different than what you originally proposed. I see a few little changes but I can't imagine she's going to have a problem with them. I'll double check and let you know for sure by tomorrow at the latest."

"Thanks." She wiped her hands on her khaki slacks and cleared her throat. "Well. I'll let you get back to work. I know you're busy."

"Do you have time for coffee?"

Paige whistled through her teeth as she unlocked the apartment door. Coffee with Jackson had been... amazing. What did he see in her? She shook her head. She wasn't going to question it. Conversations with Jackson flowed easily, like they'd been friends for years. For whatever reason, he seemed genuinely interested in her, and the feeling was mutual. Stacks of boxes greeted her as she opened the door. *Ugh. What now?*

"Whit? You home?"

"There you are. What are you doing out on a Wednesday? I thought you were always rattling around here on Wednesdays? Anyway, doesn't matter. As you can see, I've gotten some of my packing done. I'll be moving things into Elliot's storage unit for the time being, but you can expect me to be out by the end of the month."

Paige clamped her tongue between her teeth and counted slowly to ten. She sucked in a deep breath in and slowly let it out. Then repeated the process when that didn't cool the blood boiling in her veins. She forced her lips into a smile. "That's fine. But it doesn't change the rent situation. You realize that, right?"

Whitney frowned and tossed her hair. "We'll see. I talked to my dad, he doesn't think the lease will hold up in court."

Court? Whitney was really willing to take her to court over this? She couldn't afford that anymore than she could afford to lose her roommate in the first place. Or was that what she was banking on? "I guess we'll find out, if that's really how you want to handle it."

Whitney paled.

Paige fought a smirk. She'd been bluffing. Hopefully. "I'll get out of your way."

"Wait. Paige."

"Yeah?"

"Look. I'm not taking you to court. Dad just said I should try and see if the threat would get you to cave. But really, you have to see how unfair this is, don't you?" Tears welled in Whitney's eyes.

Paige's throat constricted. "I'm not trying to be obnoxious, Whitney, but I have to cover the bills and the rent. You agreed to help me do that for a year when you moved in. I know your plans have changed, but what do you expect me to do? Get evicted?"

"No. Of course not... but are you even trying to find a new roommate?"

"Yeah. But it took me three months to find you. It takes time." Paige ran her finger over the chapped skin on her lower lip. "I'll run through the numbers and see what I can do. Maybe we could lower the amount you owe? I might be able to handle a bit more. Just not all of it."

"Really?" Whitney beamed.

Paige held up her hands. "No promises, okay? But I'll take a look at let you know."

Jackson patted his pockets for the fourth time. His keys and wallet were still there. And this was getting ridiculous. It was just a date. He'd been on dates before.

"Nervous, bro? You need to chill." Zach boosted himself onto the kitchen counter and twisted the lid off a bottle of water. "Given how you two looked all day last Saturday, you're going to be fine. She's into you."

A fine bead of sweat broke out on Jackson's forehead. "Yeah. That's what worries me. What if I screw it up?"

"How do you screw up a first date? You're all spiffed up, you've got reservations for a nice restaurant, and then... what do you have planned for after dinner?"

"That's where I'm most worried. I didn't want to fall back on a movie. There's no conversation in a dark room. Plus, I don't want her to get the wrong idea. But all my other ideas seem corny."

Zach took a long drink from the bottle. "Whatcha got?"

"Bowling? Ice skating? Stuff like that."

"You're right. Corny. You're taking her to Old Town, right?" Jackson nodded.

"Why not just stroll through the Torpedo Factory and along the river? Or through the shops? There's enough there to keep you interested and it's looking like a nice enough night. So why not?"

"That's not too boring? I didn't want to come across as too cheap to plan another activity." Jackson stuffed his hands in his pockets. He may have been on dates before, but it had been too long since he'd been excited about one.

"Nah. It's good. Low key, lots of time to talk. Shows you're interested in her as a person, too."

"Okay. All right." Jackson swallowed the lump in his throat. Why was this so much harder than usual? Was it just that it'd been a while? Or was it Paige? There was definitely something about her. "Thanks."

"No problem. You'll have to fill me and Ben in when you get back. And we'll let you know which of the two of us is the conquering hero of console football."

Jackson snorted. "I don't understand why the two of you aren't doing something more useful with your Friday nights. Can't either of you get dates?"

"Let's just say I'm working some angles, 'k? Maybe I'll have something to report before much longer." Zach grinned and hopped down from the counter. "Until then, it's me and Ben taking on the greatest of the grid iron."

"Wow." Jackson's heart sped up when Paige opened her apartment door. The simple black slacks and wrap-around teal and black tank top were stunning and set off her pale, delicately freckled arms.

She grinned as she collected a black clutch and teal shawl from a chair before tugging the door closed behind her. "Thanks. I could say the same."

Jackson offered his elbow. "Shall we?"

With a low chuckle, Paige threaded her arm through his. "Absolutely. How was the rest of your week? Were you able to avoid Lisa like you wanted?"

"Ugh. She was escorted out at noon today. I've never been happier to see someone leave. Initially, I thought losing her was going to be detrimental to the support staff, but some things came up earlier this week that made it obvious we're better off." And hopefully the Senator was right and had the damage under control. No need to bring that up tonight though. "Beyond that, it was a pretty typical week with the Senator out of the office."

"Do you always call her 'the Senator'?" Paige climbed into the passenger seat of his jeep.

Jackson shut her car door and rounded the hood. *Did he?* Taking his own seat, he turned the key and snapped his seatbelt into place. "I guess I do. She's said I can call her Beatrice when no one's around. But it doesn't seem worth the risk of slipping up and being overheard by someone who'd be offended at a staffer's over-familiarity."

"Ah. So it's not her requirement. That's a little better. I'd been wondering if she was unpleasant to work for. One of those people who went off on rampages when they didn't feel they were given the respect they felt they deserved."

He shook his head. "Oh, no. She's not like that at all. I suspect she'd let us call her 'mom' if she thought she'd be able to get away with it. That's certainly the general feel she encourages—though that has its downside, too. Mom can be quite the disciplinarian when needed."

Paige laughed. "You like working for her."

"I do. I interviewed with several different offices, but the Senator—Beatrice—was the first person I felt was going to not only be able to mentor me but who would enjoy the process. We work hard but, at least in our office, it feels like she appreciates us." He paused. *When did Lisa stop feeling that way?* She'd commented on much the same thing when they'd briefly dated last year. *What had happened? With the allegations Greg had hinted at and the Senator's response, well... it had to mean Lisa was up to something. What had changed to make her willing to betray the Senator in such a way?* "What about you? Why catering instead of going to work in a restaurant or with your father?"

"Ugh. That's a question with a complicated answer."

"So? We have time." Jackson accelerated to merge with the traffic on the beltway. *Dummy. Maybe it upsets her.* "Unless you'd rather not talk about it. That's fine, too."

Paige was quiet for several heartbeats. Jackson glanced over. She was staring out the passenger window. *Way to go, Trent.* He reached across to gently touch her arm. "Never mind. Forget I asked. Instead, tell me about how you got into sustainability."

Her short laugh was devoid of mirth. "Those two things actually go hand-in-hand."

"Sorry." Well, that had killed the conversation. Had it ruined the evening, too? If so, that'd be a record, even for him. He drove in silence for several minutes, the local Christian radio station the only noise. And yet, even without conversation, the atmosphere in the car hadn't grown awkward. Maybe there was hope after all. He flicked on the turn signal and pulled onto the exit ramp that would take them into Old Town Alexandria.

As they turned onto the main street of the quaint historic area, Paige cleared her throat. "I'm sorry, Jackson. Things between me and my dad are kind of weird right now, and it all circles back around to the fact that I *don't* work at the restaurant. When I enrolled in culinary school, I think both my parents were expecting me to jump right into work with Dad and, eventually, take over. At the time, he ran a typical semi-upscale bistro. I was basically on board with that plan, too. But then I took a class on sustainable cooking and that, in combination with my Bible reading plan for the year, hit me hard. God put us here on the Earth as stewards, but we tromp around like conquerors instead, totally ignoring the effect our choices have on the land."

Jackson nodded. It was true. He certainly hadn't given it much thought before he met Paige. And even the marginal thought he'd been giving it lately had a lot more to do with wanting to understand her than a deeply rooted desire to make changes in his own life. "I can see that. So then what happened?"

"I started researching and regaling my parents with some of the horrors of modern food production." Pink crept across Paige's cheeks. "I'll admit I didn't go about it the right way at first—I jumped on the bandwagon and started ramming people at full throttle. It caused... tension."

"I bet." Jackson signaled before turning into a parking garage. He took a ticket from the machine and navigated through the narrow rows, fighting the urge to duck his head to help the jeep clear the low-hanging pipes. After he cut the engine, he dashed around to open her door. "Here we are."

Paige put her hand in his as she clambered down from her seat. Sparks shot through him. Did she feel them? He loosened his grip but didn't let go. She didn't pull her hand away.

"Anyway. Once I backed off a little, my dad started taking me more seriously and, after some prayer, he reinvented the restaurant into what it is today. It's still not perfect—but he's doing more than most of the other eateries in the area. I think he figured once he got on board that I'd stop talking about it and jump in. But by that point, I was half-way through a business plan for Taste and See and I'd gotten excited about doing something on my own. I wanted—still want—to see if I can make it work. He's disappointed. My mother's furious. She wants Dad to retire—she worries about him and the stress of running the restaurant. I think she figures that if I worked there, Dad would take it easier. But I'm not so sure he would."

Jackson winced. "That's never fun. I'm sorry."

"Don't be. It was an innocent question. Just happens that, for me, it's a complicated answer." She squeezed his hand and smiled. "Are your parents happy you're in politics?"

He chuckled. "Mom was resistant to my major in college, initially. If she gave me the 'but what are you going to *do* with it' speech once, it was six or seven times each phone call or visit home. But now that I've managed to get a job that actually uses my degree, she seems content enough."

"And your Dad?"

"Not in the picture. Hasn't been since I was two. I think maybe that's part of why Mom was so opposed to politics. She wanted me to have a stable career, something that might encourage me to be a family man." He shrugged. "I don't see politics as being oppositional to that, honestly. It seems to me that all it takes to be a family man is a will to do so. Still, I double-majored in business, so if I decided down the line that I should do something else, I have something to fall back on."

"Always good to have a backup plan."

"Do you have one?"

Paige frowned. "I guess Dad's restaurant. Though I hate to look at it like that. Plus, I like to think that Dad wouldn't put me in charge simply because I'm his daughter. He has some great people working for him. They deserve a chance to run things if that's something they want."

Jackson pulled open the door to the restaurant. "That's a very fair attitude. I don't know many people who'd feel that way. Especially in today's job environment."

"Yeah, well. Maybe my feelings would change if I needed the job. For now, though, things are going well enough that I can be magnanimous."

Jackson gave his name to the hostess. She led them through the dimly lit front room into a similar room in the back. A stone fireplace filled the back wall. Though unlit, it had logs stacked and ready for the temperature to drop. Candles flickered on each table and a quiet murmur of conversation floated through the room.

The hostess stopped at a booth in the back corner, near the cold hearth. "Here you are. Your server will be right with you. Enjoy your meal."

Paige slid onto the bench nearest the wall and flipped open the tall, skinny menu. "Have you been here before? What's good?"

"I haven't, actually. My roommate, Ben, says this is his favorite restaurant when he wants something semi-fancy. He goes on about it so much, I've been looking for a reason to come."

Paige grinned. "Did he give you any recommendations on what to order?"

"He said everything he's had is fantastic. So whatever looks good to you."

When the server cleared away the plate that had held a few smears of fudge and not much else, and topped up their coffee, Jackson leaned back against the banquette. His stomach was full, not uncomfortably so, but he definitely wouldn't be in a hurry for breakfast tomorrow. And he owed Ben a huge thanks. He'd been absolutely right about this place. He took a sip of coffee and studied Paige over the rim of the cup.

"What? Do I have chocolate all over me?" She grabbed her napkin off her lap and dabbed at the corner of her mouth.

"No, no you're fine. Can I ask you a question?"

"Isn't that what you've been doing all night? Shoot."

"Ha. Fair enough. Okay, here's the thing. You're so passionate and vocal about sustainability and making what efforts you can to, how did you put it? 'Live gently,' right?"

Paige nodded.

"How is it that you're not even registered to vote?"

"Wha—how do you even know that?"

His stomach twisted, shifting the food uncomfortably. "It's part of the checks we do on people we hire. Even if it's just for a single event. There are always people who will look for reasons to discredit the Senator or make her look bad. So we have to make sure there's nothing immediately obvious that's going to bite us in the rear."

Deep creases formed between her eyebrows as she frowned. "I'm not sure I like that. Though I guess I understand. Just one more reason I should have thought more carefully about applying for the contract though."

"Sorry. It really is standard, not personal."

Paige waved his words away. "I'll get over it. To answer your question though, I don't see the two as related. It's not a political decision, and I'm not looking for there to be rules and regulations forcing everyone to live this way."

"So you're not trying to convince people that it's a better way to do things?"

"I didn't say that. And I've already told you that I crusaded pretty hard when I first started realizing how scary the food industry, as a whole, has become. But after alienating several friends and almost losing any kind of relationship with my parents, I started to realize I was going to do more harm than good if I didn't just prove my point by living out my convictions and letting others see that. If I'm consistent and open with people when they ask, then they're more likely to be willing to consider a change in their own lives."

"Okay. I guess I can see that. But what about the rest of what government does for you? Don't you feel obligated to be involved in the process? To do your part to try and ensure that the people making and upholding the laws share your love of God and are working to keep our country in line with His principles?" Jackson took a deep breath and forced himself to back away from his soapbox and let Paige answer. Beating her over the head with his convictions wasn't the way to get her to agree to a second date.

Paige twirled a strand of hair around her index finger. "The short answer is no, honestly. God's in control and He's going to work everything to His glory. My purpose is to do what He's called me to do, not worry about things that I can't control. There are all kinds of verses in the Bible about that, from how His eye is on the sparrow, to the fact that He appoints the kings. None of those lead me to believe that I need to be involved in the process."

Jackson chewed on her response. It wasn't that he hadn't heard the same arguments before. In fact, most of the Christians that he'd spoken with who didn't vote had, effectively, the same thing to say. And it never seemed to matter that he had counter arguments.

"You're quiet. Deal breaker?"

He shook his head. "I was thinking about your arguments. But no, it's not a deal breaker. I was curious, mostly. You want to go for a walk along the river?"

"Yeah. I'd like that."

ELIZABETH MADDREY

It was a steamy summer evening, but the breeze off the water was cool enough that Paige tugged her shawl over her shoulders. They walked past the Torpedo Factory and into the local park that lined the water's edge. The sun was still hovering at the edge of the horizon and people were out riding bikes, roller skating, and walking dogs in the lingering summer dusk.

"This is nice. Thanks for suggesting it." Paige let her left arm dangle at her side. He'd held her hand on the way to the restaurant, would he do it again? Her stomach did the jitterbug at the prospect.

Jackson laughed. "I have to actually give props to my other roommate, Zach, for this idea."

"Where would we be without them?"

"Fast food and bowling."

"Oooh. Remind me to send them a thank you note." She grinned. He had to be teasing though. Surely he was perfectly capable of coming up with a fun date on his own. "So if fancy dinners and walks along the river aren't your immediate idea of a fun time, what is?"

Jackson twined his fingers with hers. Warmth radiated up her arm and into her belly. "I can come up with it when I need to, but I'm more of a casual, hang out guy. I like board games, or catching some football on TV. A picnic and some Frisbee, or a bike ride. That kind of thing. But those are all things you do once you've got a more established thing going on, aren't they? First dates need to be special—at least this one did—so I got some help."

He'd wanted it to be special? She bumped his hip with hers as they walked. "You did good. But, so you know, I like hanging out too. And I probably would've even been okay with fast food and bowling, though the way they treat the animals at the suppliers for burger joints... if you did some research, it might make you rethink ever being that hungry."

He gave her fingers a squeeze. "I'll keep that in mind for next time." Jackson stopped and faced her, his gaze meeting hers. "There'll be a next time, right?"

She stared into his eyes, getting lost in the deep chocolate pools. There were flecks of gold around the pupils, why hadn't she noticed them before? Paige nodded. "I'd like that. I'd like it a lot."

Paige frowned at the spreadsheet on her laptop. There was no getting around it, her eating choices inflated the budget. A lot. Still, there were places to scrimp. She highlighted the cell containing "beef" and deleted it. The totals at the bottom adjusted. Closer, but still not quite there. She checked the time and reached for the phone.

"Season's Bounty, how may I help you?"

"Hi, Dani, it's Paige. Could you check if my Dad can come to the phone?"

"Hey Paige, of course. Hold on."

A cheerful cello and piano arrangement filled the line. Paige smiled. Maybe Dad really had liked the CD she gave him if he was using it for their hold music. It was a nice mix of the classical feel and modern songs that appealed to a wide audience. She hadn't been sure Dad fit into that category though. Nice to get it right every now and then.

"Paige. How are you, Honey?"

Her dad's smile resonated over the banging of pans and banter of line cooks. A pang wormed through her. Maybe this would be more than a stop-gap measure after all. "I'm good. But I had a question."

"Well, if you called me, then I probably have the answer."

She laughed. "I hope so. I told you Whitney's getting married and wants to break her lease, right?"

"Actually, no. Will you be able to make rent if she goes?"

"Maybe." Paige took a deep breath. This was it, and there was no going back if he agreed. "I can, without another roommate even, if you could possibly use someone part-time on the line. I'd like to keep trying to work the catering, but I think I can do both."

"Hmm."

Her heart sank. Last time she'd asked, he was still running light in the kitchen. Had he hired more people since then? "But only if you need someone. Don't make work just because it's me. I'm not looking for a handout."

"Oh, I know."

Paige chewed her lower lip. Why hadn't she anticipated the possibility that he wouldn't have something for her? And yet, it hadn't even crossed her mind. "I'm sorry. I didn't think about the position that could put you in. I can find something else. Just forget I called, okay? I love you, Daddy."

"Wait. Wait. I didn't say I didn't have anything. But I think it'd be best if you came in to the restaurant and we could talk about it in more detail in the office. Could you come Monday morning around eight? We should have prep pretty well in hand by then and I'll have a few hours before the lunch rush starts."

Hours? What was going to take hours? She moved some papers on her desk out of the way and checked her schedule. "Sure. Monday works."

"All right, I'll see you then. And I love you too, Paige."

She hit end and set the phone down. Eyeing her budget spreadsheet again, she tweaked a few numbers but the total on the bottom wasn't changing enough. She was going to have to find a supplement to her income. At least it was Saturday. The paper would have a bigger job section to scan. Her stomach clenched. Had she been foolish to think she could start her own business? Should she close Taste and See and get a more traditional job?

Shoulders slumped, she pushed away from her desk and padded into the kitchen for coffee.

"Morning." Whitney glanced up from the magazine she was flipping through at the kitchen table. Paige craned her neck to glimpse the glossy pages. Wedding dresses. Of course.

"That it is. How's the wedding planning going?" Paige dropped a pod into the coffee machine and lined up her mug before pressing the brew button.

Whitney shrugged. "Okay, I guess. We're still looking for a venue. I can't believe the church is booked for Labor Day already. And everywhere else is saying they book a minimum of six months out, usually a year or more. Who knew?"

Um, everyone but you, apparently. Paige pressed her lips together. "Sorry. That's frustrating. If you end up needing to move the date, let me know. I can always cancel your contract. I haven't cashed your deposit yet."

"Oh no. We're getting married Labor Day weekend, it's just a matter of figuring out where. I guess we should at least nail down a reception place. Push comes to shove, we can get married at the same place."

Great. "All right. Keep me posted."

"We close on the townhouse next week."

And there it was. Paige grabbed her coffee cup, splashed in some cream and dumped in a packet of fake sugar. "I'm working on it, Whit. But I may not know for a week or two. You've paid through July. Hopefully I'll know one way or another before August, but you might want to start figuring out how you're going to work *your* budget, just in case."

"Whatever. Get it figured out, Paige."

Paige sipped her coffee, watching Whitney over the rim of her mug. "Do I need to be the one looking into suing?"

Whitney sighed, her body sagging in the chair. "No. I'll talk to Elliot, see what we can figure out."

Paige's cell phone was ringing when she got back to her room with her coffee. "Hello?"

"Morning. It's Jackson."

"Hey." Tucking a leg under her, Paige settled in the stuffed chair jammed in the corner of her room. "What's up?"

"Not much. I was just thinking about you. Thought I'd call and see how you were doing."

Tingly warmth spread through her. It hadn't even been twelve hours since he dropped her off. "I'm doing pretty good for a Saturday morning."

"The way you say that makes it sound like Saturday mornings aren't normally pleasant. What do you do with them?"

She took a long swallow of coffee. "That's when I do the books, balance my checkbook, pay bills. That kind of thing. So yeah, never really the highlight of the week. But it gets it done and I stay on top of it."

"Ah. I guess when you run your own business you need to be more proactive about that than a typical person."

Did she? "I don't know, maybe. I've always done it this way, since I got my first checking account in high school."

"You balanced your checkbook in high school? Your parents must've been thrilled."

"Doesn't everyone? I mean, maybe not in high school, but once you're on your own?"

Jackson's laughter made her smile. "Nope. I check my bank statement once a month just to be sure everything looks reasonable, but that's it. I'm not sure my roommates even do that much."

"But... how do you budget?"

"I'm pretty sure most people our age don't do that, either."

She frowned. "Do you?"

"I do, actually, have a budget. I just tend to manage it more loosely. I keep thinking about getting one of those programs that can synch with your bank online and then do reports. I just haven't gotten around to it."

"I'll send you a link to the one I like." She drained the rest of her coffee. "So since you're not busy with financial management this morning, what have you been up to?"

"Let's see. I got up, went for a run, took a shower, and called you. Nothing Earth shattering."

She wrinkled her nose. "You run?"

"Only during the pre-season."

"Pre-season?"

"For the semi-pro football team I play on? I mentioned that, didn't I? It's probably my last year, we'll see, but I love playing football, it's hard to give up."

"Hmm. No, I don't think you did mention that. Receiver?"

"How'd you know?"

She grinned. Her dad would be proud. At least she still remembered the rudiments of the game well enough to decide what a player's build said about the best position for them. Even so, it'd been years since she'd watched a game from start to end just for fun. Cater a party for people watching a game? Sure. Watch it? No time. "I'm an only child and my dad loves football. I learned to love it, too. Though I'm not such a super fan that I arrange my schedule around it. I haven't caught a game in awhile. Dad usually gets tickets to a game or two when the 'Skins are in town, but who wants to deal with all that traffic?"

"I'll get you tickets to some of my games when the season starts. Bring your dad."

"I'd like that. He'll get a kick out of it. We used to make time to hit up my old high school's games together."

"We're a little bit better than that. If you ever want to come watch a practice or one of our scrimmages, let me know."

"It'll depend on when, but I might just do that. What does the rest of your day hold?"

Jackson let out a heavy breath. "I brought some work home, and I told Zach and Ben that I'd go to the movies with them tonight. You?"

Paige glanced at the clock. "I've got kitchen time at the culinary school in an hour and a half. I need to do as much of the prep for my PC clients as I can. I booked it the rest of the day, so I should be able to get a lot done. Then, I don't know, I'll probably read and get to bed early. I like to be at the early service so it's not a rush to make lunch with my parents."

"I'll let you go then. Can I call you tomorrow? I won't be home from my sister's 'til after dinner probably, but I'd like to at least hear your voice."

Smitten. She was officially smitten. "I'd like that. Thanks for calling."

"Talk to you tomorrow."

14

Jackson grinned as he tucked his cell phone in his pocket. If he wasn't reading things wrong, she was just as interested in him as he was in her. He'd ask her out again tomorrow. Maybe they could do something a little more laid back this time. Just hang out. She said she liked that.

"Hey, man." Zach poked his head in Jackson's room while knocking on the doorframe. "You busy?"

"Nope. What's up?"

"I think you need to see this. Come on."

Zach disappeared down the hallway. Jackson raised his eyebrows. Didn't sound like a gaming issue. He pushed off his bed and ambled to the living room where Zach and Ben sat in front of the TV.

Ben looked over, milk dripping off his spoon back into the enormous bowl of cereal balanced in his lap. "Did you know about this?"

Jackson frowned and stared at the TV. The Senator's picture was in a small box to the upper left of the reporter speaking earnestly into the camera. "Turn it up?"

Zach grabbed the remote and punched the button.

" ...the Senator was unavailable for comment. However, we have a former staffer on the phone with us this morning, speaking anonymously. Hello? Are you there?"

A heavily modified voice responded. "Yes, I'm here. Thanks for having me."

The reporter smiled. "Thank you for coming forward. What can you tell us about the Senator's fundraising budget discrepancies?"

"Well, I know for certain that her last two major events brought in fifteen thousand dollars more than was reported or deposited."

"Thirty thousand dollars? That's a bit of money, and a serious accusation."

"I have proof. Before I left, I made copies of all the expense reports for the two events, as well as the post-event tallies and actual deposits."

"And who in the Senator's administration, typically, would handle these transactions?"

"Turn it off." Jackson pulled his phone out of his pocket and rapidly punched in the Senator's personal line. "That's Lisa. They can garble up her voice all they want, but there's no disguising her vindictive attitude. This must be what she was going to try and sell me on Wednesday. Thanks, guys."

"This is Beatrice."

"It's Jackson, Senator. You've seen the news?" He paced back to his bedroom, shutting the door before dropping into the chair at his desk.

The same reporter's voice droned in the background of the call. "I have. It's under control. Lisa thinks she has proof, but what she's forgotten is that I also have records showing that the only person who participated in both tallying and making deposits is her. I've got a call in to the bank now to verify that she was alone when she brought those deposits in."

"But money is supposed to be handled by at least two people at all times. There are checks in place."

"And her repeat violation of the policy is what got her fired. I really don't think this is going to come to anything, Jackson. Of course, they'll use it as an excuse to dig and see if they can come up with something—anything—they can make stick. But even still, I'm not worried. You shouldn't be either. Just do your job, follow procedures, and keep your head down."

Keep his head down. He ran a hand through his hair. "About that. I took Paige Jackson out to dinner last night. And I'd like to see her again."

The Senator clicked her tongue. "I don't think that's a problem. I'm the one who chose the winning bid, and her proposal was easily the winner. Anyone who wants to audit the selection is free to do so, they won't find anything there. And, as you've apprised me of the situation at its outset... it should be fine. We might not be able to use her consistently as the caterer, but I like to mix things up, so it's unlikely that I'd be doing that anyway."

"Okay. Thanks." Jackson straightened, his breath coming easier, as if a weight had rolled off his chest.

"I'll let you know if you need to worry about anything. Until then, just keep doing what you're doing, and I'll see you on Monday."

"Yes, ma'am."

"Dude. You totally screamed like a girl when the bad guy jumped out from behind the door. Like everyone didn't see that coming." Jackson punched Ben on the shoulder, shaking his head. "Maybe we should've gone to see the chick flick instead. More your speed?"

"Har-de-har. I happen to be sensitive. The ladies love it."

Zach laughed. "Sure they do. 'Cause they want someone they get to protect. I'm glad I'm not meeting the women you meet. I still think I ought to wear the pants in a relationship."

Ben snorted. "My pants are just fine, thank you. And it's not like either of us are in a relationship. Jackson here is the only one of the three of us with anything remotely resembling romance on the horizon. And with someone completely out of his league, at that. How did you swing that, again?"

"Good looks and clean living, boys." Jackson grinned and pulled open the door to the backseat of Zach's small compact car. "Ugh. How do you drive this thing? It's like a clown car."

"Whatever. I fill up once for every four times you do. Some of us don't have an entire disposable income to spend on gas." Zach slid behind the wheel and adjusted the rearview mirror. "Move your head, I can't see behind me."

Jackson slouched down in the seat, his knees pushing into Ben's seatback.

"Hey."

"Well scoot up. I've got to put my knees somewhere." Jackson frowned. "I'm driving next time. I don't care who wins the coin toss."

"Hey, my car's not even this bad. And if I'm driving, you can easily beat out Zach calling shotgun. He never seems to remember the rules of car seat choice." Ben tilted his chair back a notch, pressing it even further into Jackson's knees.

Jackson kicked the chair. "Seriously, man."

"Children. Would you mind not wrecking the car? I still have another year of payments on this thing. And I was hoping it'd last for at least a few years after it was paid off." Zach glared at Ben.

Ben returned the seatback and stuck out his tongue. "Spoilsport. Are we eating dinner out or getting a pizza or something at home?"

"Burgers. I want a burger." Jackson leaned forward, resting one arm one each front seat. A tiny twinge of something hit him as Paige's words about the conditions of the animals raised for food echoed in his head. He pushed it away. "If I have to be crammed back here, I ought to at least get to choose what we eat."

"Seems fair." Zach shrugged and looked at Ben. "Eat in or take home?"

"Let's take 'em home. I'll order carryout while Zach starts driving. Makes it easier to grill Jackson about his date with Paige while we eat when there's less of an audience." Ben slipped his cell phone out of his pocket. "Everyone wants their usual, right?"

Zach and Jackson nodded their assent and Jackson settled back into his seat. The car might not be so bad if you were an average size, but there was nothing comfortable about this backseat when you were tall and had done more than walk by a gym at some point in your life. He turned to stare out the window as Zach threaded through traffic. What kind of grilling were they planning? There wasn't a lot to say. And he sure wasn't interested in having them rag on him about how much he liked her. *Play it cool. Just play it cool.*

When the burgers were collected and they'd made it home, Jackson headed back toward his room.

"Hey, wait. Where are you going?" Zach plopped into a seat at the kitchen table. "You're not actually going to break Jackson's Prime Directive and eat somewhere other than at the table, are you?"

Jackson's Prime Directive? He wasn't that bad. Was he? Just because he'd fussed at them for leaving bags of chips all over the living room the first few weeks they'd lived here didn't make him obnoxious. He'd overlooked the cereal this morning, hadn't he? "I'm just putting my shoes away. I'll be right back."

In his room, Jackson sank down on the edge of his bed and took off his shoes, lining them up neatly by the footboard. He grabbed his cell and thumbed open a text message, his fingers hovering over the keys. He'd called her this morning, was it ridiculous to text her tonight? Did he care? Tapping his fingers together, he stared at the screen then frowned. He liked her. He wasn't one of those guys who tried to play some weird game of withholding attention to make sure a girl was interested. He began to type.

Hey. Just got back from the movie w/ the boys. Lots of gore—loved it. Hope you're having a gr8 night.

He slipped the phone in his pocket and took a deep breath. Time to go face the morons and their inane questions about Paige. Just as he stepped out of his room, his phone chimed. Grinning, he checked it.

Hey back. Just cracked open a new book. NO, not telling U title. Snuggled in for good reading time with a snack.

Hmm. That was a nice mental image. He tapped back.

What kind of snack? Got a burger n fries w8ing for me, but nothing sweet in house.

"He's standing in the hallway grinning at his phone like a fool. Who you texting, Jackson?" Zach's voice took on a sing-songy tone.

Heat flooded his face. Jackson dropped his phone back into his pocket. "Yeah, yeah. You better not have eaten my fries."

At the table, Jackson pulled out a chair. His phone chimed. That wasn't happening with the peanut gallery all gathered around. He grabbed the bag and dug out his burger and a skimpy cup of fries. Frowning, he reached across the table and scooped a handful of fries off Ben's wrapper. "Those are mine, I believe."

"Hey." Ben swatted at Jackson's hand. "Snooze you lose. Give 'em back."

"No chance." Jackson moved the fries out of reach and unwrapped his burger. His phone chimed again.

"Go ahead. We'll wait, won't we, Ben." Zach snuck a fry off Ben's wrapper and popped it in his mouth.

Ben shook his head and scooped up the rest of his fries, cramming them all into his mouth.

"Gross. Figure out a way to chew with your mouth shut." Jackson took a huge bite of burger and wiped his fingers on a napkin. He took out his phone.

Spiced pecans. Mixed a batch for a client, made extra for me.
You still there?

He grinned.

Got busted by Zach. Then busted Ben for stealing my fries. They both say hi.

Jackson put away his phone and took another bite. "You going to be able to swallow that mouthful anytime in the near future, Ben? Need a drink?"

"M'good." Ben's adam's apple bobbed as he swallowed. "What'd she say?"

"That she's reading and eating spiced pecans."

Zach shook his head. "You've got it bad, don't you? Already texting about stupid stuff."

Jackson shrugged. His phone chimed again.

Hi back to Z&B. Will let you go. TTY tmrw?

"She says hi, by the way. Hang on." Jackson quickly typed back an affirmative before putting his phone away. Did he have it bad? Maybe not yet, but he was well on the way. "And I don't think you realize how not-stupid it is that she can actually make, not just buy, spiced nuts."

"That is definitely a good quality in a woman. I'll have to add that to my list." Ben nudged Zach with his elbow. "So... tell us about your date last night."

Jackson stuffed the remainder of his burger in his mouth and sucked on his soda. He chewed for a minute. "It was good."

"And?" Zach leaned his elbows on the table.

"Are we girls now? It was good. Your dinner recommendation was right on." He looked at Ben then switched to Zach. "And your suggestion to walk by the river was also a hit. So thanks. And yes, I'm going to ask her out again. Tomorrow, probably, when I call. Is that enough, or did you need me to relate our conversation word for word?"

"Could you if we asked you to?" Zach arched a brow.

Could he? He took another pull from his drink, the air bubbles and ice rattle signaling the demise of his drink. He gave a short nod. "Probably."

Ben punched his arm. "You do have it bad. But since she's hot, I can't really blame you."

Zach chuckled. "Yeah. She's definitely a step up from Lisa."

Lisa. Jackson's stomach churned, his dinner settling to the bottom in a lump. "Yeah, well, that's not hard. That was her this morning. On the TV. The Senator says that Lisa embezzled funds and is now trying to make it look like the Senator misappropriated them."

Ben let out a low whistle.

"Yeah. Something like that."

"Near miss, man. Near miss." Zach stood and moved into the living room. "Now, are we taking on the big boss at the end of the game, or what?"

Paige parked at the rear of her Dad's restaurant and pressed a hand into her jumping stomach. *It's just Dad. Not a job interview. Not a real one, anyway.* Should she be looking for a real job rather than running back to Daddy? She blew out a breath. Depending on how this mysterious meeting went, that might be just what she ended up doing. One bridge at a time. Just cross one bridge at a time.

Grabbing her purse, she checked that her car was locked and crossed the small back parking lot. Only her dad's car was there. Where were the other cooks? Didn't he have people helping with prep? She pulled open the rear door and made her way into the kitchen.

"Hello?"

"Just a minute, Paige, I'm in the walk-in."

Her gaze roamed over the pristine, quiet kitchen. It should be bustling. "Where is everyone, Dad?"

"Ah." Lawrence stepped out of the walk-in freezer carrying a tray loaded with plastic covered bowls and sealed containers. He leaned back against the door until it closed with a loud click. "I've been having trouble staffing the early shift of cooks. No one wants to come in and do prep. So, for now, I've had the closing guys do as much as is reasonable and I just come in earlier to do the rest. I've got it all nearly done, but if you don't mind helping, we can talk and chop. I'm sorry. I thought I'd be ready when you got here, but they skimped on onions last night."

Of course they did. No one in their right mind volunteered to dice onions. But it had to be done. "Sure. I didn't bring my knives."

Lawrence gestured to a set of blades nestled in their own carrying case. "Choose whatever you want of mine. If you do the onions, I can finish portioning the chickens."

"That'll work." Paige found an apron hanging with several others on a hook near the sink. She tied it on before scrubbing her hands. "How long has it been like this?"

"Eh." He shrugged. "Maybe six months. We're adjusting."

No wonder her mother was mad. Instead of the more laid-back schedule he'd been slowly transitioning to, he was back at the all-hours life of the first-year restaurateur. "You don't have anyone you can get to do it?"

"I've tried promoting up. That worked out for a few weeks. But so many walk away when they finally realize what's involved in moving to a more senior position. I had actually planned to put some ads in the paper, but then you called."

The early morning and lunch shift wasn't what she'd dreamed of, but it would do. "You'd need me every day?"

"Most likely. But I had an idea that you're either going to love or hate. If you hate it, we can talk about a straight hourly position. But I think—hope—that you'll like my offer."

Paige deftly chopped the top off an onion and split it in two before digging her fingers under the layers of skin and stripping them off into the trash. As she began to dice, her thoughts raced. "Let's hear it."

Lawrence was silent for a moment, his gaze on the neat cubes that fell from her blade. "I've always admired your knife skills."

"I won't know how much flattery helps you, Dad, until I know what you're thinking."

He grinned and slapped a whole chicken down on his cutting board. "What if you took over opening and prep for lunch, worked through service, say 'til one-thirty, and handled the small bits of catering we do in the afternoon?"

Paige scooped the onion bits into a bowl and started on another. "And when do I handle my own business in that scheme?"

"What if," Lawrence paused, cleared his throat, and started again. "What if the two catering businesses merged? You incorporate Taste and See into the handful of jobs we get, and run them all from here. Then you have the benefit of a solid income and I get the help I desperately need from someone I have no trouble relying on. Everyone wins. Even your mother."

"I see." She gnawed on her lower lip. What he was suggesting made a kind of sense. There certainly was no need for two catering operations in one family. And if the jobs were going through Season's Bounty, then she wouldn't have to do all the food. Some of it could be handled by the staff during the kitchen lulls. And there'd be no more hunting around for rental spaces to cook. But what about her personal chef clientele? There wasn't time for them with that setup. Plus, wouldn't it be admitting defeat?

"You're quiet." He dropped chicken pieces from several birds into a bowl and slid it into the refrigerator.

Paige looked down at the onion she was working on. It wasn't her most even work, but it'd do. "Let's start with the morning prep and lunch shift. If I leave by one, one-thirty, I still have time to attend to my personal chef clients, website inquiries, and so forth. If you get a catering job, you sub-contract it out to Taste and See and I'll follow your menu requirements and work onsite here for my regular hourly rate."

At the sink, Lawrence dried his hands, tossing the towel over his shoulder when he finished. Leaning against the counter, he rubbed his jaw. Finally, he nodded. "All right. We'll try it and see how it goes. If either one of us decides it isn't working, we'll readdress the issue."

The muscles in Paige's jaw and shoulders relaxed and the throb that had been building at the base of her head eased. "I'm going to need at least one person to help though. You're doing too much the night before. It's going to impact quality and taste."

"I think Hector will come in if he knows he won't have to do it all. And with someone in charge who can keep him on task, what he does should actually be a help rather than a hindrance to a smooth lunch shift. Everyone else comes in around ten."

"I remember. Plus, you'll be here today, right?" Paige cleared away the last onion and wiped down her knife. "What else do we need to do?"

"Yeah, I'll stay today, introduce you around, that sort of thing. Though I think everyone knows you. Or at least knows about you." He grinned. "Let's go see if we need to replenish any of the sauces."

By the end of the shift, Paige had found the kitchen's rhythm, and her feet were throbbing right along with it. She hadn't missed this aspect of full-time kitchen work.

"So?" Lawrence carried a stack of pans to the dishwashing station at the back of the kitchen.

She blew out a breath and leaned against the counter. "It gets hopping in here, but you've got a solid team. I'm impressed."

Lawrence grinned. "High praise. It ran more smoothly than I've seen it go in months. You run a kitchen well. I was able to get some of the office work done since you had things so well in hand."

"You need to hire a manager, Dad."

"I know, I know. But I keep thinking your mother will change her mind and come back since I'm still here." He lifted his palms to the ceiling. "What can I say?"

Paige shook her head. Stubborn. But at least she came by it honestly. On both sides.

"Here." He held out an envelope. "I figured you might need your first week's pay in advance."

Paige pushed the envelope back to his chest. "No, Dad. I'm fine. Pay me with the rest of the employees."

"It's not for another week though."

"That's fine. I'm good until then. Promise."

She met and held his gaze for several heartbeats.

"Okay. But if that changes, you tell me. I've given advances before to good workers. It's not because you're my daughter."

She leaned up and kissed his cheek. "Thanks, Dad. I'm going to run, get a shower, and then see if I can still get to everything that needs to be done today. I'll be in tomorrow morning for prep."

"Hector will meet you. He doesn't have a key, so... "

"Right. I'll be listening for him."

16

"I'm sure you all saw the news this weekend." Senator Carson offered a tight smile to her staff. Jackson glanced around the packed conference room as heads began to nod. Everyone was here. She didn't have a huge group of people working for her, but they were a loyal bunch. Or were they? Who would have expected Lisa to pull anything like she did? "First, let me just say I believe we have the situation under control. The truth of the matter is that Lisa embezzled from several events before she was caught. I have proof, and an admission of sorts, that I'll use as necessary. I had hoped she'd be willing to leave quietly without a reference. Apparently, she wasn't content with our agreement. For now, please just continue as usual. Refer any inquiries to Stephanie, she's handling all the press. Questions?"

No one spoke. That was it? He'd expected more details... though maybe there weren't any.

"Okay. If you think of any, you know where to find me. Now get back to work." Beatrice smiled and crooked a finger in his direction. "Jackson, if you'd stay a moment."

When everyone except the Senator and her Chief of Staff had filed out of the room, Jackson moved to a seat closer to the head of the table.

"I suspect this next fundraiser is going to be under a lot of scrutiny. We're already talking over strategies to ensure that we preempt anything Lisa might try to pull." Beatrice looked over at Robert and nodded.

Robert cleared his throat. "I'm going to put the bids online, along with the comparison spreadsheet. Taste and See is the clear winner, so I don't foresee any pushback with our choice. But we're going to go overboard on transparency with this one."

"You don't think that'll make it look like we're trying too hard?" Jackson leaned forward, resting his elbows on the table. "Won't people wonder why we're doing this now?"

Robert sighed. "I thought I already won this argument."

"With me. But," the Senator tapped a finger against her lips, "if that's the first thing he asks? Maybe we need to spend a little more time in discussion. Jackson isn't devious. So if he's thinking this seems fishy, then a whole bunch of people are probably going to feel that way too."

"What *would* you suggest then?" Robert crossed his arms.

Great. He'd ticked off Robert. That didn't bode well for long-term job happiness. Though if the Senator was on his side, maybe he'd live through it. "Um. Why not just wait until someone asks for information and then provide it in a timely, responsive, and professional manner?"

Robert laughed. Beatrice reached over and laid a hand on Robert's arm. "No. He has a point. We have good records and we operate above board. Maybe we're not quite as squeaky clean as Jimmy Stewart's Mr. Smith, but we don't have anything to hide."

"So what, business as usual while they try to crucify you in the media?" Robert scowled at the Senator. "Do you not want to be re-elected?"

"Calm down, Robert. Of course I want to be re-elected. And no, I'm not going to just sit back and do nothing. We'll take care of Lisa. But for the August event, let's leave well enough alone. If someone asks, we'll provide whatever they need." Beatrice's gaze bored into Jackson. "Be sure you have immaculate records and that you follow money-handling protocols scrupulously."

"Yes ma'am."

"Very good." The Senator turned her chair to face Robert in a clear dismissal. Jackson slipped from the room.

Lisa better hope he didn't run into her in a dark alley. He hadn't wanted this stupid event in the first place. Sure, meeting Paige was a huge bonus, but was that even enough to offset the potential nightmare it could become?

Jackson dropped his football gear in a heap at the foot of his bed and guzzled the last half of his sports drink. It shouldn't be possible to be over a hundred degrees at six o'clock at night. And the coach shouldn't punish the whole team for one person's inability to follow the rules. Okay, sure, they were a team. But everyone had told the kid to go get his full gear, the fact that he refused should just be on his shoulders. What were they supposed to do, refuse to practice until he geared up? Idiot.

He carried the empty bottle out to the kitchen and held it under the faucet.

"Hey." Ben pushed the garage door shut with his foot. "Thirsty?"

Jackson lifted the bottle to his lips and took several long swallows before thrusting it back into the stream of water. The drink cooled his throat, but did nothing for his blood. "Ended up doing laps because one of the new guys thinks he's still back in high school. Actually, that's disrespectful to high school players. If he thinks he's coming back next year, then this is for sure my last season. It's hot. I don't mind running, but not when it's punishment for someone else being a jerk."

Ben pursed his lips. "And?"

"And nothing. Just a long, lousy practice that left me stinking so badly even I didn't want to be around me, so I showered at the field and endured the incessant ragging of the same person who put me in that condition in the first place. I haven't been that close to slugging someone since middle school." Jackson shut off the tap and lifted the bottle to his lips.

Ben watched him.

Jackson raked a hand through his hair. "And work was lousy. This thing with Lisa and the funds... I have a bad feeling about it. The Senator's not worried, but I think she ought to be. And as low man on the totem, coupled with being in charge of the next event, if things go south I'm the most logical choice for the scape goat."

"Never a fun position to be in. Is that all? No bright spots? Maybe a text or two from a certain hot caterer?"

"She didn't return any of mine. Probably just busy. I don't have a firm read on her schedule yet."

"Aha."

"Don't 'aha' me. I mean, fine, it's annoying 'cause I'd like to talk to her. But I'm not sure that I would even have brought up the work thing. She doesn't vote, I can't fathom she's interested in the latest political intrigue. Why would she be? And that makes me start to question if there's any point in trying to pursue something with her. She's interesting and fun—"

"And hot. Don't forget hot."

Jackson rolled his eyes. "And hot. But she's... she's a political Ent."

"Tell me you didn't just compare that lovely woman to a walking tree."

One corner of Jackson's mouth poked up in a wry smile. "But she is. Think about it. The Ents sat around, ignoring everything going on in the world thinking that it didn't apply to them because they were busy living their convictions. That's what she's doing."

"Yeah, okay. But it's not like she's the only Christian doing that—or non-Christian for that matter. I wasn't obsessive about voting before I moved in here. You've got to admit, it's hard sometimes to balance civic responsibility with the realities of politics."

What was hard about it? If you stood idly by while laws that ran contrary to the Bible were enacted with no challenge, you were culpable for the damage they caused. "Not really, man. You either do what you can to try to make a difference or you share responsibility for the problems. Sticking your head in the sand doesn't get you out of anything, it just gets your hair gritty."

Ben snickered. "Look, I agree with you, now. But I don't think most people who didn't grow up in politically minded families have the background to realize those implications. If you're like me, you grew up with a pastor who never mentioned politics in the pulpit. At school you weren't supposed to talk about God or the Bible because the church and state were supposed to be separate. We've, as a culture, accepted the idea that that means you can't talk about your faith in a public forum, rather than acknowledging it was originally designed to keep the government from interfering in the church."

"I don't know. She seemed pretty adamant about the idea that it was more important to live as an example and leave governing to God." Jackson peeled the label off his bottle. He'd apparently gotten through to his roommates, was it possible to get through to Paige, too? If he didn't, could he still be interested in her? How did you justify a relationship with someone who didn't share one of your core beliefs? Could you?

"Give her a chance. Go call her. I'm guessing hearing her voice will cheer you up."

"Since when do you know anything about relationships?"

Ben balled up a napkin and threw it. "I've dated."

"When? In high school?"

A dark red flush worked its way across Ben's cheeks. "College, too. The one that got away." He shook his head. "Go call Paige and leave me alone."

Paige stretched out on her bed and closed her eyes. She couldn't go to sleep quite yet, but she could rest for a minute or two. Maybe five. What a day. Her feet ached. Stabbing throbs worked their way up her calves. She'd get used to it before too long, but until then the end of the day was going to continue to be a misery.

The ring of her cell ripped through the quiet. She groaned. Maybe she could ignore it... but it could be a client. Or a new client. Or... she rolled over and grabbed the phone.

"'Lo?"

"Paige? It's Jackson... are you asleep already?"

She wiggled up, leaning against the headboard and stifled a yawn. "Not yet. I was just resting. I have a little more work I need to do before I can call it."

"Busy day today?"

"That might just qualify for understatement of the year. I saw your texts maybe ten minutes ago and planned to get back to you. Sorry."

"It's fine. I'm not bugging you, am I?"

She chuckled. "Not at all. I started back up at the restaurant today. I'm trying to make it possible for Whitney to move into the townhouse she and her fiancé are buying, but that means more cash flow than Taste and See is currently managing. So... Dad's wanted me to help out at Season's Bounty for a while now."

"Will you be able to handle both?"

Would she? It had to get easier with time, right? "I hope so. Today was rough, but that's to be expected, I think. Ask me again in a week. How was your day?"

"Long. Frustrating."

She waited. "Want to expand on that at all?"

"You remember Lisa?"

"She barged in on our meeting. Sure. I thought she left." Paige glanced at the clock and dragged herself off the bed and to her desk. Maybe if she typed quietly she could take care of some email while they talked. If she was going to be at the restaurant by five tomorrow morning, she needed to get to bed sooner than later.

"She did, but she's stirring up problems. It was on the news all weekend... you didn't see it?"

Her stomach clenched. She already had a black mark for not voting, would admitting that she didn't watch the news kill any chance of them having a future? But, bleh, she couldn't abide the idea of sitting for thirty minutes while perky people with overly-white teeth told you how terrible the world was. If you wanted to know that, you just had to walk around the city for a few blocks. You'd figure it out. "No. Missed it. Bad?"

"The Senator doesn't think so. I'm trying to trust her judgment."

Paige deleted an email and hit reply on the next. "Is there anything you can do?"

"Probably not. Well, nothing but pray. Would... would you pray too?"

Heat suffused her. When was the last time someone asked her to pray with them? Too long. "Of course I will."

"I'll let you get back to work. Sounds like you have a lot on your plate. It's good to hear your voice though."

Paige smiled. It was good to hear his voice, too. "I'm glad you called."

"We still on for Friday? I was thinking maybe we could grab dinner and hang out with Zach and Ben, watch a movie here at the house, or play a game or something? Is that too casual?"

Zach and Ben had seemed friendly enough when she met them. They had to be pretty decent if Jackson chose to spend time with them. She couldn't imagine inviting people to come and hang out with her and Whitney. Not that she and Whitney ever hung out.

"Or we can do something else. Just the two of us. Does six still work?"

"Six is fine. And so is hanging out with the guys. I was just thinking how nice it would be to have roommates who were actually friends instead of a means to an end."

Jackson chuckled. "I'll admit I lucked out. I've had enough bad roommates in my life to understand what you mean. And even though you're going to be working extra hard when you add the restaurant into the mix, maybe it's a blessing to have her out of your life."

"Hmm."

"Something to consider, anyway. Can I call you tomorrow?"

"Absolutely. Good night, Jackson."

"'Night."

Unable to stop grinning, Paige set her cell next to her computer and clicked on the next email.

Paige shuffled into the bathroom and cranked the hot water tap to full. None of the coffee she'd consumed before and during work at the restaurant today was making a dent in the fog that clouded her brain. And she had a lot left that had to be accomplished today, including her date with Jackson. She stepped under the spray, adjusting the tap slightly as the water seared her skin.

A date shouldn't be one more thing on the to-do list. It wasn't. Not really. When she could push through quivering muscles and the shadows hovering at the edge of her vision, it was definitely the bright spot that had kept her going all week. But an afternoon of gardening in the hot sun loomed between now and their time together. Maybe even a third shower, depending on how much sweat and grime was involved in the weeding and harvesting she had planned.

The haze receded. She switched off the water and grabbed her towel, still damp from her morning's shower, and wrapped it around her. She could do this. She'd made it through one week and only lost one client. And losing that one wasn't exactly heart breaking. She'd miss the income, certainly, but not having to deal with the constant litany of complaints? That wasn't going to be a hardship. With the amount of time she'd save not having to customize menus and ingredients for that one client, she could probably add two or three new people to her weekly schedule. Assuming she could find two or three new people.

Paige tugged on shorts and a tank top and eyed her flip flops. Her feet longed for the relief of open shoes, but the imminent dirt and brambles pushed her toward the sneakers. *Hang in there, tootsies. We'll wear the cool shoes tonight.*

"Well?" Whitney pushed open Paige's bedroom door and leaned against the jamb, arms crossed.

Paige blew her bangs out of her eyes and looked up from tying her shoes. "Good afternoon to you, too. Well what?"

"Elliot and I close on the town house tomorrow. Are you hosing me, or not?"

Paige bristled. Hosing her? There was no possible way to look at this situation and think that Paige was the one doing the hosing. Unless, apparently, you were Whitney. She bit her tongue and frowned at her roommate before returning her attention to tying her shoes.

Whitney sighed. "Sorry, okay? It's just stressful not knowing what's going on and whether or not we're going to be in financial trouble before our marriage even gets off the ground. You said you'd know soon… "

The responses that flitted through Paige's head weren't helpful. She pushed them aside and inhaled, pausing before exhaling. Then she repeated the process, willing her heartbeat to slow. Whitney didn't care that her stress wasn't Paige's fault, and telling her that wasn't going to be beneficial to either of them.

"Fine. Don't answer me. Just let me know when you know, okay?"

Paige waited until Whitney turned down the hall. "I've got it covered."

Whitney whirled, a hope-filled smile spreading across her face. "Really?"

Paige nodded. The numbers worked. It wasn't going to be fun, and there was nothing going into her savings account for the foreseeable future, but it wasn't as if she had friends calling at all hours begging her to go out and do things. Even if she did, she was usually too busy. Adding in the restaurant simply solidified that problem.

Whitney squealed and rushed into Paige's room, giving her a tight hug. "That's awesome. Thank you. I'll go call Elliot."

Sighing, Paige stood and grabbed a rubber band for her hair. After securing her locks in a messy knot, she grabbed a canvas bag full of other canvas bags that she used to hold the fruits of her garden, tucked her keys in her pocket, and headed across the street. At least tomatoes and zucchini made more sense than other women.

18

"You're just hanging out here? With us?" Zach shook his head and grabbed the game console remote off the coffee table. "You're either insane or brilliant."

"I'll go with B." Jackson hooked his thumbs in his pockets. "Out of curiosity, why would I be insane?"

Zach snorted. "'Cause you're bringing a hot girl to hang out with you and your two roommates who have no life on a Friday night. I mean, really, what are we going to do?"

Jackson shrugged. "I thought we could dig out a board game. We have several of those cooperative games cluttering up the closet that Ben always tries to get us to play. She seemed to think it sounded fun."

"You already told her this was your plan?"

Jackson nodded.

"And she's still letting you pick her up?" Zach pursed his lips. "Maybe she really is cool with it. Or she likes you so much she'll do whatever she thinks is going to make you happy. But that seems unlikely. She's too pretty to be desperate."

"Who? Paige?" Ben strolled in from the garage, dropping his bags on the kitchen table as he passed. "She's definitely not desperate. Why are we considering that?"

"This yahoo," Zach jerked his thumb at Jackson, "invited her to get takeout and hang with us tonight. She agreed."

"Huh. Nice to get the head's up. What if we had plans?" Ben grabbed the other controller and plopped on the couch.

Jackson raised his eyebrows. "You two? Plans? I think I'm looking at the extent of any plans you might make. When was the last time either of you went on a date?"

"No rush, bro. God's got the right girl for me out there somewhere. I'm just waiting 'til I meet her. Aw, come on, run you piece... gah. This game cheats."

Zach let out a guffaw. "Nah, you just stink at it. That's why I always win. I'm with him. When the right girl comes around, then you'll need to start scheduling your roommate hang out dates in advance. But, as it happens, I'm free this evening. Of course, I can't promise she won't throw you over for me after a few hours of my scintillating conversation."

Ben elbowed Zach in the ribs. "If she's throwing Jackson over for anyone, it'll be for me." He glanced at Jackson. "You sure you want to bring her here?"

"I was. Now... we'll see. If we don't show up, assume we went somewhere else." Jackson checked his watch. "Gotta run."

"Hey wait. You're getting food for us, too. Right?" Ben furiously worked the buttons on his controller then threw his arms in the air. "Yeah, baby. That's what I'm talking about."

Maybe eating here wasn't such a great plan. Hanging out, playing a board game, those weren't too bad. But having seen his roommates eat... "You know what? I'm going to take her out to eat. We'll head here after that. If you're nice, I'll bring dessert."

"Oooh. Are we getting food from here? I've wanted to try it since it opened but never managed to make the time."

Jackson looked at the ornate sign over the doorway, the only indication that a Vietnamese restaurant was located on the main floor of the office building. "I thought we could eat here, then head back home and hang with the guys. Best of both worlds?"

She chuckled. "I've seen guys eat before, so if that was your concern, it was unfounded. But I'm not going to complain about some time alone with you."

Grinning, Jackson slipped around the front of his jeep and grabbed the handle of the passenger door. "I was hoping you wouldn't mind. Do you like shrimp? They make a spicy shrimp that is absolutely the best thing you've ever tasted." He paused, wincing. "Though I have no idea where they get the shrimp. It's probably— well, definitely—not even local-ish. Is it even possible to get shrimp locally? We can go somewhere else."

Paige put her hand on his arm. "Relax. It's okay. And I love shrimp. Look, to be clear, I think we need to all do a better job of trying to live in a gentler manner. But I also realize that we have to do that within the bounds of reality. Not all of us, and I include myself in this, are able to chuck the life we've built and move to a rural area where we can farm and live in straw-bale houses and never again eat a vegetable that we didn't grow ourselves. It's just good to think about the fact that, even here in the suburbs, there are things we can do."

Jackson held up two fingers for the hostess. She led them to a table in the back corner of the restaurant with a window overlooking the parking lot. "Like what?"

"Like what? Oh, things we can do? Well, public transportation is an option for some, but again, not for everyone. I'm a car girl myself, because most of the places I need to go aren't accessible by bus or metro. And by the time you combine bus and metro and walking... that just doesn't work for what I need. But if I was in an office during the day and it was just a trip in and a trip out, I'd find a way to make it work."

He nodded. Most days he rode the Metro. He still drove to the station though. "I could probably ride my bike to the Metro on nice days instead of driving. It's not that far, and it'd be good exercise at that."

Paige beamed and sipped her water. "Exactly. It's exactly things like that that I'm talking about. Even if you only ride on the days when the weather's good, the difference adds up. Most people have enough room for a square-foot garden. They could grow their own vegetables and start reducing the demand for off-season produce flown in from South America. Or participate in a produce-basket program through a local farm co-op."

"Aren't those expensive? And full of swiss chard?" Jackson wrinkled his nose. His sister was always putting kale and chard into things and blaming it on the produce box they'd gotten.

She chuckled. "Some are better than others, you have to do some research. And yeah, there are probably going to be things you don't like or, maybe, don't recognize but who knows? You might end up finding a new favorite. As for the expense, it depends on what you're looking at. You're helping support a local family farm and getting produce that was allowed to ripen naturally so it retained more of its vitamins. Most of the stuff in stores has been chemically ripened and picked before its peak so that it'll make the journey without going bad."

The server appeared, as if out of thin air. "Can I take your order?"

Jackson met Paige's gaze. They hadn't even looked at the menu yet. "Do you need more time?"

She shook her head. "You had me at spicy shrimp. Whatever that's called, it's what I want."

Jackson flipped open the menu and scanned the offerings. When he found the right listing, he pointed to it. "Two."

The server nodded, collected the menus, and glided away.

"Do you think there's a special school for that? I've never been able to walk that gracefully. My parents put me in dance as a child, thinking it'd help me be less clumsy. I got kicked out. My dance teacher said she'd met elephants that were lighter on their feet."

Jackson fought a grin. "Aww. Poor kid."

She shrugged. "My parents are in the food industry. I grew up around food and learned that enjoying it was a good thing. Thankfully my genes don't tend toward obesity, but I still have to keep an eye on it. You can't be a good cook if you don't taste. And so often one taste leads to two, then you adjust the seasoning... before you know it, you've eaten the equivalent of two meals and all you've done is prep someone's menus for the week."

How was he supposed to respond to that? It didn't sound like she was fishing for compliments or saying she considered herself fat, but surely he needed to say something? "You're lovely."

The pink that washed across her cheeks drew his gaze back up to her eyes. "I wasn't... "

"I know. But it's still true." He reached across the table and clasped her hand. Electricity skittered up his arm. Did she feel it too? She didn't show it if she did, but she didn't pull away, either.

"Spicy shrimp." The server appeared out of nowhere again and gently set a plate in front of each of them. "Enjoy."

Jackson squeezed her fingers and started to pull his hand away. Her fingers convulsed, tightening her grip. "Why don't you pray before we eat?"

Jackson glanced at Paige. She sat in the passenger seat, staring dreamily out of the window as he drove her home. "Penny for your thoughts?"

She turned, a smile playing at the corner of her mouth. "Cheapskate."

He laughed. "Fine, a quarter?"

"Better. I was just thinking how much fun your roommates are. I see why you've lived together so long. You're a good mix of personalities."

Had they been together a long time? Two years didn't seem that long. Maybe it was in roommate land. "We have our moments, but generally yeah, we're a good mix. And at this point, we've got a pretty smooth routine going. I'm glad you had fun. They said I was insane for making this our second date."

"Nope. It was fun. We can hang with them again anytime."

He grinned. It had to be a good sign that she assumed they'd go out again. "I've got a scrimmage next Friday night. I can send you the info if you think you'd like to come out and see the game. It's in Fredericksburg though, so a bit of a haul, especially on a Friday."

She wrinkled her nose. "Maybe I'll wait 'til you have a game up here."

"Sure. Are you free Saturday?"

"Should be."

He signaled and turned into Paige's complex, winding through the buildings to a visitor spot near hers. He cut the engine and hit the button on his seatbelt.

"You don't have to walk me up."

He shook his head and pushed open his door. "Yeah. I do. My mother would kill me if I didn't."

Her laugh followed him around the car. "Fair enough. But I can't ask you in. I'm pretty sure Whitney's not home and, well... "

"It's fine." He took her hand as they walked up the sidewalk to the building's door. Inside, they climbed the stairs to her third-floor condo and stopped at the door. He pulled her closer, wrapping his arms around her waist. His lips tingled. It was too soon to kiss her. Too soon to want to kiss her as much as he did. He laid his cheek on her hair, the light fruity scent of her shampoo sent his senses reeling. "I had a really good time tonight."

"I think that's my line." Her arms circled his waist, her head resting against his shoulder. "Thanks."

He gave a gentle squeeze before loosening his grip and leaning back. "Saturday afternoon?"

"I have to work 'til one. But after that, I'm free."

He frowned. "Will you be up to doing something after working all morning? I was thinking we could go to the museums downtown, or maybe the zoo. Something like that. But if you've been on your feet all morning... "

"Any of those sound fun." She pulled away and turned to unlock her door.

"Talk to you tomorrow?"

"'Course. 'Night."

Jackson waited until she'd closed the door behind her and the locks had clicked before heading out. He'd never felt so alive.

Paige floated through Saturday and church on Sunday. If she stopped and was quiet, she could still feel Jackson's arms around her, holding her against his muscular frame while heat sizzled across every nerve ending. And even after the initial sizzles had calmed, there was a sense of warmth, of being home, that came from being wrapped in his embrace.

"You look lovely today, Paige."

Paige planted a kiss on her mother's cheek before sliding into the booth across from her parents. "Thanks, Mom. So do you. Hi, Daddy. Taking a break from the kitchen today?"

He grinned. "Every now and then, your mother wants barbecue. It's one of the few things I'm hopeless with. And Randy does it well, so why not visit an old friend and get some eats?"

"I'm not complaining." Paige inhaled the scent of smoked pork mixed with tangy barbecue sauce, water pooling in her mouth.

"Hey there, strangers. You've been hiding again, haven't you Lawrence?" Randy, a robust man with silver hair to his shoulders and a matching beard, would've looked more at home at a Civil War reenactment. And you could often find him doing just that, fighting under the Dixie flag and muttering about Yankees the whole time.

"If by hiding you mean busy running a restaurant, then yeah, that's where I've been. Same as you've been hiding from me, I imagine."

Randy's laugh shook his belly, straining the buttons of his shirt. "The usual all around?"

Everyone nodded. Even though it'd been a while since she'd eaten there, Randy undoubtedly remembered exactly what they all liked. He was just like that. Eat at his place more than twice and you were a regular in his book.

"Do you think he has a notebook in the back with pictures, names, and orders so he can keep it all straight?" Paige watched Randy make his way back to the kitchen, stopping at each table along the way to chat for a moment.

Lawrence shook his head. "Nope. Randy's just one of those people blessed with an incredible memory. And it's not just customers and their orders. The man is a walking encyclopedia. If it's something that interests him, or even caught his eye for more than a passing glance, he'll remember it down to the smallest detail."

"Which is, if I recall correctly, the exact reason his wife gave when she left him." Renee frowned, straightening the silverware on her napkin. "Sometimes a memory like that is more of a curse than a gift."

Paige winced. Randy didn't seem the type to bring up past mistakes and fling them in someone's face. But that seemed to be what Mom was implying. Of course, she only knew him as "Uncle Randy", Dad's restaurant friend. "I'm not sure I wanted to know that, Mom."

"Life is full of things you don't want to know but need to, dear." Renee shot a veiled look at Lawrence.

Lawrence sighed. "All right, all right. I was going to wait until after we ate though."

"What's going on?" Paige smiled at the server who delivered tall cups filled with crushed ice and a pitcher of tea that would be so sweet it'd make her teeth hurt. But she couldn't get enough of it. And what else were you supposed to drink with barbecue?

"I know you don't watch the news, but this week it's been full of Senator Carson. A former staffer is accusing her of mishandling money from fundraisers. It started out small, and felt like someone trying to get back at the Senator for something. But this morning the reports are saying there's more than just financial misconduct."

Paige's mouth went dry. Jackson hadn't said anything about more coming. Did he know? "Like what? Did they say?"

Renee shook her head. "They said they'd have the full story tomorrow. But honey, you've got to get out of doing this event. You don't want your name dragged through the mud with hers."

"Mom. I'm not going to bail on a client because of an allegation that, at this point, has nothing behind it besides sour grapes. Jackson actually talked to me about it last week when the story first broke. He's not worried, he says the Senator isn't worried. So I'm not going to worry, either."

"Jackson?" Renee leaned forward, elbows on the table.

Paige took a long drink of tea. Was she ever going to learn to keep her mouth shut? "Jackson Trent. He's the person in charge of the fundraiser. You met him, Daddy, remember?"

"Sure. He seemed nice enough. But are you really on a first-name basis with him? That seems unprofessional."

Unprofessional? "I'm on a first-name basis with most of my clients, Dad. I'm cooking in their homes, sometimes without them there. If you give someone a key, don't you think it's reasonable to let them call you by your given name? Even if I am just the hired help? Besides, Randy calls us by our names and you think it's one of the things that makes his business so successful. So what's the difference?"

Lawrence and Renee exchanged a look before her mother spoke. "Why are you so defensive, Paige?"

"I'm not defensive. I just don't think we need to jump straight into dropping a contract, one that has the potential to help me finally get the catering company off the ground, because of what may or may not end up being a big deal. And even if Senator Carson is guilty of something, I hardly see how having catered one event for her will be a huge black mark on my reputation." Not to mention the penalties in the contract if she cancelled. Paige fumed. Should she mention she and Jackson were dating? They were dating, weren't they? They hadn't exactly discussed it, but with how often they were talking, texting, and going out, that meant they were an exclusive item, didn't it? Their conversations certainly seemed to imply that they were—it wasn't as if you talked about how many kids you wanted to have and your retirement hopes with just anyone.

"I still want to know what's going on with this Jackson person." Renee looked at Lawrence, who shrugged.

Paige's shoulder slumped. "We've gone out a few times, okay? He's a great guy. I really like him."

"Oh, for heaven's sake, Paige." Renee covered her face with her hands, her head shaking. "Don't you have any sense?"

Paige scoffed. "Not according to you, apparently. Though I hardly see why it's a bad thing that I found someone who's interested in me who I also happen to find interesting and attractive. I thought your whole goal in life was to get me married off so I could start giving you grandchildren."

"To someone eligible, not someone you're working for. What kind of woman dates her employer?" Renee's fist bounced off the table, jingling the cutlery.

Lawrence laid a hand on his wife's arm. "Renee. It's not the end of the world."

"Don't you take her side. You know as well as I do how this could end up. Or have you forgotten about Mandy?"

Lawrence scrubbed a hand over his face. "No. I haven't forgotten about Mandy. Geez, Renee. When are you going to let that go?"

Renee's lips thinned as she pressed them together.

"Here we go, folks. Anything else I can get you?" Randy smiled as he put their steaming plates of pulled pork and beef brisket down in front of them.

Paige looked down at her food, her stomach churning. "Can I get a to-go box, please?"

Was it possible to have a Sunday lunch with her parents without it turning into an argument anymore? Her parents had always been fighters. And it had always left her wanting to run away and hide. Growing up, she hadn't had that luxury. You sat there, pasted a smile on your face, and ignored the fact that you felt like you were dying inside while they hashed things out. As an adult, she had the option to walk away, so she did. Not that it helped much. Paige pressed her fingers to her eyes. Was she just that bad at making decisions, or was there more going on? And what was that thing about Mandy? She'd have to find a time to ask her dad about it when Mom wasn't around. If he'd even tell her. It definitely had that vibe of "things that happened to parents before kids were on the scene," and those were rarely discussed in her presence. Most of the time, she considered it a blessing.

She stared down at the week's calendar. Only four mornings at the restaurant this week, so that was something. Hector had agreed to take Wednesday off her hands if he didn't have to go in on Saturday. It made Saturday busier, but having a day off in the middle of the week would help keep her personal chef clients happy. They'd all been willing to switch her day to Wednesday, which meant after she finished her restaurant shift each day, she had the afternoon to handle the paperwork, her garden, any food processing—she made a note to can a batch of spaghetti sauce on Monday—and maybe still get to bed at a decent hour. Was she ever going to get her own business off the ground, or was she going to get stuck with her dad's restaurant after all?

Her cell rang. She didn't recognize the number. Should she let it go to voicemail? Tempting. Very, very tempting. But that wasn't how you got new business. After almost losing the contract when she lost her charger, she even had a backup one of those now. *A necessary evil. Just answer it already.*

"This is Paige."

"Hi, Paige, it's Whitney. I'm calling from our new town house, wanted you to have the number. Also, could you go look in my room and see if I left a box of shoes in the closet? I've been digging through everything and can't find them and I just have to wear them tonight. We're going to dinner with Elliot's family for an engagement celebration and nothing else is going to go as well with this dress as those shoes."

Paige pushed her chair away from her desk. Would she ever be completely rid of Whitney? Not 'til after Labor Day. Wait. Whitney had moved out. The condo was completely hers. She could move her desk into the other bedroom and have a real office. Maybe a little reading corner with bookshelves instead of the overflowing chair jammed between the wall and her nightstand and the piles of paperbacks on the floor. "Sure. Hey, congrats on the house. No problems at closing?"

"No. It was great. I'm really glad things went as smoothly as they did, that's one less thing to stress about. And oh! We found the perfect place for the wedding, finally. And they'll let us use an outside caterer, so that's great, but I need you to fill out some forms and get them sent in."

Of course she did. "Sure. Just get them to me and I'll take care of it."

"Oh, well, I was thinking I could just text you the email address of the wedding coordinator there and you could get in touch. Eliminate the middle woman, you know? Plus, I mean, I'm really busy with decorating and everything. Okay? Are the shoes there?"

Paige sighed and opened the closet. Her eyes bulged. "There are probably twenty pairs of shoes here. I thought you got all your stuff out last week?"

"Well, I kept the essentials there, you know? I forgot the closet when we moved the rest of my stuff this morning. We'll swing by on our way to dinner so I can get those shoes and then I'll get the rest at some point. Maybe next week?"

"Can't you just take them tonight? I can help carry them down—I probably have a box you could just dump 'em in." Paige shut the closet and returned to her room. Maybe she'd do an accent wall, some kind of rich blue. Soothing but still with a pop. She rubbed her hands together.

"I guess. Let me make sure Elliot's able to leave a little earlier than we'd planned. I don't see why it can't wait, but whatever. I'll text you that email address."

The line went dead. Nice. "Goodbye to you, too. See you in a bit."

Paige drummed her fingers on her desk. Should she call Jackson and ask about the new allegations? Or wait? She didn't even know what the problem was. Step one, do some research and see what people were saying. If nothing else, not sounding like an ignorant idiot in front of the guy you liked was a good goal.

20

Jackson clenched his jaw as he strode through the halls of the Senate Office Building. He'd gotten a text late last night from his journalist friend and had passed the information on to Senator Carson, but the news this morning still had fire coursing through his veins. Anyone who would believe that she was capable of turning a blind eye to illegal toxic waste disposal was out of their mind. She was a woman who took her state, the great state of Virginia, and its ability to produce food for its residents, as well as food to be used in commerce, very seriously. Maybe she hadn't run on an agricultural platform, but that didn't mean she would condone toxic waste dumping.

People looked at him out of the corner of their eye as he zipped past. Conversations quieted, then resumed in force when he was just out of range. He should turn around and let them have it—though that would do no good. It would just confirm the rumor in their mind. You didn't get your name cleared by protesting innocence. Not in politics. You needed proof. Senator Carson had better have some or she was doomed. And he'd be sunk right along with her. It wasn't easy to recover from something like this. Everyone expected the staff to know what was going on behind closed doors, regardless of how many times it was proven not to be the case. He trusted Senator Carson. *Please, God. Don't let that make me a fool.*

He rapped on the door to the conference room where the Senator had barricaded herself with her Chief of Staff and a few other advisors.

"Come in."

Jackson pushed open the door, closing it behind him. "You wanted to see me, Senator?"

"Ah, Jackson. Perfect. Everyone knows Jackson Trent, right?"

Heads around the room nodded.

"He's coordinating the fundraiser next month. And, as luck would have it, our catering choice provides a particularly good opportunity for some positive press in the midst of the current climate. Jackson, would you give everyone the executive summary of Taste and See's philosophy?"

Jackson schooled his expression. Why did she need him to do that? She knew all the details just as well as he did. He'd tried to talk her out of using Paige. Maybe they'd laugh about that with their kids someday. He cleared his throat. "You've probably already given them the basics, but Ms. Jackson is committed to locally sourced, naturally grown foods. So her menus are all based on seasonal availability. Additionally, she's focused on sustainable living. So she strives to eliminate waste in her cooking."

"What does that last part mean?" A man, probably in his mid-forties, sitting three chairs down from the Senator leaned forward as he asked the question. What was his name? They'd met at a meeting a few months ago.

"Basically that she won't order two-hundred chicken breasts for a banquet. Instead she works to create menus that will use the whole chicken so she knows that animals aren't being butchered for a single cut of meat. There's the possibility, obviously, that the other parts are being used when you simply buy one cut in bulk, but Paige wants to know for certain, in addition to using smaller, local farms whose animal husbandry practices are kinder to the earth and the animals they're raising for food."

Around the table, several eyebrows shot up. The same man frowned. "Is she a kook? One of the nuts in the 'animals are more important than people' camp? Or today's version of the unwashed, tree-hugging hippie?"

Jackson bristled. What Paige sought to practice wasn't wacko. Sure, he'd had trouble understanding it at first, but she really was someone who was just trying to do her part, and get others to find places where they could do theirs. "Not at all, sir. She just wants people to make the changes that they can to have less of an impact on the earth. Ride bikes in nice weather instead of driving, support a local farmer instead of Chilean imports, that sort of thing."

"It's risky." Robert looked at the Senator. "Not even all of the farmers in the south and west areas of the state are going to necessarily support that kind of attitude. After all, they can get better prices shipping their crops out of state and practicing those same farming techniques that enable Chilean fruit to make it here without going bad."

The Senator shook her head. "That's not the point though. If I come across as someone looking to help the local farmers, to use them myself for my fundraising meals, then I'm not someone who would willingly allow the waterways they depend on to become polluted. That would destroy their livelihood, something I've just shown I'm in favor of nurturing."

Robert gave a subtle nod.

The Senator smiled. "Thank you, Jackson. That'll be all for now."

"Of course." He paused with his hand on the doorknob, took a deep breath, and turned. "You're not going to do anything that has the potential to damage her, are you?"

"I don't see how it would. If anything, it should help get her name out there, possibly drive more business her way." Robert tilted his head toward the door.

Jackson took the hint. Something was off, though he couldn't put his finger on what. Should he call Paige and let her know about the conversation? To what end, though? All he could tell her is that he'd been called into a meeting to explain her catering philosophy. It wasn't as if there was anything nefarious in that. Paige was the one who had given them the information in the first place, presumably to support or strengthen her bid for the contract. No, he'd let it ride. The Senator would do what's right, wouldn't she?

"Do you have a website or anything for the caterer we're using in August?" Robert hulked in the doorway, his arms full of folders.

Jackson saved the document he was editing and looked up. "Sure. Want me to email it to you?"

"Copy the Senator, too. Thanks." He stomped off.

Jackson stretched his arms over his head and leaned back in his chair. He made circles with his wrists, cringing as the bones scraped and popped against one another. He needed to remember to take more frequent breaks or he was going to end up with carpal tunnel like his sister. He slid open the center drawer of his desk and pulled out Paige's card, smiling as her face came to mind. She'd been busy the last two days, they'd only gotten a few short bursts of texting in during the day and had kept their evening phone calls shorter than usual, but she was off tomorrow. Well, kind of. At least she'd be able to sleep in a little before heading out for a day of cooking in various people's homes. He didn't like that she was working so hard. But it wasn't as if he had a right to comment one way or the other. Not yet.

His phone rang as he opened an email and began to type in the web address. He tucked the handset under his ear and kept typing. "Jackson Trent."

"Hey there. I had five minutes to call my own and couldn't think of anything I'd rather do than hear your voice."

"I was just thinking about you."

"Good things, I hope?"

"Always. In this case, Robert just stopped by asking for your website. Which made me dig out your card, which in turn reminded me of the first day we met."

"Ah. The day you decided I was some kind of nutcase who the Senator should stay far, far away from." There was a hint of laughter behind her words. She wasn't horribly far off though. Maybe he wasn't as good at hiding his facial expressions as he thought he was.

"No. That's not exactly what I thought. I thought you were pretty. Still do, for that matter. And now that I know you better, I realize that beauty goes all the way through."

"Flatterer. You're not warming me up because there's an ax falling, are you?"

Was he? With the Senator's current problems, and his reservations about what he knew of her plan to fight back, was he trying to separate himself from that in Paige's mind? "Nope. At least not one I know about. Though you've seen things are getting uglier with the Senator, right?"

"Yeah. Dad mentioned it on Sunday, so I did a little research. I wanted to know what I was talking about before I asked you about it. Should I be worried?"

She already sounded worried. Jackson could picture her chewing on her thumbnail like he'd caught her doing a few times when something bothered her. His heart ached. He didn't want to be part of anything that hurt her. "No. I really don't think you should be. The Senator's been working with Robert, and others, to come up with a strategy for countering the toxic waste allegations. I don't believe them, by the way. I just can't see the Senator sitting by, or worse, participating, in something like that."

"You're sure? I... I looked up her voting record on environmental issues. It's not exactly stellar."

His lips curved. She'd dug into voting records? Maybe there was hope for her yet. "I'll admit that hasn't been her strongest performance, but she's said it's something she wants to do better at. A lot of the time, though, those measures have other projects or stipulations attached to them that are simply untenable. So while the legislation might benefit the environment, it would also allow the creation of unnecessary projects that cost too much and do nothing. The Senator hates bills that have pork projects like that attached to them. It takes a lot to get her to support something that isn't straightforward."

Paige scoffed. "I'm surprised she's able to vote for anything then."

Jackson chuckled. "I've had the same thought a number of times. But it's one of the reasons she went into politics in the first place—and why I'm grateful she took me on as well—she's fighting it from inside."

"And how's that particular windmill battle doing? Any damage yet?"

Was the Senator being quixotic? Her opponents certainly thought so, but then, they had a lot to lose if she was successful in getting rid of hidden, unrelated projects in legislation. "It's hard to say. From what I've seen, some of her peers are starting to come around."

"Hmm. Well, that's a start, I guess." A clamor broke out in the background, full of shouts and banging metal. "Ah, I should go. You'll tell me if I need to start worrying, right?"

"Absolutely." Jackson swallowed the lump forming in his throat. He was loyal to the Senator; she'd done a lot for him. But Paige... she was important. Hopefully he wouldn't have to make a choice between the two of them.

Jackson took a long pull on a large iced coffee and checked the traffic. He darted across the street between a lumbering sightseeing bus and several taxis. Summer in DC was tourist season. Flocks of people clogged up the sidewalks and parks that would otherwise be pleasant places to grab a quick break and eat the sandwich rattling around in the paper sack in his other hand. He'd brave it today. He needed to get out of the office.

Kicking at a pigeon, he stepped up onto a map of the seas inlaid in the plaza honoring sailors who served in the Navy. The fountains on the edges sprayed flecks of water into the air, adding to the suffocating humidity. People milled around. Families posed for photos or pointed out interesting facts to bored-looking children. Office workers perched on planters, eating, reading, or talking in small groups. Under it all droned a steady hum of conversation and traffic noise. The tension in his shoulders and chest eased. Why being out in the chaos and sweltering heat relaxed him was a mystery. But it did. He found a spot on one of the planters and settled on it, setting his iced coffee next to him. He wiped the condensation off his hand and dug out his sandwich.

The office was a madhouse. It didn't seem like anything the Senator was doing to counter the allegations was taking root. Another story had run today accusing her of assaulting her opponent when she'd run for city council years ago, at the start of her political career. That was easily disproved and the retraction had aired just before noon. But the implication that Beatrice was someone who'd do anything, even resort to violence, was still out there in people's minds. Politicians could be a lot like ambulance-chasing lawyers and Senator Carson was the latest traffic accident. Her opponents were all hurrying to join the crowd and get in a jab or two while she was still the target. They knew that political scandal was like the summer weather in DC. It could blow over quickly, leaving cool relief in its wake, or it could hunker down, trapping and amplifying the heat for days, even weeks, before a major storm erupted and cleared the air.

This didn't look like it was blowing over anytime soon.

"Jackson?"

"David? Hey, man, what are you doing in the city? I thought you worked in Tyson's Corner these days."

The short Korean man sat down with a sigh. "I do, but they've got me doing customer calls all this week. Which means I'm down here, hobnobbing with government employees and trying to ensure we keep our funding."

"Ha. I thought you hated politics. Sounds like you're still up to your eyeballs in them." Jackson chuckled. He and David had been in several political science classes together in college, before David had changed to a computer science/business double major instead of business and poly sci.

"Yeah, well. At least it's only a week or so each year. You still on The Hill?"

Jackson nodded.

David pursed his lips. "Hm. How's that going?"

"You know who I work for. It's... going to get better."

David scoffed and dug into the breast pocket of his dress shirt as he stood. "Here's my card. If it doesn't get better, call me. We can always use people like you. Seriously, man."

Jackson took the card and looked at it before tucking it into his shirt pocket. "Thanks."

"Catch you later."

As David walked off, Jackson dropped his sandwich back into the bag. He wasn't hungry anymore. The business card seemed to burn in his pocket. Was he going to be buffing up his resume and looking around soon? There were already whispers in the office. People were nervous. He didn't want to find something new, but it never paid to be the last man standing on a sinking ship.

21

"Where are we headed?" Paige smiled at Jackson as he navigated the ramp onto the Beltway. Her feet were throbbing from yet another long week in the kitchen. Hopefully they'd recover a little of their usual vigor before they got downtown.

"How do you feel about history?"

"That those who ignore it are doomed to repeat it?"

Jackson chuckled. "Not opposed, then."

"I don't think you'd be very happy living around here if you hated history. I'm sure there are people who do, but they probably stay home a lot. Can I get a general era, or are you keeping me in suspense?"

"Since we were serenaded by the 1812 Overture on our first date, I thought it'd be fun to continue the theme and go up to Fort McHenry, since it was crucial in the War of 1812."

Fort McHenry. It was familiar, but if she was asked to put a pin in a map, she'd just as easily miss as hit. "I can't say I've ever been there, so that should be fun."

"You haven't? Did you go to school around here?" Jackson accelerated around a tiny four-door compact, so stuffed with people that the back half of the car nearly bounced off the ground when they hit a bump in the road.

"Must've missed that day. We took field trips to Mount Vernon and downtown to the Air and Space Museum. But I think that's pretty much it. Oh, and the amusement park down by Richmond."

"Seriously? You went to an amusement park but not Fort McHenry? Sad. Just sad. Well, prepare to be enchanted. And also to have the Star Spangled Banner stuck in your head for a while."

"Oh, goody. I can never hit that note for 'free.' Is there actually a key that makes the song singable by someone who doesn't have a vocal performance degree?"

"That I don't know. We'll ask at the visitor center."

Paige laughed. "I'm sure that'll go over well. We'll skip it and just continue to wonder, all right?"

"Fair enough. How was your Wednesday off? Well, not off. But not at the restaurant. Were you able to stay on top of everything like you hoped?"

She shrugged. "I guess. My dad says I hold myself to unrealistic expectations, so maybe that's my problem, but I didn't get everything done like I'd hoped. I did keep all my remaining clients happy, but I have eight pounds of zucchini sitting on my kitchen counter that I need to turn into jars of pickles, relish, and dip. Let alone all the tomatoes that didn't get made into marinara on Monday. I'll get to it, it's just going to eat up my afternoon tomorrow, and I was really hoping to take a nap."

"Pickles? Aren't those cucumbers?"

"Can be. Pickle is actually a term for the process, not the vegetable. You can pickle just about anything. Some are more successful than others. But I think zucchini hold their texture better than cucumbers. I'll set a jar aside for you and you can tell me what you think."

"Hmm. Maybe not a whole jar. Zucchini have never been my thing."

She shook her head. "What are you, six? You have to try something before you decide you hate it. Anyway. How was the rest of your week? I'm sorry I haven't had time to chat, or really even text. By the time I get home and get the catering work done, I'm beat."

"Don't worry about it. It's been... a long week. Have you caught any more of what's going on with the Senator?"

She'd meant to. Every night, she made a mental note to at least scan the headlines online, but by the time she was free to do it, she couldn't face even one more thing. She'd been shutting off the computer and crawling into bed with a book and, most often, falling asleep before she'd even read a full page. At this rate, she was never going to finish her current read. "No. Sorry."

He shrugged. "That's fine. You're not really missing anything. It's more of the same. Seems like everyone who can is thinking up some reason to dish dirt on her. She's swinging back at this point, and making some good hits, but it's never the best idea to be on the defensive end of something like this."

Paige caught her lower lip between her teeth. That didn't sound good. "Is the fundraiser still going to happen?"

"Why wouldn't it?"

"I don't know. I guess I thought keeping a lower profile might be a wiser course of action? Or if it's bad enough that she doesn't have a chance of reelection, would she waste her time? You know I don't do politics."

He offered a tight smile. "It's not that bad yet. It isn't as if she's being kicked out of office or considering dropping her campaign. This is just a bump in the road. In some ways, it means she's on the right track. She's made people nervous, so they're lashing out. I think she'll get through it and manage to come out on top. She usually does."

It all seemed so underhanded. Why, if you were being accused of nastiness like this, would you continue to work in that environment? To seek it out, no less? "Can a clean fighter win in something that gets ugly? I guess this just makes it clear that I really don't understand why anyone would willingly participate in politics. Especially when we're commanded to live at peace with everyone when we're able. It just seems like picking a fight."

"Maybe. But we're also told to fight the good fight. And if God created and established government, then it seems unlikely that He then expects us to step back and stay out of it. Particularly when we're living in a fallen world. And then you have the examples of Esther, Daniel, Paul and Silas and others. They were all actively involved in politics, sometimes to their own personal detriment. But they did it because God required their action. We can't afford to be like King Hezekiah, content that things were fine in his time and unconcerned for the future. God chastised him for that attitude. We have an obligation to try and look after not only the present but the future."

Paige twisted in her seat so she was angled toward him, and tucked a leg underneath her. "Isn't it better, though, in a situation where the political system is so broken, to just do what we can in our own lives to be the change we're hoping to see? If everyone actually took the time to live their convictions, we'd need a lot less governmental involvement. The poor would be cared for, the hungry would be fed, and we'd be taking steps toward making it more reasonable for people to live gently and sustainably."

"That's the ideal, certainly. But if you look back at the Old Testament, one of the reasons Israel ended up with a monarchy is that they weren't doing those things. That and they wanted to be like the nations around them. Think about it though, it isn't human nature to do that. Is it the fruit of the Spirit? Absolutely. But not everyone has the Holy Spirit, and the unsaved, even the truly good, altruistic ones, are always going to be more concerned with their own good than anyone else's. And so we need government and laws. Wouldn't you rather those were formed by God-fearing men and women?"

She sighed. He made some good points. And he didn't discount her views... just said they needed to be combined with more organized civic action. Maybe she'd figure out how to register to vote. It couldn't hurt.

"I'm sorry. I know I just hit another soapbox."

Paige chuckled. "It's okay. You do it for a living and it's interesting. You've got me convinced to register to vote, start doing at least that much. I'm not sure I'll ever turn into one of the people marching on the lawn of the White House but... it makes sense that voting is one more piece of doing my part to live my convictions. Now, tell me more about Fort McHenry."

Jackson grinned. "Well, the most interesting thing about it, at least to me, is its shape. It's what's called a star fort. Just like it sounds, it's sort of star-shaped. The design is supposed to be one of the more defensible ones, particularly when one or more sides are bordered by water."

"Who knew?"

"Right? How much trivia do you want?" Jackson glanced at his mirrors and shifted lanes.

"Let's have it. I'm always up for trivia." Paige settled back into the passenger seat as Jackson rattled off more facts about the history of Fort McHenry, the War of 1812, and the various areas they passed as they made their way north. The conversation was easy, and Paige remembered enough history to add a comment here or there.

Jackson moved into the right lane. "I think we're getting close to the turn. Could you help me watch for signs? Seems like there's always construction blocking the early warnings and I end up having to cut people off to make the exit."

"Owwww." Paige sucked on the fingers she'd just mashed in the doorway of her bedroom. Served her right for trying to move furniture while daydreaming about her date with Jackson, but she'd begged off her usual after-church lunch with her parents for the sole purpose of getting the office set up in her new spare room and she was going to get it done. With a shake of her hand, she grabbed the desk again, placing her fingers more carefully, and pulled. The cheap particle board monstrosity wobbled and skittered across the carpet, but finally it was through the door and into the hall. Now for the fun part. The spare room was at just the wrong angle to make the turn.

Ten minutes later, she sank to the floor and lowered her head to her knees. Jackson had offered to come help. She should've taken him up on it. But being alone with him in the apartment hadn't seemed like the wisest decision. Maybe that was stupid. He hadn't made any move to kiss her yet, unless you counted resting his cheek on her hair, but that could be considered brotherly. Couldn't it? Not that she wanted him to think of her like a sister. Still, she wouldn't mind an acknowledgement of the chemistry they shared on top of their deepening friendship. Or did he not feel the sparks?

She glared at the desk wedged in the doorway, blocking her exit from the room. She'd give it one more good pull and, if that didn't work, give up and call her dad. Rubbing the knuckles she'd scraped, she grasped the desk legs and leaned backward. Maybe gravity would work in her favor. The desk shuddered and screeched into the room, leaving a deep gouge in one side of the door's frame. Great. Just great.

Paige positioned the desk under the window and stepped back. Perfect. Now for the rest of the stuff. When her arms were full of miscellaneous desk items, the doorbell rang. A loud knock followed it. She dropped her load on the desk's surface and hurried to the door. Peeking out, she grinned and turned the locks.

"Hey. What are you doing here?"

Jackson lifted a shoulder. "My youngest nephew decided to start projectile vomiting after lunch. So, I didn't stick around. After I went home and cleaned up, I remembered you were setting up your office today. Figured maybe I could help?"

She laughed. "You're about twenty minutes too late to be really useful."

"Oh." He visibly deflated. "Well, I won't bother you then."

"No. Wait. I... come on in." Paige widened the door.

"You sure?"

"I'm sure I'd like you to come in. I'm not sure it's a good idea." Heat burned her neck and cheeks.

Jackson paused two steps into her apartment and frowned. "Do you want me to go?"

"Augh." She mentally kicked herself. How stupid was she going to be? Better to just get it out there in the open, right? She took a deep breath. "No. I like you here. And being alone with you. But I, are you, are we…"

A smile played at the corners of his mouth, his dimple flickering in and out. He pushed the door closed and stepped closer to her, one arm snaking around her waist, the other curving around her neck. He lowered his lips toward hers, stopping just before they touched.

Paige's heart hammered in her chest. Every nerve ending was on fire. Her hands moved to his waist of their own volition, fingers curling into fists. She floated in the chocolate sea of his eyes as his gaze locked with hers.

"To answer the question I think you were trying to ask," Jackson's voice was husky and his breath minty on her face. "Yes, I feel it too."

He lowered his lips to hers.

Before the fireworks arcing through her body had finished, Jackson eased back. "I've wanted to do that since our first date."

"Me too."

He ran his thumb across her cheek and released her completely, tucking his hands into his pockets and stepping away. "I probably would have waited another couple of weeks. I didn't want to rush you."

"I don't feel rushed. I may not have a ton of experience to go by, honestly, but I have enough to say I think we're doing all right." She cleared her throat. Was everything that came out of her mouth when he was around going to be moronic? "Anyway. Can I get you something to drink? A snack? I already moved the desk, so it's really just about organizing now. I ramble when I'm nervous. Sorry."

He chuckled. "Why don't we sit in the kitchen? Would that be less awkward?"

"Sure. Yeah. This way." Paige crossed the living room and entered the kitchen. "I haven't made the zucchini pickles yet, so I can't offer you those. I do have some spread though. Want to try it?"

He shrugged and pulled out a chair at the table. "Sure. Sounds good."

"Lemonade or iced tea?"

"Tea. Can I help?"

"Nope. Just sit there. It won't take long." Paige opened the cupboard that held glasses and pulled two out. Maybe a tall glass of iced tea would drown whatever was hopping around madly in her stomach. *It's Jackson. You're alone with him at restaurants and in his car. There's no reason to be nervous about him being in your house.* Except that she'd never been alone with an attractive man in her home before. Her parents had drilled it into her that it was a slippery slope from there to teen pregnancy, drug addiction, and homelessness. Extreme, certainly, but it had kept her on the straight and narrow for twenty-six years, so it couldn't be completely bad.

"You okay?"

With a firm mental shake, Paige turned and plastered a smile on her face. "Yeah. Sorry. Daydreaming. Here, can you pour?" She set a box of crackers, the glasses, and tea pitcher on the table before opening the fridge and grabbing a jar of her zucchini spread. "All right, dig in."

Jackson pushed a glass of tea across the table toward her. "This is good. What kind is it?"

"Mint. I grow mint," Paige gestured to the pots in her kitchen window. "So you basically mix it with hot water and sugar. But it's always embodied summer to me. My mom and I used to pick mint on summer afternoons then set out a jar of water filled with the leaves in the sun to brew."

"That's a nice memory. I don't think my mom and I ever did anything like that. Though she was always working, keeping us in bread and clothes. Next time I get home, I'll have to see if we can figure out a way to make some together. I think she'd like it."

"Where's home, remind me?" Paige scooped out a dollop of spread and slathered it over a cracker. She put it on a plate and pushed it toward Jackson.

He took a bite. "Mmm. You're sure this is zucchini?"

"A few other things too, but yeah, primarily. You like it?"

"I do." He reached for the jar. "And home is Florida. I try not to go in the summer. I never loved the heat. Neither did my sister, for that matter. So when she came up here for school, I followed. At least this way we have each other. Mom misses us, but she understands. She talks about coming up to visit, but my sister doesn't have room and, well, can you see her bunking down with the guys? I've offered her my room, but so far no dice. She says she's waiting for a good reason to make her next trip."

"So she's happy there?"

He nodded. "Seems to be. Feeling less anxious?"

Heat flooded her face. "Yeah. Sorry about that."

"It's sweet, actually. You've really never had a guy over?"

She crossed her arms. Was he making fun? She must seem like a complete rube. "Not by himself."

"Hey." He reached across the table and pried one of her hands loose, lacing his fingers through hers and giving them a gentle squeeze. "I'm just surprised. I don't make a habit of having women over, myself. Even if the guys are home."

She relaxed her shoulders, the corner of her mouth tipping up. "Okay."

"Want to show me your garden?"

"You really want to see it? It's just a pretty typical garden."

He shrugged. "You've got me curious."

She pushed her chair back and stood. "Sure. Come on."

Jackson stood and reached for her hand. He gave a quick tug, pulling her to him. Before she could blink, his lips had once more descended to hers. Just when she was sure her heart was going to beat out of her chest, he eased back. "Lead the way."

22

By Thursday, the tingles from having kissed Paige were beginning to wear off and the gloom hovering in the halls of the Senator's office was inescapable. Had he missed another breaking story? Jackson's mind had been wandering back to Sunday afternoon entirely too often, so it was possible. He flipped through the meager pile of response cards on his desk. The event was in three weeks, shouldn't there be more people committed to coming by now? Or did people procrastinate?

Collecting the stack, he pushed back from his desk and stepped into the hall. Robert would know. Where would he be right now? The Senator's door at the end of the hall stood open, so it was unlikely he was in there. Jackson headed for Robert's office. Empty. He tapped the cards against his leg. Something was off. He looked more closely. The print of people picnicking along the river by, oh who painted that? Robert was always correcting people. Seurat. It was gone. As were the frames that had decorated the edge of Robert's desk, the photos of his wife and four children replaced frequently to document their changes. What was going on?

Jackson headed to the reception area. Donna would know. She might spend the majority of her day behind a desk up front, but her finger was on the pulse.

"Hey, Donna."

"Morning, Jackson. Crazy around here today, isn't it?" She swiveled in her chair.

Was it? Better to act like he knew what was going on. "Yeah. Um. Have you seen Robert? I wanted to ask him something."

Donna shook her head. "You've been distracted all week and it finally caught up with you. Is it that caterer? I've seen the way you two look at each other when she drops by. Nice looking girl though. I think I approve."

Heat burned up his neck. "Mm. Yeah, well, we're seeing each other. The Senator didn't think it would be a problem."

"Can't see why it would be. You're not in charge of the money decisions. Anyway, if you'd been paying attention, you would've heard Robert and the Senator arguing all week. And this morning, he came in with a box, packed up, turned around, and left."

Jackson's mouth dropped open. "He quit?"

Donna nodded. "The Senator's furious about it, too. Told him not to bother asking for a reference. But I figure she'll come around after she's cooled off some. Still, if he's gone, I can think of two or three others who aren't going to be far behind."

Yeah, so could he. Did he need to be one of them? David's card was filed at home, should he call tonight and at least find out what the opportunities were? Gah. That was something to worry about later. Right now, he needed to find out how worried he should be about the fundraiser.

"What did you want to ask him? Maybe I can help you figure out who to ask?"

Jackson held the handful of response cards up. "It seems like we should have more people coming than this. There are only three weeks to go. But I wasn't sure. We were somewhat late getting the invites sent, so maybe people are trying to figure out their schedules?"

Donna eyed the stack and shook her head. "That should be four times thicker than it is, at least. Does the Senator know?"

"Uh-uh."

"You need to tell her."

Jackson's stomach clenched. The one thing his mentor through college internships had drilled into him was to avoid being the bearer of bad news whenever possible. "Yeah. All right."

Donna's "good luck" trailed down the hall after him. More out of habit than anything, he glanced in his office as he passed. The

Senator was leaning over his desk, scribbling. So much for putting off talking to her.

"Were you looking for me?"

She straightened and nodded, her lips set in a grim line. "I was. Come on in and close the door."

Nothing quite like being ordered around in your own office. Jackson did as instructed and scooted around his desk to sit in the chair.

With a lifted eyebrow, the Senator lowered herself into Jackson's guest chair and crossed her legs. "I imagine you heard that Robert is no longer with us."

Bless Donna for knowing the news and not minding catching him up. He nodded.

"With him no longer assisting, I'm going to need you to do a little more on the press management side of things. Everyone seems to have glommed on to the toxic waste fiasco. That's the only story in all of this that has any staying power so far. So, it's the issue we need to target and, as luck would have it, we've got the perfect way to do that already in place. The caterer."

Jackson drew his eyebrows together. "Paige? What about her?"

The Senator waved her hand. "She's all natural, sustainable, good Earthy. Would someone who turns a blind eye to toxic waste go out of her way to hire a caterer with those principles? No, of course not."

"She was the lowest bid. It wasn't her principles that got her the contract."

"You and I know that, but no one else needs to. Besides, who says she was the lowest bid?"

Jackson opened his desk drawer and pulled out a fat folder. "This does. It's all the bids we received—I thought we put this up online for everyone when Lisa first started this snowballing mess?"

"Always intended to. Turns out it's good that Robert let that ball drop. Hand me that?" She reached for the folder.

Jackson gripped it. "I can get you copies."

"Give me the folder, Jackson."

"I'm not... "

She stood and wrenched the folder from his hand with a stern glare. "I'll handle the bids. You just make sure that when a reporter calls you looking for information about your girlfriend, you tell him all about how environmentally friendly she is. Got it?"

Jackson swallowed as she stomped from his office. What was going on? It was one thing to fight back. He understood that. Supported it, even. But this... seemed like something else. And until he figured out how he felt about it, he wasn't going to be taking any calls from reporters.

"So now I don't know what to do. Should I tell Paige?" Jackson scraped the last grains of rice off his plate and looked at his roommates. They'd at least have an idea of what to do. Even if it wasn't particularly helpful.

Zach pushed his plate toward the center of the table. "Why wouldn't you? Seems to me they're looking to, effectively, give her some free press. Isn't the whole point of this for her to get her catering business of the ground? I can't fathom why she'd object."

"I keep coming back to that, myself. But still, something feels... off. She's so anti-politics. I just don't think she'll be happy being splashed around in the papers and associated with the Senator. Especially not right now." Jackson frowned. "But at the same time, if I tell her and she reacts like I think she will... how do I stop it from happening? I don't think I can."

Ben balled his napkin up and dropped it into the middle of his plate. "I don't see why not. Just don't do the interview."

"Okay, that keeps *me* from doing it. But it doesn't stop it from happening. Someone else will, maybe even the Senator. And it'll all be 'a source close to the Senator' or whatever, so it's going to look like it's me." Jackson sighed. This was impossible. "I need to give her a heads up, don't I?"

"I would." Zach shrugged. "I don't think she's going to be as unhappy as you do, but if I was going to be in the paper, I'd want to know."

"And if she gets upset and says I need to make it not happen? What then?"

Ben laughed. "Then you're in the dog house, dude. Seriously. I think I fall on the other side of the fence on this one. I wouldn't say anything and do whatever you can to keep her out of the papers. Then, if it does happen and she gets mad, at least you can say you tried to avoid it. Maybe offer up the free publicity angle, too."

"Isn't that dishonest?" Jackson stared at his empty plate, looking for answers. No mysterious messages were appearing in the streaks of gravy though. "It feels dishonest."

"That's 'cause it is." Zach glared at Ben. "You need to tell her."

Ben stood and started collecting plates. "He's probably right. Between the two of us, he's had more successful relationships. The last time I was serious, really serious, about someone, she disappeared off the face of the earth after two months. And I did everything I could think of to track her down."

"Yeah, no one I've dated has gone into witness protection to get away from me." Zach grinned.

Ben kicked Zach's chair. "For that, you're on dish duty."

"But it's Jackson's night."

Jackson held up his hands. "Hey, if the cook says you have dishes, I'm not going to fight him. Thanks, man."

Ben pointed at Jackson. "That frees you up to call Paige."

Just great. Fresh out of excuses, Jackson headed to the back patio. He settled in the hammock strung between two of those stately trees and hit the speed dial for Paige.

"I was just thinking about you." Paige's voice held a smile and sent waves of warmth through him.

"Good things, I hope?" He pulled up a mental picture of Paige's living room and pictured her there, reclined on the beat-up blue thing she called a couch.

She laughed. "Don't you just wish you knew? How was your day?"

"Uck. Let's start with your day, instead." He was a chicken. A big, fat, yellow chicken that made the children's show mascot look stringy by comparison. And he wasn't ashamed to admit it. At least not to himself.

"That good? Okay, well. I was hoping you'd have a great story to kick things off, because I'm guessing my day was right up there with yours." She sighed and papers rustled in the background. "Let's see. Now that Hector has figured out that the morning prep to lunch shift isn't actually terrible, he's asked to take it over completely. Since Dad wasn't sure what my intentions were, he said okay. Which means I'm cut back to two days at the restaurant, which is what I initially asked for."

He furrowed his brow. "If it's what you wanted... isn't it a good thing to get it?"

"Yeah, I guess. Except that I've lost one personal chef client and it's not as if I'm rolling around in excess clients. So it's going to be tight unless I go ahead and try to find a new roommate, which I really don't want to do. I don't have the luck with roommates that you do."

"Maybe you'll get more catering business soon?" *Like when the Senator runs a newspaper article about you?* He couldn't push the words past his lips.

"Yeah, maybe. I guess I'm really counting on the fundraiser for that, now. What are the numbers like? Will my initial estimates still be enough? I thought with all the extra press she's getting there might be more people trying to get a front row seat in case something happens."

That was an angle he hadn't considered. It'd be nice if it played out, particularly since in all the fuss over the article he hadn't managed to tell the Senator about the low numbers. "Not so far. We should be good with your plans. We're actually a little lower than I'd expected right now."

"Uh-oh. Should I change my food orders? I probably still have time to do that, but I'd need to do it immediately."

Jackson swung a leg over the edge of the hammock and gave a push. Should she? As it stood right now, there'd be a ton of leftover food. But they could always package it up and send it to the local homeless shelter. That's what they'd done in the past. In addition to making the Senator look good, it was nice to know the food was going to people who'd appreciate it. "Nah. It's always better to have extra, isn't it?"

"Probably. All right, I won't worry about it. There are still three weeks to go. Who knows, you might get a big influx of replies any day now."

He could dream. "Anything else? Not that that's not enough."

"Actually, yeah. I can't seem to get it through Whitney's head that she has to actually move all her junk out if she's going to stop paying rent. She was supposed to come get all her shoes last week. I told you about that, right?"

"Right."

Paige scoffed. "So I finally got around to trying to move things into that closet and what do I find?"

"Shoes?"

"Ding ding. And not just shoes, I swear she brought extra stuff over and added to the pile when she came to get that one pair she was missing."

"You're right, you have terrible luck with roommates."

"Ha. Thanks."

"So what will you do?"

She sighed. "I don't know. Part of me wants to haul it all down to the curb and let her know it's there, so she better come get it before other people do. But that's not very Christ-like... and as much as she drives me to my absolute wit's end, I need to at least try and do the right thing. So I'll go with the other part of me that says I don't *have* to have the closet space. Just let it be."

"Do you have her new address? I could come over and help you just take it there this weekend." As the words left his mouth he winced. He really couldn't. He was going to be busy with football all day tomorrow, and then the usual family madness on Sunday.

"As tempting as that is, she seems to have conveniently left that off all the paperwork for catering her wedding. Next time I get a hold of her, I'm going to have to get that info. Besides, weren't you traveling with the team Saturday?"

"Yeah, I forgot about that when I offered. But I'll make time if you change your mind."

"You're sweet. Now, how about your day? Oh, hang on, I should grab this other call."

Jackson drummed his fingers on his leg, the subtle hum of summer insects coming out for the evening filling the air. How was she going to respond? They were off to such a great start, he didn't want this to end things before they had a chance to get off the ground.

"Hey, Jackson, I need to run. It's my mom. She's taking Dad to urgent care, thinks maybe he's coming down with the flu. But she worries, so it'll be better for both of them if I'm there. Knowing my mom, she'll be the one they end up having to treat because she'll have a full-blown panic attack."

"Okay. Text me later and tell me how he is. I'll be praying." He dropped the phone on his chest and stared into the patch of twilight visible through the leaves. There wasn't a good time to tell her. Not really. He wouldn't have had a chance to find out about her day if he'd just jumped in with it. And... the justification sounded lame even to him. He sighed. What was he going to do?

23

Paige shuffled into the kitchen. It was weird to still be at home at eight in the morning on a Monday. Even though she'd only worked at the restaurant for two weeks, she'd settled into a groove. An exhausting groove, but a groove nonetheless. Now she'd have to see if she was able to handle the randomness of two mornings a week. The only requirement she'd given her dad was not Wednesday. Now that she had her personal chef clients settled, she wasn't going to rearrange them again if she could help it.

Her phone chimed an incoming text as the coffee gurgled to a stop. She tossed in cream and sugar and perched on a kitchen chair. Whitney? Why was Whitney texting her? Maybe she needed another pair of shoes.

Did u c this?

Paige frowned at the link to the national newspaper that was also their local paper. It was something about the Senator from the few words of the title in the hyperlink. But they'd been running two or three stories on the senator every day for the last week and a half. Why was Whitney texting her this one? She poked the link and sipped from the steaming mug as the link loaded on her phone's browser.

She skimmed the first line of the article.

Wait, what?

She went back and re-read more carefully. Blood thundered in her ears. She set her mug down with a thunk, barely registering the coffee that splashed over the lip and onto her hand. How could he not have told her this was coming?

"Despite recent allegations regarding the Senator's lack of concern for the environment, her choice of caterers for her upcoming fundraiser tells a different

story. Until you look closer. Generally, contracts are filled by selection of the lowest bid that meets the required criteria. For this dinner, to be held on the lawn of George Washington's Mount Vernon on the 22nd of August (tickets still available, call the office for reservation information), the Senator chose philosophy over price. Unfortunately, it wasn't the philosophy of sustainability touted by Paige Jackson's catering company Taste and See so much as the time-honored political tradition of hiring those who are connected. In the case of Ms. Jackson, the connection comes in the form of a romantic liaison with one of Senator Carson's senior staffers, Jackson Trent. Mr. Trent is the point of contact for the August event... "

Paige threw down her phone. She couldn't read anymore. Bile crawled up her throat. Tears burned her eyes. All she'd wanted was a chance—one stinking chance—to show people who could afford to hire caterers that she was a viable alternative. Against her better judgment, with Clara's encouragement, she'd thrown her hat in the ring. Clara. Paige closed her eyes. A hot tear slipped down her cheek. What must her mentor be thinking?

The phone buzzed against the table. Jackson. She shook her head. Another tear worked its way free. She swiped 'deny,' sending the call to voicemail. He didn't deserve her tears. They'd pass soon enough and then they'd talk. Oh, they would talk.

The phone buzzed again.

"I saw it, Clara."

"Oh, Paige. I'm sorry I ever suggested this."

"It's not your fault. I'm the one who submitted the bid. And I'm the one who agreed to go out with Jackson. He said it wasn't a problem. I was dumb enough to believe him."

"So it's true?"

Her shoulders slumped. "We weren't dating before hand, not the way the article makes it sound. But yes, we've been dating for five weeks."

Paige's cheeks burned. She was falling for him. How stupid was she?

"Tsk. It's not the first time someone's been taken advantage of, won't be the last. What will you do?"

Practical. That was Clara. "I don't know. The contract's designed to make it hard to cancel. I may try to get out of it, but I don't think it'll work. Besides, I've already ordered, and paid for, the food. What would I do with all that food if I didn't have the event?"

"You should call the reporter, offer to tell your side of things. Surely you have some dirt to offer that would take the focus off you?"

She chewed her lower lip. She could probably come up with a few things Jackson had said about Lisa that might be newsworthy but... what was the point? "No. I'm not stooping to their level."

"Good girl. I'd be disappointed if you did."

Paige let out a mirthless laugh. That was Clara, always testing, looking for places to teach. "I'll keep my head down and cook. The event's in two weeks, surely by then I'll be old news and I can get on with my life."

"And if it isn't?"

She didn't want to think about it. "It'll have to be."

"And your heart?"

The memory of Jackson's kiss was seared into her brain. Her lips tingled, even as a new flood of tears burned a path down her cheeks. "Will mend."

"I'm here if you need me."

"I know. Thanks, Clara."

Her voicemail signaled the arrival of another message. She wiped her eyes and stood. Let him keep calling.

By noon, Paige had ruthlessly weeded her garden and was up to her elbows in canning projects. Her phone had so many voicemails from Jackson she'd finally just turned it off. She didn't need to hear it buzzing, and she wasn't going to answer. All her clients had managed to get through, so it wasn't as if anyone else was going to be calling. Her tears had dried up somewhere between harvesting tomatoes and peppers. Now her blood simmered in time with the batch of marinara cooking on her stove.

She swiped hair out of her face with her arm and frowned. Was that the door? Wiping her hands on her apron, she checked the dials on the burners and scooted into the living room. There it was again, definitely a knock. Maybe Whitney had finally come for her stuff. She wrenched open the door. Her heart stopped, then took off at twice its normal speed.

"Jackson." She shook her head and began to close the door, swallowing the lump in her throat.

"Paige. Please." He put his hand on the jamb. "Hear me out."

She imagined slamming the door on his fingers. Her stomach twisted. That wasn't her, no matter how much he deserved it. "Talk."

"Can I come in?" His brown eyes were wide, pleading. She'd been taken in by them before, though.

"Only because I have stuff on the stove. Close the door behind you." She stalked back to the kitchen, not checking to see if he followed. He came up behind her and touched her shoulder. She spun, her hand flat against his chest, and pushed. "You don't get to touch me. Not anymore. Go sit over there, say your piece, and then get out."

Jackson backed away, his hands up. "Okay."

Something—pain?—flashed in his eyes before she turned back to the stove to blindly stir her sauce. She blinked away the tears. She wasn't going to cry while he was here.

He cleared his throat. "I didn't know the article was going to come out today."

"So you knew there would be one. But you didn't think maybe I deserved a head's up?"

"No. I knew the Senator wanted there to be one. I told her I wouldn't be the one talking to any reporters and that I thought it was a bad idea. I was going to tell you Thursday, but you had to go with your mom to urgent care."

She scoffed. "So it's my fault. Oh, wait, you could've mentioned it at any point all weekend long."

"I should have. Though even if I had, the article she talked to me about was nothing like what got printed today. It was supposed to be about your efforts in sustainability. I honestly thought it'd be free advertising for you."

Paige spun, the spoon in her hand dripping splotches of blood-red sauce on the floor. "Oh, I got some great free advertising today. I've had two clients call to inquire if asking me out would get them a discount, and what other services I provide. And another cancelled her contract with me because she couldn't, in good conscience, continue employing someone with questionable ethics. So that's three of my, oh that's right, three steady clients now gone. So thanks for that."

Jackson closed his eyes. "I'm sorry."

"You should be." She turned back to the sauce and turned off the heat.

"Paige... "

"I don't know what else you think there is to say, Mr. Trent. I looked over the contract and as I don't see any way out of it that wouldn't end up bankrupting me on top of everything else, I'll cater your event. But I don't believe we have anything else to say to one another. If you have updates about the dinner, you can send them to me via email. Now, if you'll excuse me, I have to get this into jars. You know the way out."

Out of the corner of her eye, she saw Jackson stop in the kitchen doorway and open his mouth. With a sigh, his shoulders fell and he closed it and shook his head. When his footsteps faded and the door clicked shut, Paige slid down the front of the cabinets to the floor and wrapped her arms around her knees.

24

Jackson slammed the door to his jeep and banged his fists against the steering wheel. Was there any possible way that could've gone worse? At least if she'd refused to talk to him he could have held on to a shred of hope. Now though, she'd been pretty clear about where things stood between them. Would it be different if he'd said something last week? He sighed. There was no way to know, not for sure. But if she'd told him to stop the article and he hadn't been able to—because there was no question, he wouldn't have been able to— how would that be any different? She'd still hate him.

The air caught in his lungs. She hated him. He closed his eyes and rested his head on the wheel. How was he supposed to live with that? Taking a deep breath, he shoved the key into the ignition. He wasn't going to. Not without a fight.

He barely noticed the drive downtown. His muscles were on autopilot, his thoughts racing. Grinding his teeth together, he nodded curtly to Donna. She held up a finger, her mouth opening. He shook his head and stomped past, down the hall to the Senator's office. Knocking once, he pushed open the door.

"I'm in a meeting, Jackson." The Senator inclined her head toward the man sitting across the desk from her. He looked familiar. It was the same man as in the previous meeting. *Where* did Jackson know him from?

"This can't wait." Jackson crossed his arms over the heart that threatened to beat out of his chest.

The Senator gave him a long look, one eyebrow raised. "All right. I'll join you in your office. This won't take long, excuse me."

Jackson spun on his heel and marched to his minuscule office. At least it wouldn't take long to clear out. Tiny daggers began sawing at his insides. He didn't want to lose this job. But how could he keep working here when he no longer believed in the woman in charge?

The Senator shut the door and leaned against it. Everything about her demeanor was casual, like this was just another day. Maybe to her it was. "What's on your mind, Jackson?"

"Well, let's see. How about we start with the article in the paper this morning? I know you engineered it. What I want to know is if you planned for it to turn into a hatchet job on Paige's reputation—and mine, for that matter—or if that was just a side effect."

She shrugged. "Reporters are a tricky breed. I gave him the information I wanted him to use. He dug more than I anticipated. Really, if you want to be mad at someone, you should be mad at him, not me. After all, I told *you* to take his call. Maybe if you'd done as instructed the article would've turned out differently."

Would it have? Jackson shook his head. Unlikely. The press was eating up a scandal, even one that began with trumped-up nonsense, surrounding Senator Beatrice Carson, the long-running darling of socially liberal conservatives. No reporter was going to be dumb enough to stick to just what she wanted said and look like they'd been paid off by her. "Don't try to put this on me. I told you I thought it was a bad idea. And now, instead of making you look like someone who cares about the environment, you've ruined the business of someone who actually practices what you preach."

"What do you mean?" Beatrice frowned. If he didn't know better, he'd think the flicker of concern in her features was real.

"Please. Like you couldn't see this coming? The few clients she had have either dropped her or propositioned her. And since, despite how the paper painted her, Paige doesn't trade sexual favors for business, she had to break those client's contracts. Leaving her with nothing. How do you think that'll go over if she takes it to the press?"

The Senator's eyes widened. "You have to keep that from happening."

"How am I supposed to do that, exactly?" Jackson perched on the edge of his desk.

"Use your masculine wiles. In fact, I imagine this could be very good for your relationship. You can swoop in, like a knight on a white horse, and offer comfort. Convince her it'll all blow over. That kind of thing." She waved her hand dismissively. "Really, I'm not sure why you're as riled up about this as you are. I thought men liked to be rescuers."

Jackson clenched his jaw. "Let me just ask you this: if you were Paige, would you be sitting around boo-hooing, waiting for the man that was used to paint you as a loose woman to come and rescue you?"

"Probably not. But—"

"But nothing. You're not as unusual as you seem to think. I'm pretty sure Paige wouldn't spit on me if I was on fire right now."

Beatrice smiled. "Give her a chance to cool off."

"If she got any colder, she'd be sinking cruise ships, so I don't really see that happening." Jackson cocked his head to the side. "Do you believe in anything you say or is it all just part of the political machine to you?"

She straightened and tugged on the hem of her suit jacket. "Get out. How dare you accuse me of being some kind of heartless politician."

"It's not an accusation, it's a realization. And I'm just one of the dupes who fell for the act. I thought you were one of the good ones. I'll have my resignation on your desk within the hour."

"You're home early." Zach put a thick yellow highlighter in the middle of his text book and closed it. "You sick?"

Jackson dropped the box holding the few personal items he'd had in his office onto the kitchen table. Even though the summer session had finished last week, he'd figured Zach would still be at school setting up his classroom or doing something to get ready for the new year that'd be starting soon. "I could say the same for you. Shouldn't you be in faculty meetings or something?"

Zach chuckled. "We do actually get a week and a half off before all that madness starts over again. Which means I can do my prep here in the comfort of home instead of in a classroom. And you didn't answer my question."

Jackson blew out a breath. "I quit."

"Ha-ha. Look, if you don't want to tell me, that's fine. I'm just surprised to see you. Want me to head back to my room so you can watch TV?"

"I'm serious. Didn't you see the article in the paper this morning?"

Zach's gaze traveled to the paper beside him on the couch, still folded neatly in its plastic bag. "I brought it in, does that count?"

"Yeah, well, you should take a look. It's on the front page and hard to miss. I'm going for a run." Jackson grabbed his box and trudged down the hall. What he ought to do is call David and see if he was serious about having job openings. Or contact some of the people he knew on The Hill and see about any openings in other offices. Tossing his work clothes over the chair at his desk, he tugged on shorts and a t-shirt and swallowed around the catch in his throat. His stomach roiled. He'd been so sure Senator Carson was above board. That's why he'd chosen her in the first place. How was he supposed to trust anyone in politics now?

Jackson sat on the bed and tied his sneakers. *And this is why Pai—some people—don't vote.*

Jackson tucked his hands in his pockets and looked up at the pastor's house. It wasn't quite what he was expecting—just a simple, single-family colonial from the eighties in a typical suburban neighborhood. It fit though, when he stopped to think about it. Pastor Brown was the main reason Jackson still went to the enormous church. That and the fact that his roommates liked it, so tagging along with them was easier than striking out on his own. Still, maybe this was a bad idea. Even if the pastor said it wasn't an imposition, it surely had to be.

The door opened. Grinning, Paul Brown stepped out onto the stoop. "Mary's beginning to wonder if you're here to talk to me or just case the place."

Jackson let out a short laugh. "Sorry. I—you've got to be busy. I don't want to intrude on your personal time."

"Don't be ridiculous. Come inside. I don't say I'm free unless I am. I learned very early on in ministry that you have to be scrupulously honest, with yourself and your parishioners, if you expect people to trust you. All you're interrupting is an evening of me falling asleep in my easy chair while Mary watches a show about decorating. Really, you're doing me a favor." Paul glanced over his shoulder into the house. "And, since I mentioned someone was coming by, I happen to know she has cookies in the oven. You don't come in, I don't get a cookie."

This time Jackson's laugh bubbled up from his chest, easing his tight shoulder muscles as it rolled through. "Well, if you put it that way. I don't want to stand between someone and a cookie."

Paul stepped inside and gestured for Jackson to enter. "Jackson. It's Jackson, right?"

Jackson nodded.

"Come on into the study and tell me a little about yourself. I think I've seen you in the pews, usually with two other guys about your age?"

"Yeah. That's Zach and Ben, my roommates." Jackson glanced around the study, taking in the leather couch and matching chairs, the solid desk that was clearly made for serious work, and the shelves and shelves of books. A few popular fiction titles caught his eye, mixed in with thick theological tomes. He sat on one end of the couch, trying to take up as little room as possible. "We've been coming for... three years now? You actually got me some of my first house-sitting jobs, when I was in college. Not sure if you remember that."

Paul settled into a chair, crossing his legs. "Sure, sure. Of course. It's been a while. How're your sister and her family doing? I haven't seen them lately."

"They're doing all right. Still crammed into their tiny apartment, but I think they actually like it. There've been a few times they could've moved and they chose not to." Jackson shrugged. Who could understand his sister? He loved her and appreciated everything she'd done—and continued to do—for him, but her choices weren't likely to ever make sense. "They switched to a smaller church closer to home maybe eighteen months ago. Said it was easier to get everyone there on time."

"That makes sense." Paul brightened at a light tap on the study door followed by Mary's head. "Come on in, Hon. You remember Jackson? He house sat for Kevin a while back."

"Of course, though I don't think we actually ever met." Mary set a plate of cookies on the coffee table. Steam rose from them in little wisps. "Can I get either of you a drink?"

Jackson shook his head. "No, thank you."

"I'm good. These look wonderful. Thanks." Paul leaned forward and selected a cookie, bouncing it in his fingers a few times. "Still hot. Just the way I like 'em. Dig in, Jackson."

Mary shook her head and left the room, chuckling.

Jackson looked at the cookies. His stomach churned. "I'm okay. They smell great though."

Paul pursed his lips. "So what brings you out tonight, Jackson?"

Where was he supposed to start? Might as well begin at the beginning. Jackson launched into a tale of getting the fundraising event dumped on his desk, hiring Paige, asking her out, the immediate connection he'd felt with her, all the calls and texts that left him feeling like he'd known her his entire life, and ended with today's newspaper article. "When I asked the Senator about it, it became clear, to me at least, that she wasn't the person I thought she was. So I quit."

Paul's eyebrows shot up. "What do you mean by her not being the person you thought she was?"

"I thought she was someone committed to making a difference and standing for the principles she espoused during her campaigns. Not someone who would throw innocent people to the wolves in an attempt to draw attention away from something negative about her. At this point, I don't even know if she's innocent in the whole toxic waste thing. Or the funds that have gone missing. She blamed Lisa but... who do I trust?" Jackson's shoulders sagged. This was all so pointless. What was he hoping the pastor was going to do? Give him a magic pill that fixed it all?

"Politics are tricky, whether you're on The Hill or in the pulpit. I always hoped that I'd be able to avoid them. Then God gave me a church outside Washington D.C. that keeps growing." Paul chuckled. "And some days it's all I can do to not run screaming from the building because of the politics that try to swamp me. Here's what I've found though. If you remain true to the calling God has placed on you, you'll navigate the storm."

Jackson ran a hand through his hair. "What if... what if you're not sure what that calling is anymore?"

"Mmm. Do you feel like what's happened this summer is leading you out of politics? You no longer have a heart to make a difference for God by working in government?"

A tiny spark in his chest began to burn. "Not exactly. That's just what I want to do, phrased more concisely than I've ever managed. But hasn't today proven that it's not possible? This isn't a Capra movie and I'm not Jimmy Stewart."

Paul chuckled. "Of course not. But is working directly for a legislator the only way you can make a difference?"

"No. My roommate, Ben, works for an international charity. They do a lot of lobbying as well." Lobbying. That was a possibility he hadn't really ever explored, though he'd had plenty of dealings with lobbyists as they came to talk to the Senator. "There's no guarantee you'll make an impact that way though. And you have to be much more issue-specific."

"Well, seems to me there's no guarantee when you work directly on The Hill, either. And it'll always boil down to issues. The question is, are you willing to continue to fight the battles God put on your heart, or are you going to turn your back and run?"

Jackson sighed. When he put it that way... "Point taken."

"Now will you have a cookie?"

"Yeah, I will. They smell good."

Paul grinned. "They are good. While you eat, why don't you tell me more about Paige?"

"Thanks for letting me share your spot." Paige shook the red and white checked tablecloth and folded it in half.

"My pleasure. I think we increased our sales by quite a bit. Having your preserved foods was a big draw. If you want to join us for the rest of the farmer's market season, I'd be happy to have you." Mr. Gorman flipped one of the tables onto its side and folded in the legs before sliding it into his pickup.

"Really? That'd be a lifesaver." Paige dropped the tablecloth into the empty boxes piled up by her small table. She'd sold all of the jars she brought and had orders to ship during the week. If her garden kept producing the way it had been, she might just make it through 'til the fall. Then... well, she'd have to see what happened then. If she didn't get the contacts and clients she needed at Senator Carson's fundraiser, she'd probably have to face the facts and close Taste and See. But for now, at least she wouldn't end up homeless.

Mr. Gorman slid the next table into the bed of his pickup. "It's a deal, then. We'll see you next Saturday. You need help getting any of that to your car?"

Paige eyed the stack of boxes and folding card table and shook her head. "Nah. I should be okay. I really appreciate this."

"Don't mention it. We have to stick together. And if you find you need more produce to keep up with the demand, let me know. We'll work something out." He smiled and hopped into the cab of his truck, giving a cheery toot of the horn as he drove off.

She folded the table, grabbed the boxes by a handle in one hand and the table in another, and plodded across the hot asphalt toward her car. The bank bag under the tablecloth in the top box dragged down one end of the cardboard and her muscles strained to keep them from tipping completely. But that bulging bag would go a long way toward building up her rent fund for September. The contract cancellation penalty from one client had been split between the other two who she'd had to fire, so that was a wash. But at least it hadn't depleted her anemic savings any.

Jackson hadn't called all week.

I'm not thinking about him, no matter how much I miss his voice. Paige gave herself a firm mental shake and popped the trunk of her car.

"Need a hand?" Zach materialized at her elbow with a grin. "I thought that was you. You didn't hear me calling?"

Paige's heart accelerated and her gaze darted around. Was Jackson here, too? Why hadn't she dressed up some? Though sitting in the sun to sell jars of food didn't warrant business attire, jean-shorts and a tank top weren't what she'd pictured for her next encounter with him. "I... sure. The table's tricky."

"He's not here, by the way." Zach hoisted the table and wiggled it into the tiny trunk of her sedan. "It's just me and a colleague. She's still chatting up one of the baked goods vendors, something about using nut flours instead of wheat for a special order. I was having a hard time following the conversation when I saw you, and excused myself. You doing all right?"

She lifted a shoulder. "Sure. These things happen, right? Thanks for the help with the table. I should get going."

Zach nodded.

She waited. He looked like he was about to say something. When he didn't, she offered a tight smile. "It's good to see you, Zach."

"Yeah. You too."

She tossed the boxes in on top of the table and slammed the trunk. She wasn't going to ask about Jackson. It didn't matter if he was a miserable puddle of goo that could hardly get out of bed every morning. Not that she'd believe that, even if Zach said it. Guys didn't feel that way, not about her. It was her own stupid fault that she'd broken her rule and kissed him so early in their relationship. He'd acted as if he cared. Why shouldn't she have believed he was really interested?

Well, it wouldn't happen again.

"What are you doing here, Daddy? Where's Hector?" Paige tossed an apron over her neck, tied it at the waist, and scooped her hair up into a baseball cap.

Mopping at the beads of sweat on his brow, Lawrence leaned over to grab another chicken out of the cooler at his feet. "Hector's got the flu. Called me this morning. I know you've been busy with your canning. I didn't want to bother you. Wednesday isn't your day to work."

"Daddy." Paige frowned at her father. It wasn't that hot in here yet, and piecing chickens wasn't that taxing. "How are you feeling? You don't look well."

"Eh. I'm fine." He swiped an arm across his forehead and continued butchering the birds. "If you want to start on the shellfish, that'd be a big help. Your mother called you, I take it?"

Paige nodded. Seeing her dad, though, she didn't blame Mom quite as much. "Why don't you sit and rest a minute and I'll finish the chickens before I start on the shrimp."

"I said I'm okay, Paige. Just do your job."

Paige stiffened. The last time her father had yelled at her like that, she'd been twelve and had been caught using his ceramic kitchen knife, very nearly slicing off a finger with it. She nodded, shrinking into herself. Did everyone she loved think so little of her? In the walk-in, she grabbed the box of whole shrimp, hefted it to her shoulder, and strode back out to the kitchen. She dropped the box on the counter and went to wash her hands. "Everyone else still on the schedule to come in?"

"As far as I know." Lawrence's breathing was heavy. He set the knife down and dropped his chin to his heaving chest. "I'm sorry for snapping. Your mother has been hovering and it's making me crazy. I was glad when Hector called out, if only to have a chance for some peace. I shouldn't have taken it out on you."

"She's just worried, Daddy. And... I can kind of see why. But if you say you're fine, I'll trust you." She pulled the head off a shrimp and tossed it into a bowl. They were getting low on seafood stock. She'd put a batch on after she got the prep work finished. With the flick of her knife, she slit the back of the shell, slid the meat out, and pulled the vein loose. She dropped the vein in a trash bowl and added the shell to the pile of heads for stock. Only the rest of the box to go. "I was able to hook up with Mr. Gorman at the Farmer's Market on Saturday. He was delighted to share his space. I sold everything I brought and spent Monday and yesterday filling orders. I should be able to get enough done between now and Saturday to make another good sale. Thanks for the suggestion."

"Good. Good. If you want more hours here, I can probably—" His breath hitched and he coughed, dropping his knife to the floor with a clatter. "Paige?"

Paige looked up in time to see him stagger and crash to the ground. "Daddy."

She dropped the knife and ran to his side, wiping her hands on her apron. "Daddy?" Paige lowered her ear to his chest and pushed her fingers into the junction of his jaw and neck. There had to be something. She fumbled in her pocket for her cell phone and punched in 9-1-1, oblivious to the tears rolling down her face.

"9-1-1, what's your emergency?"

"My dad. I need an ambulance. I can't find his pulse. You've got to send someone."

"Okay, can you give me your address?"

Paige rattled off the restaurant's address with instructions for how to get to the back door, hit the speaker button on her phone and set it on the floor. She searched her memory for the CPR technique she'd learned in culinary school. Her fingers palpated along his ribcage to the middle, did you press there? Or go up a handsbreadth? Up. You had to go up. She moved her hands to the middle of his chest, locked her elbows and pushed. "I'm starting CPR, I think, it's been so long since my class."

"Stay calm, I'll talk you through it."

Paige struggled to hear over the buzzing in her head. Her dad couldn't die. Not now. Not like this. When the EMTs burst into the kitchen, one gently led her aside. She vaguely saw him end the connection with 9-1-1 before pressing the phone into her hand. She jolted when the paramedics zapped her father with the defibrillator and buried her face in her hands as they strapped him to the gurney and rushed him into the ambulance.

26

"You're only telling me this now?" Jackson frowned at Zach. Five days. Zach had seen Paige five days ago and sat on it? "How'd she look?"

"She looked good. Casual. Cool. Confident. Looked like she'd sold all of her canned goods, too." Zach paused the game and glanced up. "And I didn't mention it because you said we weren't allowed to talk about her. Remember?"

Jackson sighed. "Yeah, all right. I just wish... "

"Ha. You know what they say, 'if wishes were horses, beggars would dine.'"

"I'm not quite sure that's how it goes." Ben sauntered in from the kitchen with a plate holding a sandwich that would make a long-running cartoon character proud. "You're implying that beggars would choose to eat horses. I'm kind of thinking that's not what they'd wish for."

"Whatever." Zach snatched a pickle that was poking out of the side of Ben's sandwich and crunched into it. "He knew what I meant."

"Strangely, I did, which is both fascinating and somewhat frightening." Jackson raked a hand through his hair. "I'd forgotten how horrible it is to sit around waiting for job offers."

"Nothing yet?" Ben worked the sandwich into his mouth, somehow managing a bite that covered all four inches of its height.

"Nope. Though I did get one email back saying that they were interested and would be getting back to me soon. Whatever 'soon' translates to." Jackson flipped a chair around and straddled it. "On the positive side, the gym's pretty empty during the day, so I don't have to wait to get the weights I want."

"You should take up a video game. All that working out isn't good for you." Zach grinned. "Trust me, I'm a teacher."

Ben snickered. "I can just see the parent emails if that little nugget got loose into the wild. Speaking of... have you seen the latest on Carson?"

Jackson opened his mouth to correct Ben. She was, after all, still a Senator. But she'd lost any claim to respect at this point. He shook his head. "I skimmed some headlines but didn't see anything new. What'd I miss?"

"She was spotted having dinner, multiple times mind you, with one of the big wigs from some lobbying firm. And they were looking pretty cozy, at that. Her husband was nowhere to be seen."

That was it. That was the guy. Jackson shook his head. "Huh. I won't jump on the bandwagon immediately, but that guy was around the office a lot in the last few weeks, so it's possible. How could I have been so wrong about her?"

Ben took another bite and chewed for a moment. "She's a person, Jackson, just like the rest of us, and prone to making stupid mistakes. It's not as if being elected, even when you're re-elected over and over, somehow makes you less prone to sin."

"I'd say the latter leaves you slightly more prone to it, if you're not careful. All that power? She probably started off with all the best intentions and then Washington got a hold of her." Zach paused the game again. "Which sounds like I'm advocating Christians staying out of politics, but I'm not. I don't think it's inevitable. I just think Christians who choose that path need to always keep at the forefront of their mind that their career choice has put them directly in the path of a spiritual battle. And Satan would like nothing better than to cause another Christian to crash and burn on a public stage."

"Or get them to give up entirely." Ben set his empty plate on the coffee table and reached for the second controller. "If he can keep Christians out of the world of politics and focused on the tiny sphere of other Christians, that's almost as good as discrediting us, cause then we're not doing any good out in the world anyway."

Ben's words followed Jackson through the next two days. He wasn't giving up on politics. Pastor Brown had helped him see the good he could still do there. But hadn't he given up on Paige? Two weeks ago, if you'd asked him if Paige was the woman God had for him, he would have said yes. Then he'd let her walk away. It was time to change that. Maybe he was too late, but he had to try.

He hopped down from his jeep and looked around. Who knew there was a farmer's market this close to their house? Judging by the steady trickles of people working their way from the parking lot to the booths, a lot of people. Was it just not advertised? Maybe he didn't know where to look? He'd stroll around a bit first, then corner Paige. Hopefully a few sales would put her in a good mood and she'd at least be willing to hear him out. He sniffed. A mixture of fresh popped corn, sugar, and salt hung in the air. Step one, find the kettle corn stall.

The salty-sweet snack was covered in buttery-goodness. Jackson hadn't had fresh kettle corn since he was a kid. He grinned as he dipped his hand back into the sack. There were all kinds of vendors here, not just people selling tomatoes and green beans. He stopped and squinted at the sign on a white box truck. Buffalo? You could buy buffalo to cook at home?

"What's it taste like?" Jackson sidled up to the table and smiled.

"Like beef, but leaner. Some say it's gamier, but that could be because they're not used to grass-fed beef. We'll have samples out in another hour, if you want to swing back by."

"Can you grill it? Like burgers?" It was probably a dumb question. If the meat was ground up, you could probably make burgers out of it.

The man chuckled. "Absolutely. Might need a bit more egg to hold it together in patties. Leaner, like I said."

"I'll take a pound. I'm on roommate dinner duty this week. Usually I order pizza, but I can handle burgers." Jackson dug out his wallet, swallowing at the final price. It wasn't cheap, but if it tasted good, it was worth it to say he'd eaten buffalo burgers. He nodded his thanks to the vendor and continued his stroll, stopping here and there for a sample. Finally, he saw the Gorman Produce truck where Zach said he'd seen Paige.

Jackson poked through the boxes of vegetables displayed under the Gorman canopy. This was more what he expected from a farmer's market. He grabbed a few ears of corn and a fat, purple tomato to round out the menu for roommate night.

"I heard you had someone selling preserves last week. I was hoping they might be back?"

Mr. Gorman shook his head, a concerned frown creasing his forehead. "Pity, that. Try back next week though. Paige, that's the gal's name, said her dad was getting out of the hospital today or tomorrow."

"Hospital? What happened?" Jackson took the plastic bag of produce and his change.

"I didn't get all the details, but it sounded like he had a massive heart attack. Nearly died. Paige was alone with him at his restaurant when it happened."

Oh, Paige. Jackson closed his eyes. "That's terrible."

"It is. But if he's getting to go home, sounds like he's on the mend. Definitely a good sign. I'll let her know you asked after her. There've been a number of folks dropping by. I think it'll do her good to know she's got some loyal customers already. There was a nasty bit of press about her catering company a few weeks back, none of it true. But it's put the poor gal in a bind, business-wise. I'm glad to be able to share my stall space. Plus," he grinned, "her jars bring a lot more business my way. It's a good partnership all around."

Jackson nodded and held up his bag. "Thanks."

He wandered off, his thoughts spinning. What must that have been like? Terrifying. It had to have been terrifying. And he hadn't been there for her.

27

"Are you sure, Dad? I really think you should see about staying another day or two. You almost died." Paige's voice caught as her mind flashed back to the slow-motion replay of her father falling to kitchen floor.

He grunted and leaned over to pull on his sock. "You don't get better in a hospital, Paige. This is where sick people come to die. Since I'm not going to do that last part just yet, I'd rather recover at home. Besides, it's too hard for your mom to come see me here. At home she can dote and not panic because I'm hooked up to machines."

"But what if—"

"Don't start what-if-ing. That never solves anything. The facts are that the doctor agrees that I'm well enough to go home, and so that's what I'm going to do." He held out his hand and didn't speak until Paige put hers into it. "I appreciate that you're concerned. I'm not taking this lightly. I know I have a lot of recovery left to do. It's just going to be easier to do at home. And I can't sell the restaurant from in here."

"Sell the restaurant? Why would you do that? I can keep it going until you're able to come back."

"No, Paigey-girl. The doctor says going back is absolutely out of the question. It's too much stress for my heart. So it's time to sell."

Sell. He hadn't even asked if she wanted it. On the one hand, it was good that he took seriously her desire to have Taste and See. On the other... she didn't exactly have a catering company left anymore. "How much are you going to ask for it?"

"I need to do a little research yet."

"Will you tell me before you put it on the market? I don't have much saved, but maybe I could qualify for a loan."

He drew he brows together. "You'd buy it? What about your catering company?"

She shook her head. "You never did read the paper, did you Daddy? Probably why I was never very interested in keeping up with politics either. Taste and See is all but dead. The Senator offered me up as fodder to get the vultures off her back. In addition to not seeming to work, it effectively made me look like someone willing to trade favors for business, which cost me all my clients. I'll do her event on Saturday and that'll be it."

"Didn't you have a wedding to do, too?"

"If Whitney actually gets married, yes. At this point, I'm not holding my breath. Even so, the restaurant could handle that just as easily. She was supposed to get me an email address so I could get some forms for the venue they were using, but never did. I guess I need to follow up with her on that. But closing for a private party might be even better than trying to cater somewhere else." Paige shrugged. She'd suggest it to Whitney.

"If you're serious, I'll give it to you."

Her heart lightened, then sank. "How can you afford to do that, though? Don't you need the money from the sale for retirement?"

"Nah. That was never my plan. *You* were always my plan. But I didn't want to force you into it. I wanted you to want it to be your plan, too. Is it?"

Was it? She'd started Taste and See because she hadn't wanted to simply fall into her dad's restaurant without trying to do her own thing and because sustainability had become important to her. But Season's Bounty had changed into a place she was proud of, a place she'd be thrilled to call her own. It wasn't her own business from the ground up, but it was still hers. Hers and her dad's. "Yeah. I think it is."

He smiled and pulled her close, pressing a kiss to her forehead. "Then it's yours. I'll have our attorney draw up the papers. How does a dollar sound?"

Paige laughed. "That's a price I can afford."

Was he ever going to stop calling? Paige swiped 'deny' on her phone, sending Jackson to voice mail. Again. He'd stopped for a few days and now he was back at it. As much as her heart ached to answer it, she wouldn't give in. Besides, he knew he was supposed to email with any work-related business. And she'd made it clear that was all they had left to discuss. The few emails she'd had from the Senator's office were all from someone named Donna. Why would he call but not be brave enough to do his own emailing?

She shook her head. There was no understanding the male mind. Better not to try. Pushing thoughts of Jackson away, she ignored the new tear in her heart and focused on the spreadsheet breaking down the prep work for the Senator's event on Saturday. Just six days away. There was a lot to do, but it was all manageable. Especially now that she could use the restaurant's kitchen, and staff, to help. Dad had put her in charge until the sale was complete. Hopefully everyone would stay on. Minimal turnover would keep things running smoothly. As much as she hadn't wanted to go running back to Daddy for a few shifts when things started getting tight, it turned out to have been a good thing. She had a much better idea of how things ran, who the key personnel were, and so forth. It shouldn't be quite as traumatic to take over as it would've been coming in cold. *Thank you, Lord.*

She checked the time. Nearly six. After she'd gotten Dad home and settled, Mom had shooed her off, saying not to call 'til after dinner. Probably better to wait until tomorrow, all things considered. Which left her... with nothing to do and no one to talk to. Why had she never been the kind of girl who collected female friends? Her gaze drifted to her phone. The weeks with Jackson had been some of the least lonely in recent memory. *Why had he ended up being a jerk?* Her conscience twanged. If what he said was true, he wasn't entirely responsible for the character assassination. But still, he should have told her what was coming. True, he was quick to apologize... but that didn't solve anything.

Would I have been at the restaurant when Dad got sick, if it wasn't for that article? Paige pressed her lips together as tears burned the back of her eyes. Probably not. It was a Wednesday, the one day she absolutely wouldn't have been able to fill in, no matter how much her mother begged. She swallowed. If she hadn't been there... how long would it have been until someone found him? Too long.

Maybe the reporter had done her a favor. Maybe she'd at least hear Jackson out. But not 'til Saturday. They could talk at the fundraiser, when she'd be busy enough that she wouldn't be tempted to let him kiss away the rest of her reservations.

"Thanks for meeting me." Whitney pulled out a chair and sat at the small table for two shoved in the corner of the crowded coffee shop.

Paige offered a weak smile. What alternative was there? She was still supposed to be catering their wedding and she didn't have any information about it beyond the initial questionnaire she gave clients. "Of course. Did you bring the forms for your venue? You never did text me the coordinator's email address."

"About that... "

Paige stifled a yawn. Every muscle in her body cried out for a hot bath and bed. "Look, Whit. If you don't want me to cater, just tell me. I'm not going to be upset and I won't keep your deposit. I've only been in charge of the restaurant for two days and I'm maxed out."

Whitney's face crumpled. Tears glimmered in her eyes. "Are you backing out on me?"

"No. That's not what I'm saying." Her shoulders fell and she gave in and massaged the back of her neck. "I thought it's what you were trying to say. I made a commitment, I'll keep it."

"You're the best." Whitney cleared her throat. "Here's the thing. We still don't have a venue."

"I thought... "

"I know. So did I. But I guess Elliot forgot to send in the deposit like he promised, so when I called yesterday to talk about a few details, I got the 'we don't have that date available' speech. At first, I thought they just misunderstood and thought I was trying to book it and they had their wires crossed. But it was me with the crossed wires."

Paige winced. She could just imagine how well the conversation with Elliot went after that phone call. Poor guy. Though Whitney's anger was also justified. With just over two weeks 'til Labor Day, their options were getting slim. "So what will you do? Can you get married at the townhouse?"

"I guess we're going to have to. If people laughed us out of the building when we had two months to plan, I can only imagine their reactions if we called to ask about booking with just two weeks to go. Is there any way you could come over and help me figure out how to make it work? It isn't as if we're inviting hordes of people, but... it's a townhouse."

"What's the yard like?" Paige didn't want to spend another evening away from an early bed if she could help it. How had her dad managed the restaurant all on his own those first few years? Early mornings, late nights... she was never home. Some of her mother's resentment made a bit more sense now, though why hadn't Mom said anything? Or just spent more time at the restaurant? Dad had always loved it when she was there.

Whitney groaned. "It's not one of the top selling features, let's just put it that way. It's on our list to fix up in the spring. It'll have to be inside. Besides, Labor Day weekend? It's gonna be hot and sticky. That's fine for a barbecue, not quite so awesome when you're dressed up."

Paige took a long swallow of hot chocolate. Coffee would taste better, but she didn't need to be up all night. Four o'clock came awfully early in the morning. "I have an idea."

"I'm all ears. At this point, unless it involves standing in the middle of the Beltway, I'm probably game."

"What if you rented out the restaurant? We could close for the day on Saturday. If you're really not inviting tons of people—"

"Forty-three. We have forty-three people coming. And no, I don't know why Elliot's younger sister couldn't find a date. She's sweet and pretty, but she won't even consider finding a plus one to make it an even number."

"That's doable." Paige took a napkin out of the dispenser on the table and dug in her purse for a pen. She sketched a rectangle that was about the shape of the main dining area at the restaurant, marked the doorway, and flipped it around to face Whitney. "Our maximum occupancy is one hundred two. So if we split the space in half— maybe you could look into renting those garden trellis things and you could decorate them—"

"Sure. A few vines or flowers woven in... that could be pretty."

Paige nodded and drew lines dividing the room. "We could set up chairs here for the ceremony. Then you could move over here for the reception. It still wouldn't be crazily fancy, but you can decorate however you want, provided it's removable, and I think it'd work out fine. I'll put together a smaller menu based off our usual menu if you give me an idea of how much you want to spend per person. But I still can't do the cake. I'm just not a baker."

"The cake's handled. Thirty minutes ago the cake, my dress, and Elliot's tux were the only things we knew for sure. This is great. It's perfect." Whitney took the napkin and folded it in half. "How much will it cost?"

Paige frowned. She knew the general formulas you were supposed to use for this type of thing, but it didn't seem right to go crazy. Still, she'd need staff to work, and there'd be no tips, plus the operating costs of being open. "What's your budget?"

Whitney named a figure.

"Does that include food?"

Whitney sighed. "I'd like it to. We can probably add a little more if we need to."

"Let me work something up. I think we can figure it out." It wasn't going to be a huge money-maker for the restaurant, but it wouldn't be a loss either.

"Thanks, Paige. I know I haven't really treated you well the last two months... I'm sorry."

"It's okay. I hear wedding planning is stressful." She forced a smile. It wasn't as if Whitney was the only one who'd treated her poorly. Her heart yearned for Jackson. Whenever there was a spare minute, she found herself staring at his number in her phone, considering calling, replaying his pleading voicemail just to hear him again. "I've got an early morning tomorrow, but I'll try to carve out some time to put numbers together for you. We get a little lull after lunch and I usually spend it in the office. That work?"

Whitney nodded and stood, her chair screeching along the floor as she did. A few heads turned their way, but the din of the evening coffee crowd continued.

Paige followed Whitney to the door, her heart stopping as a familiar jeep turned into a parking spot two cars down from hers. *Oh, please don't let him see me.*

Jackson hopped down from the driver's side while Zach and Ben piled out of the passenger doors. The three aimed toward the coffee shop. Zach and Ben were laughing. Jackson wore a smile that didn't quite reach his eyes. He looked thinner, wan. Passing under the streetlights, shadows under his eyes jumped into view. A trick of the light. Had to be. Why would he be losing sleep?

Zach pulled open the door, holding it as Whitney walked through. Trying to shrink into invisibility, Paige followed, refusing to meet his eyes.

"Hey, Paige."

She bit back a groan. Whitney hurried off to her car, oblivious to Paige's predicament. "Zach."

"Paige, hey there." Ben elbowed Jackson in the ribs.

"Hi, Ben." Paige's gaze locked with Jackson's. Her heart galloped in her chest as all the air was sucked from her lungs. She stepped out onto the sidewalk, turning toward her car. Tears pricked her eyes. Even with the changes, he looked good. Too good. "Nice to see you."

Jackson's fingers brushed her elbow. "Paige...?"

She crossed her arms. "I have an early day tomorrow."

The flash of pain in his eyes nearly did her in. But this wasn't her fault. None of it was. That article... his comments in her apartment rang in her ears, as did her resolution to talk to him at the fundraiser. Now, seeing him, every muscle itched to throw herself into his arms and let go. He'd understand about Dad, and the restaurant, and all the conflicting thoughts circling in her head. He understood her better than anyone ever had. But he still hadn't stopped the Senator. Maybe he didn't understand her as well as she'd thought he did. She shook her head and bolted for the desolate safety of her car.

28

The wall he'd built around his heart crumbled when their eyes met. Paige. She was it for him. It didn't matter how fast things had happened, or what kind of ribbing he was going to get from the guys. God had arranged for him to meet the perfect woman and he wasn't going to let her get away. Not without a fight.

As she turned and ran, his heart bled. Would he be able to win back her trust? She still cared for him, he'd seen that... but would she let herself admit it? Pain as fierce as the day she'd kicked him out of her apartment stabbed through him. He followed his roommates into the coffee shop. Maybe they could help him figure out how to win her back.

"Here. While you were mooning over lost loves, I got you a latte. With an extra shot of girly vanilla in it." Zach slid the huge paper cup across the table to Jackson.

Jackson peeled off the lid and sniffed. "Just like I like it. Where's the whipped cream?"

"Really? Why don't you give me your man card now and we'll all avoid the embarrassment later."

Ben scooted out a chair and sat. "Who's turning in their man card?"

"Jackson. He's over there whining cause I didn't get whipped cream on his... what are you drinking?"

Red spread up Ben's neck and across his cheeks. "Skinny decaf white mocha with extra whipped cream."

Zach buried his head in his hands. "I'm rooming with two women. When my mother finds out, she's going to have a heart attack and die. Why can't the two you just drink coffee? Plain, manly coffee."

"He's never tried it, has he?" Ben snickered. "Here, scoot your cup over, I'll share my whipped cream."

"What's the point of making it skinny if you're going to add extra whipped cream?" Jackson grinned as Ben scooped a generous dollop of fluffy white goodness into his drink.

"It's all about maximizing taste and minimizing calories. You don't really notice the skinny, especially not with whipped cream."

"Can we *please* talk about something else before the two of you start discussing the relative merits of shoulder bags over clutches?" Zach blew across his coffee and took a long sip.

Jackson furrowed his brow and looked across at Ben. "Is this like backpacks versus a wallet? They're not really comparable."

"Ha. Good one." Ben cocked his head to the side. "Oh, you're serious. You get to keep your man card, girly drink or not. And is no one going to mention the whole awkward thing at the door? 'Cause I can keep pretending I wasn't part of it, if that's what we're doing, but it seems like maybe Jackson might want to talk about it?"

You could always count on Ben to cut through the small talk and get down to it. "I was working up to it, then Zach made fun of my drink."

"Oh sure, blame the guy who *bought* your four dollar drink. Classy."

"I'm sorry, are we on a date?" Jackson dug his wallet out of his back pocket, pulled out a five and tossed it on the table. "We good?"

Ben snorted out a laugh and began to cough, a tiny dribble of mocha working its way out his nose. He wiped at it, still coughing. Zach snatched the money then reached around and pounded Ben's back.

"You all right?" Zach tucked the bill in his pocket.

"Yeah. Will be." Ben cleared his throat and wiped watering eyes. "So. Paige? I wasn't the only one who felt the sparks in the air, right?"

One corner of Jackson's mouth poked up. He'd felt them. He just hadn't realized people around them could as well. "No. But I'm not sure what to do about it. She won't answer my calls. I'm not sure how you talk to someone who's freezing you out."

Zach tipped his head back and drained his coffee. He set the empty cup down with a thunk and held Jackson's gaze. "Turn up the heat."

Jackson's phone roused him from a deep sleep. Groaning, he fumbled around on the nightstand for his cell. He cleared his throat. "Jackson Trent."

"Jackson, it's Donna. Please don't hang up." The secretary's voice was panicked.

He rubbed his eyes and wiggled to a sitting position. He'd hear her out. He owed her that much. She'd saved him numerous times when he was still learning his job for the Senator. "What's up?"

"The fundraiser on Saturday. I'm in charge of it now and I get only the briefest responses from the caterer when I ask her questions. It seems like she has things under control, but... I don't know. Is there any way you could check in with her and make sure?"

"You're kidding me, right? She won't even take my calls anymore. That article killed whatever chance we had at making something happen. Or at least set it back a good bit. I've got the beginnings of a plan to try and win her back, but I'm not wasting them to help the Senator. Not even for you."

"All right. It's just... attendance is going to be really low. Do I need to tell her? Is it too late for her not to buy and prepare so much food? The Senator wants me to tell her the price is lowering based on attendance, but that wasn't in the contract. I looked. So I'm not going to be the one having that conversation with her. But if the Senator's going to try and pull a fast one, doesn't she deserve to know?"

Jackson scrubbed a hand over his face. At least Paige couldn't blame this on him. Was she strong enough, business savvy enough, to hold the Senator to the contract, no matter what? He'd seen the invoice for the food, there was no going back at this point. And Paige's contract hadn't been hugely padded. It wasn't as if she could afford to have it cut and still turn a profit. "You've got to warn her. But, for your own sake, you need to do it under the radar."

"I know. That's why I was hoping you'd talk to her." Donna sighed. "What do you suggest I try?"

"I don't know. But if you can, it's going to be better to keep my name out of it." Jackson swung his legs over the side of the bed and stood. He stuffed his feet into his slippers and shuffled down the hall toward the kitchen. It was quiet. Zach and Ben must already be at work. "And Donna, watch out for yourself, too. You deserve better than to go down with the Senator."

"Already on it, Jackson. Thanks, though. You having any luck?"

"I'm tugging on some lines. Think it's time for a shift in focus though."

"You're not leaving politics, are you? You're one of the good ones. We need people like you to stay the course."

He grinned. It was good that someone thought that way. "Not leaving, no. But I'm applying at a few PACs, people who are committed to the values that I think matter and whose sole purpose on The Hill is to promote them. Maybe it's not as glamorous as effecting change from within, but I need to be able to look myself in the eye. After finding out how wrong I was about Senator Carson... I don't want to go down that road again. At least not right now."

"Mmm. When you land somewhere, give me a call on this number with all your info and I'll do what I can to make sure you get Senator Pinkerton's ear whenever you need it."

Jackson paused with his hand on the coffee. Senator Pinkerton? That was a good step up. So far at least, Pinkerton had managed to be consistent in his votes and he stayed out of the papers. "Good for you, Donna."

"Well, it's not official yet. But I'm sure enough that I'm telling a few people. I'll send Paige an email from my personal account and just give her a head's up. If Senator Carson wants to get mad about it, she can run the event herself."

Jackson chuckled. "There you go. Hang in there."

"You too."

He hit end and dropped his phone on the counter, his eyebrows lifting as he saw the clock on the stove. Ten fifteen. On a weekday? He shook his head and poured steaming ambrosia from their insulated carafe into his oversized mug. The heavenly smell lifted his spirits. He, Zach, and Ben had spent an hour last night plotting various ways to get Paige to come around. Ideas were still percolating. Several had promise, but he'd let her get through the Senator's event first. It was bound to be stressful under the best of circumstances. After what Donna said, Saturday was definitely not going to fall into that category.

Paige dropped her phone in the pocket of her black slacks. Hector said he had everything under control. So why did he keep calling? He'd run dinner before when her Dad had been in charge. This was no different. Not really. She smoothed her white chef's jacket. It was stiff and scratchy. If she was going to wear something like it with regularity, she was going to have to find one that wasn't quite so horrible. But that could wait.

She walked the length of the buffet, stopping to check temperatures on the dishes. Everything was exactly how it was supposed to be. So why was her stomach in knots? Jackson. It had to be Jackson. She'd see him tonight. Would he be wearing one of those fitted suits like he did at the office? Probably. She pressed her lips together. Attraction was one thing, but if he didn't respect her, there was nothing for them to do but part ways.

Her inner voice chided her. It was true, he hadn't overtly done anything disrespectful. But he should have told her about the article. Even in her head it sounded weak. That was something you had a fight about, sure. Maybe you'd even break up. But to not take his calls at all and at least give him a chance to explain? It had made sense at the time. Now, with a cooler head... she sighed. Hopefully it wasn't too late.

She stopped at the end of the buffet, by the array of plated desserts, and adjusted the position of the restaurant's business cards. It was weird not to see the Taste and See logo that she'd worked so hard on, but this was where God had her for now and she was working on readjusting her dreams. Maybe it wasn't something she'd started herself, from the ground up, but it was still a wonderful business. And since Dad had reinvented the restaurant into sustainable fare... it was hard to complain. It was just what she would love to have started on her own down the line. So why complain that it wasn't hers from the start? It was hers now.

"Ms. Jackson?"

"Yes? Oh, hello Senator Carson. It's good to meet you in person." Paige extended her hand. *Liar, liar. I could have gone decades without ever having to meet you face to face.*

"Everything looks lovely. I've got your final check here and wanted to give it to you now, before things got busy."

Paige schooled her expression as she accepted the envelope. "Thank you. Let me just double check that it's correct and I'll get the final paperwork for your signature."

"There's no need for that." Senator Carson started to turn.

"Oh, but there is. It's best for both of us that we have an official document indicating that we both agree the initial contract has been fulfilled. It won't take a moment and, as you said, it's nice to have it out of the way before things get busy. That way you don't have to wait around for me to finish cleaning up when things are said and done."

Paige wriggled her finger under the envelope's flap, breaking the seal, and slid the check out. She pressed her lips together. Thankfully, Donna had warned her that the Senator might try something or she likely would have just tucked the check away and it would've been too late. "Ah, there seems to be a slight discrepancy. The final payment, due on the night of the event, was to cover the difference between the initial deposit and the agreed upon contract price. You're several thousand dollars short."

The Senator straightened, looking down her nose as she spoke. "Owing to the current political climate, I'm sure you've seen the papers, the attendance is much lower than anticipated. I've adjusted the payment accordingly."

Paige shook her head. "The contract wasn't on a per-person basis. It was bid as a flat fee based on the estimates you provided. I'm sorry there'll be fewer in attendance, but that doesn't change my costs or allow you to break the contract. I hope you have your checkbook with you, Senator, because none of this food is getting served until I've been paid in full."

Senator Carson's face contorted, her eyes spitting fire. She leaned into Paige's personal space, so close their noses nearly touched. "Look, you. I don't know who you think you are, but you're not getting a single penny more. Frankly, I'm surprised you upheld your contract once Jackson left in his silly snit over how the papers treated you. But just because you did, doesn't mean I have to. We're re-negotiating the payment, and the check you have in your hand is the new price."

Jackson had quit? Her heart soared, and then plummeted. She'd been so horrible to him. And he'd been telling the truth. She willed away the tears clawing their way into her eyes. First things first. Paige cleared her throat. "I'm glad you acknowledge that I'm an ethical businesswoman who keeps her commitments, regardless of the work environment. I wish I could say the same about you. I'll give you one more chance to prove that you have even the tiniest bit of integrity behind all that political polish. Honor the contract you signed, now, or I'm taking the check as a cancellation fee and packing up this food."

"Ha. What will you do with it? You can't sell it to anyone else at this point." The Senator crossed her arms with a smirk.

"No, that's true. But there are any number of homeless shelters between here and home that will most likely be quite happy to have a donation." Paige's voice rose, her blood boiling. Who did this woman think she was? How had Jackson worked for her as long as he had? There had to have been signs, right?

The silver-haired woman who had been manning the front desk the times Paige stopped by the Senator's office hurried over. "Hi, Paige, right? I'm Donna. We've been coordinating over email lately?"

"Yes, of course. Nice to meet you." Paige scowled at the Senator. "Well, Senator?"

"Donna, take care of this. Ms. Jackson is unwilling to accept final payment of her contract and is threatening to take the food and leave. If you can't make her see reason, contact my attorneys. I have guests to attend to." Senator Carson stalked off, her ankles wobbling as her heels sank into the lawn behind Mount Vernon.

Donna watched over her shoulder until the Senator was on the other side of the banquet area, then she pulled an envelope out of her pocket. "Here's the rest of the payment you're owed. I was able to convince the comptroller that there'd been a calculation error. Thankfully the Senator hadn't gotten rid of the original contract, so I had it as proof."

"You'll understand if I check?" Paige flipped open the envelope and swiftly added the totals in her head. It seemed right. "All right. Thanks... won't you be in trouble?"

Donna shook her head. "My resignation is sitting on the Senator's desk. She'll find it the next time she goes in. I just had to wait until I had an official offer. I'm not sure how Jackson's been managing the past two weeks. Maybe, being single, he has more savings than I do. Doesn't matter. I'll just be glad to be done with the witch. She had us all fooled."

How was that possible? "Thanks for this."

Donna touched her arm. "I can tell you don't understand, but the Senator used to be someone I respected and looked up to. I'm not sure what happened, to be honest. Maybe it has to do with this man she's supposedly having an affair with. But whatever it is, the changes came on suddenly. If Lisa had kept her mouth shut, I don't know that any of us would have seen her for what she's become. But now? There's no one left in her corner. Don't judge those of us who tried to believe the best of her because of who she used to be."

Paige stared up at the ceiling of her bedroom. She should get up and go to church. But every muscle in her body ached. What a week. How had her dad managed to run the restaurant by himself for so many years? She really needed someone in the office full-time. Or a head chef. Doing both was insane. It wasn't as if she had a huge personal life, but she did still want to keep her garden and put the produce up for the winter. And Mr. Gorman had called four times about the Farmer's Market. That wasn't going to happen again anytime soon. Still, it was nice to know people had been back looking for her. Maybe she could squeeze in some time to... oh, who was she kidding? Anything she managed to can now was going to be for her own use. There sure wasn't time to process extra. At least the Senator's event was over.

Stretching her arms up over her head, she headed to the kitchen. She'd get some coffee and then... God would understand if she skipped church. Wouldn't He? Heaviness settled over her shoulders. Sunday meant church. She wasn't sick, not really. But not having to go anywhere, or maybe just scooting across the street to her garden for a bit, it sounded like heaven. And yet... shouldn't she want to be in church? Was it okay to choose to worship at home, by herself, every now and then, or did that somehow diminish her as a Christian? She sighed. The only answer in her head was her mother chastising her not to forsake the gathering of believers. But was one skipped church service really forsaking? Or was it just taking a break?

She stared at the coffee machine. It didn't have any answers either. Dropping the pod into the top, Paige aligned her cup and hit the start button just as her cell rang.

"Hi Daddy. Shouldn't you still be asleep?"

"Don't you start, too. Your mother's going to drive me up a wall with all the resting I'm doing. Seriously. It's one thing to take it easy and recover, but this has crossed a line."

"Daddy. You could've died."

"So, what, you all kept me alive so I could die of boredom instead?"

Paige snickered in spite of herself. "It can't be that bad."

He sighed noisily into the phone. "It really can. She won't let me go get myself a drink of water, for crying out loud. Look, she's going to be mad at me for asking, but I really want to know how things are going at the restaurant. You doing okay?"

"It's good. But I understand a little of why you ended up so stressed out. Why didn't you tell Mom you needed her to be in the office? She's been puttering around home, doing nothing, for over a year and I don't know how you've managed to keep it all going."

"It's complicated. She wanted to retire. I wasn't going to say she couldn't. I think she was hoping it would make me want to retire, but I wasn't ready... I'm still not ready, to be honest. So... "

Uh-oh. Her dad's tone could only mean one thing. He had a crazy idea and was going to try and make her complicit in it. "Just stop there, Dad. I'm not doing anything that jeopardizes your health. Or makes Mom angry, which would jeopardize my own."

"What if I get the doctor's permission?"

"And Mom's."

"I might need your help with that, but okay."

Paige collected her coffee and sat at the kitchen table. "All right, let's hear it."

"Let me be clear, I'm not trying to say you can't handle things. But, I know how hard it is to manage both the kitchen and keep up with all the paperwork. What if I came in, one, maybe two days a week for a few hours to handle the office stuff?"

Paige took a long drink of coffee. How amazing would that be? He could probably do ninety percent of the job in that amount of time. Which meant she might be able to use the downtime in the kitchen to handle inventory and staffing problems. "Mom will never go for it."

"If she does, would you be open to it?"

"Of course. But it's easy to say that. I'm serious, you'll have to drug Mom to get out of the house. And that'll only work once. You didn't hear her the whole time you were in the hospital. She blames the restaurant for all of this." *And me, for not having stepped into a full-time role there sooner... she might have a point on that last one.* Had her pride almost cost her dad his life?

"Let me handle your mother. There's one thing she loves more than she hates the restaurant, and that's you."

Paige scoffed.

"Paige." Her Dad's stern reprimand sent her back to middle school when her relationship with her mother had started turning complicated. "She loves you. I'll admit she doesn't always show it in the best way, but if you seriously don't believe that, the two of you need to sit down and really talk to one another."

She sighed. "I know she does. I just wish she acted like it more often. It's hard to have to rely on knowing something like that in your head when your heart is getting kicked around and reminded of all the places where you don't quite measure up."

"Aw, Sweetheart. You need to listen better. You'd think after twenty-six years you'd know your mother."

"Fine. I still don't think she'll let you. But if you can get her to agree, and the doctor says it's okay, I could use the help. In the office *only*."

"Perfect. I see the doctor tomorrow and I'll start working on your mother after that. So probably not 'til next week. Can you hold out that long?"

"Yeah. I'm making it work."

"That's my girl. I'm proud of you and I love you."

Maybe he really was proud of her, but it was hard to take at face value when his sole purpose for calling was to offer to help. Didn't that mean he assumed she was floundering and couldn't handle it? *Or he knows how hard it is to do both and wants to help.* Why was it so hard to listen to the optimistic voice in her head? "Love you, too."

Paige set the phone down as it chimed. A new voicemail? The call waiting hadn't rung, had it? She punched in her password and listened.

"Hi, Paige. It's Jackson... again. Um, I heard about your Dad, and the restaurant, and a lot of other stuff, actually, from Mr. Gorman at the Farmer's Market yesterday. I stopped by, hoping to see you. Last week he said he thought

you might be back this week. But with the restaurant, I guess you're probably too busy. And I'm rambling. Sorry. Look... I hope the event went well for you last night. I'm sorry I couldn't be there for you. Again. Apparently." He paused, cleared his throat, and barreled on. *"Would you please—please—come to dinner with me? You probably don't have much time off, but the restaurant's closed on Sundays, right? So dinner tonight? Six o'clock? Let me know. All right. Well... bye."*

30

Ben reached across Zach and grabbed Jackson's phone out of his hands with a scowl. Heat crept up Jackson's neck and he focused his attention—or at least as much of it as he could muster—on Pastor Brown's sermon. Why hadn't Paige picked up this morning? Was she still that angry? There were other options. She could've been in the shower, out in the garden, already at church, though he'd checked the website for her church and that one didn't seem likely. It might have absolutely nothing to do with him. Or she really could still be *that* mad.

Jesus, please help me. If she's still upset and unwilling to even hear me out, take away the feelings I have for her. 'Cause I know you can't have a strong marriage that honors You when one person is unwilling to even talk about problems and freezes the other out. But... I... I think I love Paige. Please at least give me the chance to find out for sure if she's the woman you have for me.

Zach's elbow jammed into Jackson's side as the congregation rose to sing the benediction. Had he spaced out the entire service? He shook his head as he sang the familiar words. He *was* glad to be part of the family of God... it was just too bad that it was so much like an earthly family, warts and all.

"Dude." Ben extended Jackson's phone. "It's like sitting with the high school kids. What's up with you today?"

Jackson tucked the phone in the pocket of his jeans. "Sorry. I left a voicemail for Paige this morning before we left. I keep hoping she'll at least text me back. I—I asked if she'd have dinner with me tonight. One last chance to try and clear the air and see if we can't get things back on track."

"What happened to the plan?" Zach frowned.

"I don't want play games. I want her to forgive me and for us to be together. But if she's not willing to do that, then I guess I'd rather know now and move on with my life." Jackson turned as a hand dropped onto his shoulder. "Hi, Pastor Brown."

"Morning. I was hoping I'd catch you. Am I interrupting?" Paul's gaze flicked to Zach and Ben.

"Nope. We're on our way to class. We'll save you a seat." Ben jerked his head toward the exit on the other side of the pew. Zach rolled his eyes and followed.

Paul chuckled. "Come with me. I have someone I'd like you to meet."

Jackson followed behind the pastor as he wove his way toward the front of the sanctuary. Progress was slow, with a pause every few feet as someone stopped Paul to shake his hand and compliment—or complain about—the sermon. Didn't seem like anyone was shy about expressing their opinions, though Paul remained gracious the whole time. Never appearing dismissive or hurried. The pastor really did understand politics.

Paul stopped at the front row next to a man who was probably in his late forties or early fifties, if the tiny streak of grey at his temples and wrinkles around his eyes were anything to go by. "Jackson, I'd like you to meet Don Ballentine. Don, this is Jackson Trent. I talked to you about him last week."

Don stood, his gaze appraising, and extended his hand. "Nice to meet you. Paul here has a lot of good things to say about you."

A little star-struck, Jackson gripped Don's hand. "The pleasure's mine. I didn't realize you attended here. I'm so impressed by your organization. You do some amazing things for the country."

Don chuckled. "Thanks. I've got a good bunch of people helping to make that happen. But I'm always looking for more."

Jackson's heart leapt. Was Don offering him a job? The Ballentine Coalition was one of the first websites he'd checked when he decided to shift focus, but there were no openings listed anywhere. At least not that he could find. What was he supposed to say?

"Tell you what." Don fished in the pocket of his suit jacket and extracted a business card. "Give me a call in the morning, my direct line's at the bottom there, and let's set up a time to chat. See if you might be one of those good people I'm always looking for. Paul insists you are, but I like to make those kinds of decisions for myself. Have to say, so far, I'm impressed. Most people start fawning all over me and rattling off their experience and qualifications when I say I'm always looking. I like a man who knows that sometimes you have to wait and see if an offer's really being made."

Jackson accepted the card, his heart hammering in his chest, he'd been about to do just that. This was his dream job. Even when he'd worked for Senator Carson, the idea of working for the Ballentine Coalition was one of those things that people whispered about in the halls. "Thank you, sir. I'll do that. And thank you, Pastor Brown. This is... awesome."

Don clapped Paul on the back. "Looks like I owe you. Again."

"My pleasure. You know that." Paul checked his watch. "Let's scoot out the side door here so they can start the next service on time. I'm going to run and get some water and slip back in while everyone's singing."

Jackson shook out his hands and jumped up and down in place. "All right, ladies, are we playing some football, or what?"

Zach, Ben, and some of the other guys from church all laughed but slowly morphed into two opposing lines at the center of the field behind the church parking lot.

"Hike." Zach tossed the ball between his legs to Ben.

Ben caught it and backed up a few steps, his head swiveling.

Jackson broke out of the mass of bodies on the line and waved. "Ben, over here."

Ben's gaze locked with his as he cocked his arm back for the throw. Two guys from the other team smashed into Ben, one high, the other low. The ball dropped to the ground next to Ben.

"Sorry, man." The first guy stood, brushed himself off, and reached out a hand to Ben.

Jackson jogged over. Ben didn't look good, his skin was devoid of color and his knee was already visibly swelling.

Ben drew short, choppy breaths. "I can't... my knee."

Jackson knelt by Ben's side and lightly ran his hands over Ben's knees. He winced. "Did you hear a pop?"

"I don't... maybe. Why?" Ben struggled to prop himself on his elbows.

"We need to get you to the ER for an x-ray, maybe an MRI. With how you were hit and the swelling, I'd bet money you tore your ACL."

"How is it that you're the idiot who still plays football for real, on a team, and I make it not five minutes into a 'let's toss the ball around after church' game before I'm out for the season?" Ben licked his lips. "And as much as I'd like to sit here and say you're over reacting about the ER, I want an aspirin. Or six hundred. Help me up."

Jackson and Zach helped Ben to his feet and, one on either side, started toward the car.

"I could carry you, if you wanted." Jackson grinned. "Sweep you up in my arms? It'd be good practice for the next time I run into a damsel in distress."

"Ha-ha. I oughta kick you."

"Don't. You'll hurt your other leg. And I'm not offering to carry you." Zach stopped and waited as Ben maneuvered into the back seat of Jackson's car. When he was settled, Zach shut the door. Jackson hurried around the front of the car.

"At least it's close, right?"

Zach nodded. "Drive fast. I can hear him gritting his teeth from here."

"It's either that or cry like a baby. Got a preference?"

Jackson tuned out the banter of Zach and Ben as he zipped onto the Beltway. The hospital was close to home, so it wouldn't take long to get to, but he remembered the agony of that injury—and his hadn't been torn, just sprained. Maybe Ben would luck out, too. He dropped Ben and Zach off at the entrance and went to park the car. Why did they have valet for regular visits but not the emergency room? It was one of life's more bizarre questions.

Ten minutes later, Jackson jogged through the double sliding doors and scanned the waiting area. He spotted Zach leafing through a newspaper.

"They got him back already?"

Zach shrugged and set the paper aside. "Apparently we hit a lull. I didn't think this ER was ever quiet. Nice to know there's a possibility of getting in and out in under a week."

Jackson chuckled. "Don't count on it."

"Oh believe me, wasn't planning on it."

Jackson flopped into a chair and pulled another around to prop his feet on. He pulled his phone out and frowned. "You have any bars?"

"Nope. I'm pretty sure it's one of those places where they inhibit signals to keep you bored to tears while you wait. After all, if you enjoyed it here, you might just keep coming for fun. There's a guest wifi, but I couldn't get mine to connect."

With a sigh, Jackson slid his phone back into his pocket. If Paige hadn't called by now, she probably wasn't going to anyway. And being offline would keep him from stressing about the call with the Ballentine Coalition tomorrow. Had he even mentioned that to his roommates? They'd be stoked for him. "Hey, did I tell you what Pastor Brown did for me today?"

Ben stumbled as he eased into the house on crutches.

Jackson squeezed past him and kicked the kitchen rug out of the way. "Go slow. Let me make sure there are no other hazards in the way. Couch or your room?"

"Couch. I hate crutches." Ben picked his way across the kitchen. "I'm going to have to take tomorrow off, at least. Maybe the next day. And even then... do you think you could drive me downtown?"

"Of course. You're not riding the Metro like that." Jackson dropped two of the tiny square pillows that came with the couch onto the coffee table. He'd never understood their purpose before. Apparently couch manufacturers anticipated the need to elevate body parts and sent along matching cushions.

Ben lowered himself to the couch and used his arms to lift his mid-thigh to mid-calf brace-encased leg onto the cushions. "Thanks."

Even without a crowd, it had taken three hours for the x-rays and MRI to confirm the torn ACL. Ben had left with a brace, crutches, an appointment with a surgeon tomorrow, and strict instructions for elevation and icing. For the first time, Jackson was glad he wasn't working. Ben was going to need someone to tote him around for a while, especially since it was his right leg that was injured.

Zach came in with a steaming mug and a bag of frozen peas. "Here. Zapped a can of soup. Figured that might hit the spot about now. You want some, Jackson?"

"Nah. I'm going to go do some prep for this call tomorrow morning. Ballentine... do you know how cool that would be? No more having to justify the little things here and there because, in the big picture, you're making a difference in the right way. And yet, still a chance to be involved—maybe even more involved since I wouldn't be tied to a particular person's agenda—in the crafting and passing of legislation. The only thing better would be getting elected myself, though I don't really feel that's a call for me. At least not right now. But holler if you need me to help with anything."

31

Paige frowned at her cell phone. She'd left a message for Jackson after church, agreeing to dinner, and sent a text around three-thirty. No response. Now, at twenty to six, she wasn't sure what to do. Should she just nuke some leftovers and call it a night? Why would he ask her out and then disappear? Whatever. She had an early day tomorrow. She'd reheat the mac and cheese she'd made for the cooks last night and head to bed. She could read for a while and still get plenty of shut-eye.

By eight, she was snuggled up in bed, devouring the pages of a thriller. Her phone rang, splitting the silence. She jolted, her heart hammering in her chest. Eyes still glued to the book, she put the phone to her ear.

"Hello?"

"Paige, I'm so sorry. You have no idea—"

Jackson. That would teach her to get caught up in a book and forget to check the caller ID. She slipped a business card in between the pages and closed the book. "Stop. Just take a breath and give me one good reason I shouldn't hang up right now."

"Ben tore his ACL after church. There's no cell coverage in the emergency room and my phone only just received your text."

She'd noticed the lack of cell coverage when she was at the hospital with her dad, but her phone always chirped and chimed the minute she got to her car, updating all the emails, texts, and calls she'd missed. "Tell Ben I hope he heals quickly. But Jackson, I... I don't think I have time for this right now. You said you talked to Mr. Gorman, so you know the gist of things. I'm taking over the restaurant for my dad—he's selling it to me, actually. So it's my restaurant now. And between handling day-to-day operations and the influx of catering that I'm hoping will come from the Senator's fiasco last night, I just can't. No matter how much I might want to. So please. Just stop calling."

"Paige. Please don't do this."

Her heart broke again at the pain in his voice. Everything in her screamed to give him a second chance. And yet, what she'd said was true. She was busy, with hardly a spare second to herself. And those few shreds of "spare" time needed to be spent in her garden and getting set up to have produce over the winter. There was no point in growing all this food if she wasn't going to get to eat it. She didn't intend to change everything she believed and start buying internationally shipped vegetables just because she'd gotten busy. "I'm sorry, Jackson. I really am. But I have to listen to my head on this. Take care of yourself."

She pushed end then powered off her phone. Knowing Jackson, he'd call back. She didn't have the strength to continue to resist him. A tear slid down her cheek. She wanted that second chance more than anything she'd ever wanted before. But now was the time to be practical. She wasn't going to let her dad down—she'd put everything she could into the restaurant and not only keep it going, but make it thrive.

"Paige, it's your mother."

Paige fought the urge to scream. The lunch rush was over and there was an hour, maybe two, before the dinner crowd was going to start trickling in. She needed to get payroll figured out and cut checks for three suppliers. What she didn't need was a long conversation with her mom. "Hi, Mom. This really isn't a great time..."

"I'll be brief. You've got to get your father out of the house. He's driving me insane. I know he can't go back into the kitchen, that's too much stress. But is there anything he could do at the restaurant? Even one or two days a week so I could have five minutes to myself?"

Paige rubbed her temples. If it wasn't so ridiculous, she'd laugh. "I could probably use him in the office. Paying bills, that kind of thing. Would that be too taxing, do you think?"

"I'll talk to his doctor when we go this afternoon—oh, shoot, we need to get going if we're not going to be late. You're amazing, Paige. Thank you. You have no idea."

Paige set her phone down and returned to the accounting software. The numbers swam across the screen and she dug her knuckles into her forehead. She could do this. She'd taken business classes. It was just like her catering company... on steroids.

She painstakingly entered the bills, separating out the costs into the appropriate divisions and then, after double-checking the bank balance, wrote out the necessary checks. Payroll would have to wait until tomorrow. She had until Friday, but she didn't want to put it off 'til the last minute. If it was anything like paying a few bills, she was going to need every spare second to get it figured out. Why hadn't Dad hired someone to do this? It couldn't possibly cost *that* much, could it?

Paige tucked the sealed and stamped envelopes into her purse. She'd mail them on the way home tonight.

32

Don Ballentine stood as the admin escorted Jackson into the conference room. The call on Monday morning had gone well enough that on Wednesday, Jackson had dropped Ben off at work, with strict instructions to take it easy and call when he'd had enough. Then he'd made his way to the Ballentine offices for an official interview. Lizards skittered around the walls of his stomach. *Get a grip, Jackson. You've been on interviews before—even important ones.*

"Morning. I'm glad you were able to make it today. We've got a fairly critical position open that I think you'd be great for." Don reached across the table to shake Jackson's hand.

That was a good way to start things off. The lizards settled down to an occasional wriggle. "Happy to do it."

"Before I get into all the details though, tell me about why you left Senator Carson's office. Even though she's having some problems right now, I believe her heart has, at least in the past, been in the right place. She's done a lot of good over the years."

Jackson nodded. "Yes, sir. I agree. I still respect her voting record and the principles she holds when it comes to her legislative efforts. Ultimately, I feel she crossed a line by attempting to use someone essentially unconnected to her as a means to deflect negative media attention. I argued against it directly, but she went ahead and used my name as well. She ruined someone's business. And, in the interest of full disclosure, my relationship with that person."

Don tapped his pen against his lip. "The caterer?"

"Yes."

"Hmmm. I'd wondered how that turned out. I saw it didn't appreciably help Beatrice, but I'm sorry it damaged the young woman's business. Will it recover, do you think?"

"You know, it's turned out to be one of those Romans 8:28 things. At least for her professionally. Losing her clients—or firing them herself when they asked her to lower her morals the way the article implied she already had—freed her up to take over her father's restaurant when he had to retire suddenly. As for us." Jackson shrugged. "She finally took my call on Sunday but only to tell me, in no uncertain terms, to leave her alone. So I guess that's that."

"All things considered, that seems like a good reason to change jobs. I wanted to be sure you're not someone who walks away at the first hint of trouble. I assume you know that the Ballentine Coalition is frequently attacked by the press. Usually they keep their personal scrutiny to me and leave the staff alone, but occasionally things happen. I need people who are committed enough to their ideals that they'll weather the storm. And I think that's exactly what you did. There was no good way out of that situation and sometimes, you have to walk away. Are you praying for Senator Carson?"

Jackson blinked. Pray for her? The thought hadn't occurred to him... and that said enough right there, didn't it? He shook his head, heat creeping up his neck.

Don offered a slight smile. "Understandable. But you need to start doing just that. She's been one all of us here are focusing our prayers on right now—she's clearly under attack, and faltering with the weight of it. Never forget that prayer is the most critical political tool we possess. Yes, voting and political action and living a life consistent with the philosophy we preach are important, but if we're not praying, we're trying to do it all on our own power and we're destined to fail."

Jackson's breath caught in his chest and weight settled across his shoulders. Had he ever had that mindset when it came to his political work? "Yes, sir."

"With all that—and believe me, I can imagine the situation in all its full drama, despite your factual retelling of events—you still want to be involved politically?"

"I didn't at first. And to be honest, there are times I still struggle with it. But I can't get away from the idea that God didn't give us government only to wash His hands of it and walk away. He expects us to be involved in government just as much as He expects us to be involved in providing for our food and shelter. So it's just one more area where we're to be salt and light. I'd hoped, for a day or two, that I'd reach a point where I'd have peace about my part being reduced to voting and living consistently. Or as consistently as you can. But I keep coming back to the fact that I'm called to be more deeply involved than that. So I've been taking the job search more slowly, trying to find somewhere that'll be a better fit than Senator Carson ended up being."

Nodding, Don flipped open the file in front of him and removed a stapled packet of papers. "Take this home. Read it. *Pray* about it. And give me your answer as soon as you can. I'd love to have you on board."

"Congrats, man." Ben shifted his crutches so they weren't banging against the door every time Jackson hit a bump.

"Thanks. It's amazing to think that I've been offered a job at Ballentine."

"You're saying yes, I take it?"

"Probably. Don was pretty clear that I should pray about it and he's right. I don't spend enough time doing that. And I've felt guilty about that in the past, just not enough to make serious changes, I guess. But that stops now. And maybe... maybe it'll help with the Paige situation."

Ben shook his head. "From what you said about your last phone call, there's not much of a situation there. I'm sorry, by the way. I'm kind of responsible for that mix-up."

Jackson shrugged and whipped the jeep onto the highway. "If I'd known she was trying to get in touch, I would've rescheduled with her. She would've understood. If I'm going to blame anyone, it'd be the hospital for blocking cell signals. Or, well, maybe me. I should've given her more than a few hours to respond."

Ben chuckled. "I'm glad you didn't. Another week of you obsessing about her returning a call would've gotten really old. Especially since I'm spending more time at home until surgery."

"You're not going in again tomorrow?"

"Nope. They gave me a laptop and told me to stay home, work when I could and rest when I couldn't. Next week's surgery can't get here fast enough."

"Yeah. I don't think I'd be excited about surgery. Ever."

"If it gets rid of the nagging pain that's chasing me around right now and back on the path to recovery, I'm for it. Even if I have to do physical therapy afterward."

"Which you will."

"Yeah, I know. And once I'm back to normal, just so you know, I won't be playing football with you all anymore. I don't need to go through this again... let's go with ever."

Jackson grinned. "Fair enough. You can be the cheerleader. You'd look okay in a short—"

"Don't you dare go there." Ben punched Jackson's arm. "Speaking of that, though, don't your games start soon?"

Jackson groaned. "Yeah. We have our pre-season games this Saturday and next. The season starts in earnest after Labor Day. Honestly, even without all the annoying commentary from you guys, I think this'd be my last season on the team. The new guys are killing things—there's just something about their spirit. It's... ugly. All the fun is gone."

Ben frowned. "If the season hasn't started yet, couldn't you quit now?"

Jackson sighed. He could. He'd even considered it. Practices were brutal recently. Not physically, that had stayed the same. But mentally it was all he could do to keep from letting some of the new team members have it. He'd even gone so far as to talk to the coach about it briefly. And gotten brushed off. The new players were good, he'd give them that. And that seemed to be all that mattered to Coach. "I guess. It just seems... unsportsmanlike. Like I'd be letting the team down. And even if it's not the same team I joined, it's still my team. Don't I owe them that?"

"Maybe that's something else to start praying about. Seems to me that if you're miserable, you've lost the whole point of being on the team. And there are other things you could do with all the time it's taking up."

Like what? If Paige was out of the picture—and it seemed like she was—he had entirely too much spare time to dwell on it. The new job might eat up some of that free time but then what? "I don't think I'm ready to take up knitting."

Ben scoffed. "Interesting that *that's* where your mind goes. Wonder what a shrink would have to say about it."

"Well? Seriously, what would I do with all that extra time?"

"I'm betting you'd find something—maybe even something with a little bit more substance to it. Weren't you all gung-ho about putting in a garden? Or was that just about Paige?"

"No. No, that's still something I'd like to do. Though you're right to some degree, it'd be a lot easier and more fun if Paige was helping." Jackson sighed as he turned into the driveway. "I'll pray about it."

Jackson smiled at the Season's Bounty hostess. "Just one."

Her eyebrows lifted minutely, but she nodded. "Right this way. Have you dined with us before?"

"Once, a few months ago." Jackson sat and accepted the menu. "It was great."

The hostess smiled. "We have a new owner, but she's the previous owner's daughter and hasn't made any substantial changes. Your server should be along shortly. Enjoy."

Jackson frowned at the hostess' retreating back. Did Paige want them telling everyone there was a new owner? It kind of set you up to look for things that were different or wrong. It was... off-putting. Like an advance apology. He'd mention it to her. If she ever let him. Maybe coming here was a bad idea. But it had sounded reasonable when Ben suggested it. You go in, have a meal, ask to give your compliments to the chef, and when she comes out you make your case one more time. Simple. Too simple?

Too desperate?

He flipped open the menu. He wasn't desperate. Right. And everything in here was imported from Argentina instead of sourced locally. There were a number of changes in the entrees. That made sense. They were getting to the end of summer, seasons were changing. What did they do for vegetables in the dead of winter? They didn't get a ton of snow in Virginia, but hard freezes and cold temperatures were common across the state. Greenhouses, maybe? It was another question he'd love to ask Paige. She could probably give him a mini-course in winter gardening. He'd hang on every word.

His heart ached. It shouldn't be possible to miss her this badly—they'd only dated for a month. And yet, she drove so many of his thoughts. He craved her opinion on the job offer from Ballentine and whether or not he should quit the football team.

"Can I take your order?"

Jackson smiled and tugged his thoughts back to dinner. Friday night out to eat on his own. Why hadn't he dragged Zach and Ben out with him? He rattled off his choice and glanced around at the other tables. Couples and families were trickling in. There were only a few tables open. Did you need reservations as it got into more popular dinner times? Did they even take reservations?

His food arrived in short order. It looked and smelled amazing. Flavors that he hadn't expected washed over his tongue. Who knew beets could taste good? Before long, he was scraping up the last dribbles of sauce.

"I brought you a dessert menu, just in case. The ice cream is made in small batches in the Winchester area. They do special order flavor profiles for us, so it's a real treat. The special this week is basil."

Jackson wrinkled his nose.

The server chuckled. "I'll bring out a sample. I think you'll be surprised."

"Okay. I think I'd also like the fruit tartlet."

"Sure thing."

When was he supposed to ask to give his compliments to the chef? After dessert? Was he supposed to do it before? He ran a hand through his hair. This was ridiculous. He should just eat dessert and go home. She said she didn't want to talk to him, let alone have any kind of relationship. He needed to respect that, didn't he? It wasn't as if there weren't willing interested women at church. *But none of them are Paige.*

"Good evening. I just wanted to stop by and see if you'd enjoyed your meal."

Jackson looked up into the smiling face of Paige's father. "Mr. Jackson. It's good to see you up and around. I... I thought you'd retired?"

Lawrence frowned for a moment, then grinned. "Trent. Though I've forgotten your first name, I'm afraid."

"Jackson."

"Ha. Well, I'm surprised that slipped my mind. How nice to see you back again. As to your question, I am retired. I'm back on a part-time, purely volunteer basis to help in the office. And get out of the house. The Senator's event was last week, wasn't it?"

Jackson nodded. Either Paige hadn't told her dad about them or he was a very good play actor. "It was, though I'm no longer working for the Senator. I left after she authorized the article about Paige. I'd asked her not to. Argued with her, in fact. And when it was clear that she valued saving face above anything else, it was also clear that it was time for me to move on."

Lawrence nodded, gesturing to a chair. "May I?"

"Please."

When he was settled in the chair, Lawrence rested his elbows on the table and tented his hands under his chin. "Can I ask you a question?"

"Sure." Jackson fidgeted in his seat as Lawrence's gaze bore down on him.

"Are you still interested in my daughter?"

A derisive chuckle wormed out before he could stop it. "Yes, sir, I am. That's why I'm here. I was working up the courage to ask to give my compliments to the chef."

Lawrence pursed his lips. "That might work. But it's also busy, and bound to get busier before the night's through. So while she'd probably come out and accept your thanks, she'd be back in the kitchen before you could say two words to her."

Jackson's shoulders fell. "At least I got a good meal out of it."

The server appeared at the table with a small bowl of light-green ice cream and an enormous, tart covered with glossy fruit. "Can I get you anything else?"

"Would you like to share this tart, sir? I had no idea it was going to be so huge."

Lawrence grinned. "I never say no to Paige's fruit tart. Would you grab me a fork, m'dear?"

"Of course." The server dashed away, returning shortly with a clean fork and another small plate. She set them down and disappeared behind the swinging doors leading into the kitchen.

"Would you say you give up easily?" Lawrence cut a thick wedge out of the tart and slipped it onto his plate.

What was it with everyone asking him that? First Don Ballentine, now Paige's dad. "No, sir, I wouldn't. But I also believe you have to respect other people's wishes. And your daughter's made it very clear that she's not interested in me anymore."

"That's just hurt talking. Trust me. I know my daughter. If she's not in love with you, she's well on the way. But you banged up against her biggest hurt and she's running scared."

"What do you mean?"

Lawrence set his fork down and held Jackson's gaze. "Ever since she was little, well before she was old enough that her mother and I would've considered letting her date, boys would ask her if she wanted to go out. When she said no, that she wasn't allowed, they'd laugh and say they were joking, making her feel like a fool for answering them seriously."

"That was probably just their own hurt or embarrassment talking." Jackson frowned. "I guess I'm not following."

"Oh, I imagine you're right. And that's exactly what I told Paige. I think she believed me. She's dated a little, here and there, but always seemed to keep her heart out of it. Mostly looking for someone to hang out with, a friend who happened to be male, I guess."

Jackson nodded. "Isn't that the way you get to know someone? Hang out? Be friends?"

"Of course. But she'd always find something—big or small—that doomed the relationship. Her mother and I wonder if it's because we're different enough that our disagreements can be noisy and messy. We always made sure she saw us make up, that she understood that it was just how we settled things between us. Honestly, we consider it healthy—there's no chance of the sun going down on our anger." Lawrence cracked a smile, then shrugged. "Maybe Paige is hoping to find someone who's so perfect there'll never be any chance of a major fight."

Jackson's heart sank. "So I'm out of luck? I don't think you can get much more major in the fight department than this."

"That's the thing. Even though you're different, and you've had this hiccup, I can tell she misses you. I don't think she's ever missed anyone she kicked to the curb before. Plus, I'm reasonably sure she's smart enough to know that a relationship with someone who never disagrees with her would bore her to tears inside a month."

"Small comfort." Jackson pushed the tart aside and dipped a spoon into the ice cream. It was definitely basil flavored.

"Is that the basil?"

"Yeah."

"It's interesting, isn't it?"

Jackson chuckled and set down the spoon. "Interesting is a good description. I think I'm more of a sweet ice cream guy. But maybe savory will work for some people."

Lawrence cleared his throat. "Back to Paige. I suspect you could wait around and see if she comes to her senses. Though I'll warn you, she can be stubborn and it might take a while."

"Or?" There had to be an "or," didn't there? Some other alternative that didn't involve waiting for an indeterminate period of time.

"One thing my girl isn't, is stupid. You just have to get past stubborn and make her listen to you."

"How do I do that? She's asked me not to call her anymore. You said here at work is probably a bad idea. And email's too easy to just delete. I'll try anything—smoke signals? Morse code? Just tell me what."

Lawrence studied him before giving a brief nod. "Here's what you're going to do..."

Paige finished wiping down the counters and dropped her washrag into the bucket of bleach-water. The kitchen was, officially, clean. Until Monday when it all started back up again. They still had a few people make comments under their breath about the restaurant being closed on Sundays, but the day off... Paige needed that. So did her staff. Even if most of them got at least one other full day off during the week. There were enough other places to get brunch that she wasn't going to sweat it.

"All set?" Lawrence lowered himself to the banquette of the chef's table.

"What are you still doing here, Dad? You should've gone home hours ago. I didn't even want you to come in today. Mom's going to kill me."

He waved her words aside. "Your mother is fine. I've kept her in the loop. And, as a bonus, since I did stay 'til closing, I managed to get everything caught up, so I should be able to just work two, maybe three days next week to stay on top of it all."

How had she gotten that behind in two weeks? She frowned. "Was it really that bad?"

"It wasn't all you. I'd been struggling to keep on top of some of it myself. You're right, I never should've let your mother retire completely. Even if she'd come in for a day a week, it would've made a huge difference." He shrugged. "Live and learn, I guess."

Paige rinsed her hands before crossing the kitchen to wrap her father in a tight hug. "I'm happy you get the chance to keep doing both."

"Oh, Paige. I'm sorry."

She shook her head. "Don't be sorry. I'm just glad I was here, Daddy. I'm not ready to lose you."

He squeezed and released her. "If I get my choice, I'm not ready to go. I still have hopes of seeing you with a few kids of your own."

"A few? Uh-uh. One, maybe two. Being an only was never a problem for me. And everyone I know who has siblings does very little other than complain about them. Sure, it's nice to have someone to play with. But that means there's someone to fight with, too."

"Given it some thought, have you?"

She shrugged. It wasn't something she'd done much thinking about one way or the other until she'd met Jackson. When she'd thought they had a future together, the idea had seemed worth a little consideration. And it was a pleasant way to occupy her mind while she pulled weeds. Now? She'd be happy to push those thoughts back into the tiny, locked corner of her mind where they'd been before. But they just wouldn't go. It was hard to forget someone when you saw their name every time you signed your own. "A little. Not so much anymore. Anyway, there's no point in worry about it now. So you might try and reconcile yourself to having more time with me, with no promise of anything else."

"No chance of things working out with your young man, then? I thought maybe... "

"Daddy, no. We're too different. He's caught up in politics—though I suppose to be fair, he did make me rethink some of my positions on voting and the like. And after the debacle with Senator Carson, doing my part to keep people like her from being in charge doesn't sound like such a bad thing. I still plan to spend most of my effort on living in a way that's consistent with what God wants. But I'm not opposed to doing my part, small though it might be, to work for His purpose on a larger scale."

Lawrence grinned. "I'm proud of you, Paige."

"Thanks, Daddy."

"Don't give up on love too quickly though, okay?"

"I haven't given up on love—not the idea of it, at least. I just don't think Jackson's the right one for me." *Liar.* There should be flames shooting off her pants with the boldness of that untruth. Jackson was the *perfect* guy for her. But how could she trust him? Even though she'd reconsidered her thoughts on voting, who was to say he wasn't going to use her as another example of his boss' progressive attitude in the future? Not that he'd been responsible, really. She could admit that to herself. But he hadn't stopped it, either.

Lawrence drew his lips into a thin line. "Did I ever tell you that your mother didn't agree to marry me the first time I asked her?"

"No. How on earth have I never heard that story?"

He chuckled. "It's not my finest moment, or your mother's for that matter. We don't speak of it, really."

"Well? What happened? Why on earth would she say no? And why would you go back and ask again after that?" Paige settled on the opposite bench and leaned in. Maybe this would give her some insight into her mom, something to finally help bridge the gap that had started in her teens and seemed to widen with every passing day.

"Mmm. As is generally the case, it was all a big misunderstanding. I'd asked her to come to a play with me. When I showed up at her dorm, she wasn't ready. I waited for fifteen minutes, but I'd already bought our tickets and they were very strict about seating people once the show had started. And it was one of those things she was willing to watch but that I was almost desperate to see. So I left a note with the desk attendant, telling her I'd leave her ticket for her, and then I went on ahead."

Paige winced. "Ooooh."

"Basically. Your mother didn't come. When I explained, she said she understood so I didn't think anything more of it. When I proposed a few weeks later, she said she'd leave an answer for me at 'will call' and flounced off."

Paige snickered. "I can totally see Mom doing that."

"Yeah, she's always been feisty. It's one of the things I love about her. Anyway, I groveled a little, finally got her to agree to go see another play with me. When we got to the show, I'd arranged it with a friend to leave the ring at the ticket window. I sent her to get the tickets and, when they pushed that little velvet box through the window, I asked again."

"Risky, throwing her words in her face like that."

"True, true. But she wasn't quite as... rigid then as she is these days. Anyway, she must have decided I was clever, or funny, or something because she went ahead and said yes."

Paige sighed. It was a lovely story. She'd heard the part about the will-call before, but never the part about it being his second try. "That's sweet. Though I'm not sure why you're telling me."

"Don't write someone off just because they make a mistake, Honey. You owe it to yourself, and to him, to be sure you're letting go for the right reasons."

Paige ruthlessly yanked weeds from the garden plot. Her dad's words played through her head. Was she pushing Jackson away for the wrong reasons? Could she change her mind at this point though? She'd told him to stop calling... and he had. Was she past the point of having a choice in the matter?

She sighed and sat back on her heels, pushing her bangs out of her face. It might be the last weekend of August, but it was still hot and sticky. She needed to plant her beets, turnips, and some more spinach if she was going to have a fall harvest. The seedlings weren't quite ready yet—she'd been too busy to nurture them along like she usually did. Maybe next weekend. Or maybe not. Next weekend was Labor Day weekend. Whitney's wedding was Saturday. And Dad had already warned her that there were some catering jobs lined up over Labor Day. Maybe the Senator's event hadn't been a complete waste of time.

Which meant the seedlings needed to go in today, ready or not. They'd be okay. Probably. She gathered the bag of weeds to empty onto the communal compost pile and her basket of harvested vegetables. She stood, leaning back to work the kinks out of her neck and knees. She'd go home, double-check the weather for the week, and bring the seedlings back over. Maybe Mr. Kim would be out of his plot and she could sneak a peek at the cold frames he'd set up down one side of his garden. The idea of extending the growing season a little longer was appealing. If the cold frames weren't too difficult to put together. She'd done a little research online and didn't think they looked too bad, but seeing some up close would be even better.

She unlocked the door and stepped in. Blissfully cool air washed over her. Air conditioning. How did anyone live without it? Her conscience pinged. There had to be some alternatives that were better than just opening windows and praying not to die. But until she found something that actually kept her cool, it was a creature comfort she wasn't giving up.

"Hey."

Paige stared at Whitney, who reclined on the couch flipping through a magazine. What was she doing here? How did she get in? Hadn't she given back her key when she moved out? Obviously not but... she shook her head and plodded into the kitchen to set the basket of produce down and get a glass of water.

"You okay?" Whitney leaned against the door jamb between the living room and kitchen.

Paige filled a glass and took several long swallows, eyeing her former roommate. "Yeah, I'm fine. Just trying to figure out what you're doing here."

Whitney smiled. "Oh, I got bored at the town house so figured I'd come over and see how things were here. Elliot's off at his bachelor party for the day and everyone else was busy, but I knew you'd be puttering around the apartment. Wanna go shopping or something?"

Puttering around the apartment? Was she an eighty-year-old spinster with six cats? "I've actually got a pretty full day. I need to get some seedlings planted and watered in, then start on some catering-event schedules and staffing plans."

Whitney's shoulders fell. "Oh. Okay."

Paige fought a groan. They hadn't done anything together when Whitney had lived here, why would she choose to start now? Still... "Do you want to help?"

"Those notes you left for the catering business this weekend looked great, Paige. Thanks." Lawrence leaned against the food window, his hands tucked in his pockets.

"I needed to know we had the staff to cover all the different bookings. If that end of things keeps picking up, I might have to break down and hire a catering manager to handle it." She'd die a little inside if she did, farming out her dream to someone else because she was too busy. But the restaurant was her dream now.

He cleared his throat. "About that."

"Dad." She wiped her hands on a towel before flipping it back over her shoulder. "Tell me you didn't accept another job. We don't have anyone else who can work an offsite event on either Saturday or Monday. Being busy is good, don't get me wrong, but I'm still planning to have the restaurant open on Monday, so I don't have extra people to play with like I do on Saturday."

"It's for Sunday."

She sighed and shook her head. "Call them back and tell them we're closed, and that includes our catering, on Sundays."

His gaze bored into her back as she returned to dinner prep, refilling the ingredient trays that had been diminished by the busier-than-usual lunch shift.

"What?" Paige set her knife down beside a pile of minced garlic.

"It's just that this client was hard to turn down."

"I don't care who it was, Dad. We're not open on Sunday."

"What about favors for friends of the family? Do we do those on Sunday?"

She returned to the garlic, chopping up several more cloves and scooping them into the tray before sighing. "Who is it?"

"Friend of a friend. He needs a romantic dinner for two. It shouldn't take you too long."

"It shouldn't take *Hector* too long. He's always hinting about needing extra hours. I'm sure he won't mind giving up his Sunday afternoon and evening for something that simple."

Lawrence shook his head. "He wanted me to do it. Since I can't, I promised it'd be you."

Really? What was he thinking? She could be busy. Have a date. Well, okay, he knew that was unlikely. But there were all kinds of reasons he shouldn't have promised before checking with her. It wasn't even that she minded. Not really. It was just the principle of the thing. "Fine. Any preferences?"

Lawrence grinned. "That's my girl. No. No preferences. Just something designed with romance in mind."

34

"You're home early. I thought you had practice tonight." Ben looked up from his laptop as Jackson stomped into the living room.

"Oh, I had practice tonight." He dropped his bag of gear with a clatter. "And about half-way through, Coach pulls me aside and says that they're going to start the new guy. At first, I didn't understand why he was telling me. The guy's a linebacker. I don't care who they have on the line, long as they have someone there running interference. Then coach is all, 'he's got really good hands and is fast for his size, so we're going to give him a shot' and 'it's good to shake things up now and then, keep the older players fresh.' And then I realize, they're starting this kid in my position."

"Oooh." Ben flinched. "Has he said anything about not liking how you're doing in practice?"

"Not a word. He even went on about how great I was doing and that's why they had to make a decision to give other guys a chance, 'cause they were never going to have to pull me on merit. So I asked if I'd at least get to play in the second half. That's usually what they do when they give someone new a chance at starting, is let the other guy come back in at the half—sometimes sooner if the new guy really flubs things up. And coach says no. So I ask if this is just for the pre-season game or a permanent thing. And he just stands there clearing his throat and finally says that decision isn't final yet. So I made it final. Reliving my glory days, as the two of you so kindly put it, is officially over."

Jackson grabbed the bag of gear and stormed down the hall to his room. He tossed the bag into the closet, sliding the door shut on the mess it made as the contents spilled out all over the floor. He'd clean it up later—on the way to throwing it out.

Stripping off his clothes, he stepped into the shower and turned on the spray. Cold water bit his skin, doing little to cool his temper. When he'd joined the team, he'd played for two seasons before moving into a starting position. It hadn't mattered that he'd been All-State in high school and had been scouted during college. And he hadn't cared, either. It was the way the team worked—you earned your spot. Sure, there were a few who came out and wowed everyone with their skills. That could bump up the timeframe. But this kid was fresh off a high school team and had never played receiver, he'd been on the line since day one. What made the newbie decide he wanted to change spots now? And why on earth had Coach gone for it?

Jackson adjusted the knob and leaned his head against the shower wall. Cold water shifted to hot. It wasn't as if his identity depended on playing football. But to leave that way went against the grain. Should he have stuck it out? Was Coach counting on him quitting? His stomach twisted. Was this just how they decided to ask him to leave the team?

He shut off the water and grabbed his towel.

Dried and dressed in running shorts and a t-shirt, he went back out into the main part of the house, slipping through the living room to the kitchen. Water bottle in hand, he went back to the living room and perched on the arm of the couch.

"Want to talk about it?" Ben shifted his laptop and used both hands to adjust the position of his leg.

"Not really. I'm just frustrated. It was a really horrible ending to an otherwise amazing day."

"First day at the new job went well?"

Jackson nodded. "It was great. Honestly, it's like someone tapped into my dreams and created a job tailored specifically for me. The few interactions I've had with people from Ballentine left me thinking that I'd love working there, but it never seemed possible. In some ways, it's easier to get a position directly for a Congressman.

Obviously, it's just my first day, but it's off to a really, really good start. How's the knee?"

"Achy, but okay. Honestly, I miss going in to the office. But with surgery on Friday, I'm trying to make sure I follow all the rest and blah blah instructions."

"Blah blah instructions. Nice. Be sure to tell the surgeon that's what you think of them."

Ben shrugged. "Maybe after he's done."

Jackson grinned. "Good choice. I thought I'd order a pizza. You want in?"

"Zach won't be home for dinner?"

"He texted, has some kind of teacher thing at school. Guess since the kids come back next week they're all scrambling to get ready."

Ben nodded. "All right. No mushrooms."

Jackson smiled at the older woman manning the baked goods table as she handed him his muffin and change.

"You came to a Farmer's Market to buy a muffin?" Zach shook his head. "I thought you were supposed to come here for stuff that was good for you. Fruit. Vegetables. You know, things farmers make?"

"We'll get some of those, too. But I'm hungry now. And these are delicious. You should get one. Maybe something to eat would keep you from being so cranky."

"Cranky? *I'm* cranky. That's rich." Zach picked up a muffin covered in nuts and dug into his pocket for his wallet. "You're the one who's been stomping and sighing around the house all week."

Jackson took a bite. Had he? "Sorry."

"Is it all the football team? I guess I didn't realize it was that important to you."

"Not all of it. I miss Paige. And I don't know how I'm going to get her to talk to me. Or if I'm going to manage it at all." Jackson grabbed a toothpick speared into a cube of cheese off a sample tray as they walked by.

Zach shook his head. "Good luck with that. You've been praying about it?"

Jackson nodded.

"That's about all you can at this point. Have you ever been attracted to a coworker?"

"I dated Lisa last year."

"Yeah, but she asked you out. Would you ever have approached her? Or anyone?"

Would he? Jackson pursed his lips. Workplace relationships were tricky at best, against the rules at worst. And if things ended badly, well, you were stuck running into your ex all the time. Even though he and Lisa had never been serious, there'd been several awkward moments after he'd finally explained that he wasn't interested. "Probably not. Why?"

Zach shrugged. "It's nothing."

"Oooh. Who is it? Have we met her? Dude. You've been holding out... all these late nights aren't actually school functions, are they?" Jackson dug his elbow into Zach's ribs. "Spill it."

Zach hunched his shoulders. "There's nothing happening... yet."

"Who?"

"Do you remember Amy?"

Jackson frowned. He'd only been to two plays at Zach's school. His schedule with the Senator had made evening activities difficult a lot of the time. It had felt like she waited until he had plans to spring something on him. Maybe she had. That was going to change. "I don't think so. What's she teach?"

"She runs the after-school program for kids whose parents aren't home until late. She gave me that Indian recipe a few months back and, well, that kind of kicked off some conversations. We've become friends but I get the feeling she'd like it to be more. And... I'm not opposed to that."

Jackson stopped in front of a display of cut flowers in every color. "How long do you think these'll last?"

The man behind the table smiled and offered a slip of paper. "If you keep them in water, with a crushed aspirin at the bottom, they should be good for at least two weeks. Trim the stems and keep the water fresh and they'll go even longer."

Jackson skimmed the instructions. He could do that. "Could I get a good-sized bouquet of those peachy-pink roses?"

"What are you getting flowers for? You really think you'll keep them fresh long enough for Paige to decide to talk to you again?"

Jackson shrugged and gave the man his credit card. "Maybe I think we need to try and add a few feminine touches around the house now that, apparently, you're going to start dating someone."

"So you don't think it's a terrible idea?"

Jackson smiled at the hope in his friend's voice. "I'm probably the wrong person to ask, given my track record, but no. If it doesn't work out, it could be weird. But if you're friends, well, maybe it'll be something you can laugh about."

35

Paige waved goodbye to the last wedding guest and flipped the locks behind them. Whitney and Elliot were safely married and off to start their new life together. The ceremony had been lovely and full of the promise of Christ and His bride and how marriages on earth are designed to mimic that relationship. She'd only thought of Jackson six or seven times during the homily. The reception had gone well and even Whitney's parents had approved of the food. Since they'd turned up their noses at everything she'd served when Whitney had invited them over for dinner at the apartment, Paige would chalk it up as a win.

She grabbed a bin and started loading up dishes from the nearby tables.

"I'll get it." The bus boy reached for the tub, ignoring the half-full tub he had at the table beside hers.

"Don't be silly. If we all pitch in, we'll be out of here sooner. I'm pretty sure everyone's ready to get home."

The kid looked like he wanted to argue, but he gave a jerky nod and returned to his work. How old was he? Seventeen? She'd have to check his file. He'd done very well and would be an asset on future catering gigs, if he was interested.

Servers worked to remove the wedding decorations and move tables back into their usual spaces. Another ran the vacuum. Paige carried her full tub back to the kitchen and set it in line for the dishwasher before moving into the main cooking area. Hector was mopping the floor. The counters and appliances all sparkled.

"Looks like you're almost done."

He nodded. "We started right after the desserts went out. I sent Jorge home when the food was put away. Hope that's all right?"

Technically that wasn't his call to make, but it didn't matter. Not really. "Yeah, sure. Just give me a heads up in the future, in case we end up needing all hands for clean up."

"Sure, sure. Sorry." He dunked the mop into the bucket and wrung it out as he pushed it toward the cleaning supply closet.

"Hey, Hector?"

"Si?"

"Any chance you're free tomorrow night? There's another catering thing that my dad scheduled—I'm still not clear on why, when he knows we're closed on Sundays—but I thought you might be interested in some overtime?"

Hector turned, a tiny smile on his face. He shook his head. "Sorry, but no. My wife has gotten too used to me being home on Sundays to try and explain that to her. Even if it would be extra money."

"All right. Thanks." Well, it'd been a long shot anyway. None of the others were trustworthy enough to handle things on their own. Not yet. And a dinner for two didn't warrant a big crew. Plus, it would probably be fun. She could try out a few new ideas and maybe have a few minutes to sit and read in between courses. There was no reason her own broken heart should keep her from helping nurture someone else's romance.

Paige clutched the steering wheel as she navigated the narrow, twisty road bordering the Virginia side of the Potomac River. Great Falls was beautiful, but only when you knew where you were going. The tall trees and fences that lined the front of the estates blocked not only the best views, but also hidden turns and stop signs. She'd already blown through one. Thankfully no one had been coming from the other directions.

She squinted at the street sign in the distance. Finally. She took the turn and sighed as an enormous white stucco house—mansion, really—came into view. Who did her Dad know who lived here? Friend of a friend, he'd said... so not Dad's friend? That made a little more sense. Still, who could it be? She turned into the long, curving driveway, pulling around the far side of the house like the email her Dad forwarded had asked. *Probably the servant's entrance.*

Paige parked and pulled a large box out of the back seat as the screen door on the side of the house opened.

"You must be Paige, from Season's Bounty, right?"

"That's me. Hi."

"Great." The woman, probably in her late fifties, wore khaki capris and a gauzy black top that swirled around her. "I'll show you where you can set up and get started. There's an outdoor kitchen just over here."

Paige followed the barefoot woman, lugging her box. Hopefully it wasn't far. They passed an octagonal pool the size of her apartment, stairs that led down to tennis courts, and finally arrived at a covered area that could easily accommodate a dinner party for twenty. A granite counter-top formed a large U. Cooktop, grill, and two sinks were all present and accounted for. "Wow."

The woman smiled. "My husband goes a little overboard sometimes, but this was one thing I was fine letting him get just right. We probably don't use it as much as we should, but it's fabulous for parties. There's a refrigerator under the counter on the left, you'll find place settings and table linens in one of the drawers. If you can just pop whatever you use into the dishwasher by the sink and run it when you leave, I'll come down and put everything away tomorrow. I had them set up a table and chairs by the retaining wall. It's a lovely view out over the river. I thought it'd be conducive to a romantic meal. Just follow the path."

"Okay... won't you and your husband be eating?"

She laughed. "Oh, dear. No. He's watching a football game. I don't think I could get him out of the house if it was on fire. Your guest'll be down around six."

"But... " Paige stopped. The woman, who had never introduced herself, was half-way up the stairs to the house already. Fine. Dinner for two mystery guests, coming right up. Step one, set the table. She slid the box of ingredients on the counter and rummaged around in cupboards and drawers for what she needed. There was a crystal vase tucked in with the plates. She turned and eyed the sunflowers and asters in the beds lining the walkways. Maybe.

She scooped up the table decorations and followed the path past a hedge row that separated the covered area from a semi-circular grassy expanse. A small table with two chairs was centered at the edge of the curve. She looked out across the rocky cliff and the river. Her breath caught. *Definitely the right spot for romance.*

Paige set the table, adjusting the angle ever so slightly to improve the view. She put two stems of asters in the vase for a little something extra and nodded. Perfect. Now all she had to do was put together a meal that would make the view pale in comparison.

36

"Are you sure this isn't too casual?" Jackson brushed at the black slacks that he'd paired with a lime green polo.

"She's going to be in catering clothes, right? You don't want to be all fancy in a suit with her in work clothes."

"You sure, Zach? I mean, I also don't want her to think I'm not taking this seriously. Like it's not a special event."

Zach laughed. "You're over-thinking this."

"Totally over-thinking it." Ben crutched into the room and lowered himself to Jackson's bed. "You look fine. And chances are, she's not going to focus on your clothes. I'm going to throw it out, one more time, that this seems risky. What happens if she sees you, dumps soup in your lap, and storms off?"

Jackson frowned. She'd listen to him. She had to. Didn't she? "I'm not going to chase that thought process right now. If she runs off... well, I guess I'll be talking to her Dad about a discount on the meal."

Zach chuckled. "Atta boy. Think positive."

Ben scoffed. "Not that I'm not rooting for you, you understand."

"Yeah. I know. It's a long shot. But it's all I've got."

"We'll be praying." Zach pointed a finger at Jackson. "Don't forget those flowers you bought yesterday. They're stinking up the kitchen."

Jackson laughed and offered a mock salute. "Yes, sir."

Jackson rang the bell and smiled when Marilyn opened the door. "Thank you so much for doing this for me."

Marilyn pulled him into a tight hug. The scent of honeysuckle filled his nose. "Anything for you, Jackson, you know that. You were the brightest student in my class and made the year I took off from running the law firm a worthwhile experiment. Even if it did turn out that I can't stand teaching. Still, if none of that was true, the idea of this?" She fanned her face. "Who can turn down the chance to be part of something so romantic?"

"You think it's romantic?" Jackson swallowed to reintroduce a touch of moisture into his mouth. "It's not idiotic?"

Marilyn chuckled. "Incredibly romantic. And that Paige, I can see why you like her. She's lovely. Seems very down to earth, too, which is good. I snuck out a little while ago, and from what I could smell on the top deck, you're in for a treat."

"Assuming she doesn't dump it in my lap."

"If she does, you come on back up to the house and I'll fix you something." Marilyn pursed her lips. "Do you really think she'd do that?"

He sighed. "I don't know. I want to say no. I'm trying to believe that she feels the same way I do and is just trying to keep from getting hurt. But I just don't know."

Marilyn put her hand on his cheek. "I'm proud of you for taking a big step and putting your heart on the line. You're made of sterner stuff than a man who runs at the first hint of trouble. Just remember that, and you'll be fine."

"Thanks." He took a deep breath, his heart slowing to normal. "Remind me which way I go down so she doesn't see me?"

Paige added a final garnish to the plates and stepped back. Glancing over her shoulder to make sure no one was watching, she tugged her cell out of her pocket and snapped a photo. It was some of the best plating she'd ever done. It'd be good for the catering page on the restaurant website. The client had requested a single course with dessert. Not exactly typical for a romantic meal. Weren't you supposed to want to linger over several plates of food? Or maybe they just didn't want the server coming in and out a lot? It didn't matter. Made her job easier. She'd brought along her book and this was a lovely place to sit and read while she waited to serve dessert. It wasn't as comfortable as being at home, but it was a pretty good second place.

She put a silver cloche over each plate and checked the time. Perfect. She took one plate in each hand and headed down the short path to the clearing. A man stood looking out over the river, his hands in his pockets. Peach roses had been added to the vase of asters, a nice contrast to the purple. A breeze ruffled his hair. Paige's breath caught. He made a striking picture and, in the orange light of the sunset, it looked a little like Jackson. Couldn't be. She breathed in and willed her heart to stop pounding. She glanced to the side. Was she early? Where was the man's date?

She cleared her throat. "Should I take these back to keep them warm?"

The man turned and stepped toward the table. Her eyes widened. "Jackson?"

He nodded. "You can go ahead and put the plates down."

Her stomach sank. It was him. Having a romantic dinner. With someone else. Tears pricked her eyes. True, she'd told him to stop calling, but who knew he had someone else already waiting in the wings? Blinking rapidly, she put the plates in front of each chair and turned to go.

"Paige. Wait."

She stopped but didn't turn. A tear escaped. She brushed it away. "Will your date be here soon? You don't want that to get cold. It won't taste nearly as good."

"She's here."

Paige spun, gaze searching the clearing. She could at least get a look at whoever had replaced her so easily. Then she'd leave. They could get their own dessert. Surely the woman at the main house would understand and be willing to come down and tell them. She scanned the area. There was no one there but Jackson. "Where?"

Jackson closed the difference between them and looked into her eyes. "Right here."

His breath was warm on her face. The slightest hint of peppermint washed over her. She swallowed, a thousand and one bees buzzing in her ears. "Me? You did this for me?"

His arms slipped around her. "You told me not to call. But I wanted—needed—to talk to you one more time."

Paige's head spun. Heat spread up from where he held her and her lips tingled in anticipation. She swallowed, but her voice was still a croak. "So talk."

His lips curved, dimple winking. "Why don't we sit down? I happen to know the chef is very talented."

She blinked as he released her and pulled out a chair. She sat, frowning at the covered plate. This wasn't for her, it was for some romantic date—a friend of a— "You got my Dad in on this?"

Jackson removed the cover from his plate and breathed in the steam as it curled into the evening sky. "It was his idea, actually. I bumped into him at the restaurant. He talked me out of my plan and suggested this, instead."

Paige turned to look out over the river, wrestling with Jackson's words. Her dad knew? And he talked to Jackson enough to give this his blessing. So... Dad at least thought whatever Jackson had to say must be worth hearing. It also meant that Dad understood the feelings she'd been trying to ignore. She uncovered her plate and picked up her fork. "Okay."

Jackson chuckled and cut into the beef tenderloin. "I could give you the full explanation of the newspaper debacle, and I will if you want me to. But before I do that, I want to say I'm sorry. I don't know what I should have done differently—if there even was anything I could have done to get the Senator to pull the story—but I should have told you."

"Stop." Paige reached across the table and rested her fingers on the top of his hand. "You said everything you needed to say that day at my apartment. I just wasn't ready to hear it yet. I'm sorry you quit your job."

"Don't be. It was time for a change. Maybe I hadn't realized it, but now I do. You made me rethink, and remember, why I wanted to be in politics in the first place. I want to make a difference, to work to have the laws of the land align with the law of God. To put even a splash of substance back into the culture and help steer us back toward being a Christian country. Working for Senator Carson, I'd lost that. More than that, though, you helped me remember that it's not just about government. The littlest things I do can make a big difference, too."

Paige looked down at her plate. So much from one argument? "Still... I could have handled it better."

"I think we both can say that." He turned his hand over, catching her fingers and lacing them with his. "I want a second chance, Paige. Please, tell me it's not too late."

She swallowed. He was worth the risk, no question. No amount of busyness or force of will had erased him from her heart. Paige nodded. "We can start again."

Jackson pushed back his chair and stood, walking around to her. "I don't want to start over, though I will if that's what you want."

Paige frowned. "What?"

Jackson gave her hand a light tug. She stood, her chair tipping over. He wrapped his arms around her and lowered his lips so they almost touched hers. "Starting over means going backwards. I want us to go forward, Paige. To pick up where we left off, stronger for having weathered a storm and confident in the knowledge that we can work through what comes our way. Maybe it won't always be smooth sailing... "

She chuckled. "That's a guarantee. But you know what? I'd rather weather stormy seas with you than skate easily through life on my own."

Jackson touched his lips to hers. Electricity sizzled through her. As it faded, it left something deeper, and much more substantial, in its wake. Love? It was probably too soon to tell. But she was looking forward to finding out for sure.

Author's Note

Thank you for reading *A Splash of Substance!* I hope that you enjoyed getting to know Paige and Jackson. I would appreciate it if you'd help others enjoy it too by leaving a review on Amazon and Goodreads and telling your friends about it. Any success my books have is owed to readers like you who take the time to tell others about my stories. Thank you, from the bottom of my heart. Paige and Jackson will continue as side characters in the next two novels in the Taste of Romance series: *A Pinch of Promise* (June 2015), *A Dash of Daring* (November 2015), *A Handful of Hope* (Spring 2016), and *A Tidbit of Trust* (Fall 2017).

Living in the Washington D.C. area, politics are a somewhat inescapable part of life. I believe it's imperative that Christians do what they can to not only live out our principles and convictions, but work to promote those same Biblical tenets as the law of the land. At a minimum, I hope Paige and Jackson have encouraged you to continue in serious prayer for your leaders at all times.

I continue to owe a huge debt of gratitude to my husband and sons for giving me the time to write, my sister for her unflinching support and encouragement, and my critique partner Jan Elder for catching all the time I use the same word six times in two paragraphs. Thanks also to Valerie Comer for letting me mention the setting of her Farm Fresh Romances, Green Acre Farms. It was reading her novels that first got me thinking about sustainability in even the smallest way. If you're looking for another good series, hers are delightful.

More than anything, I'm grateful that God continues to give me words and makes it possible for me to write them down.

I'd love to hear from you! You can connect with me on Facebook (www.Facebook.com/ElizabethMaddrey) my webpage (www.ElizabethMaddrey.com) or via email. To stay current with news and occasional giveaways, please subscribe to my newsletter (links on Facebook or my webpage).

Sources for Additional Reading

If the topic of Christians in politics is one that interests you, here is a small sampling of sources to consider looking into.

- Anderson, Bruce et al. Watchmen on the Walls: Pastors Equipping Christians for their Civil Duties. 2014.

- Barton, David. 2014. www.ipledgesunday.com

- Colson, Charles. Against the Night: Living in the New Dark Ages. 1999.

- McDowell, Stephen. "Choosing Godly Officials." Providential Perspective. Vol. 28, No. 1, October 2014.

- Myers, Jeff. The Political Animal. 2012.

- Myers, Jeff (presenter). The Political Animal. Summit Ministries, 2014. Video course.

- Genesis 6, Genesis 9, Romans 13:1, II Kings 20:19, Esther 4:1-17, Judges 6:25-32, Daniel 1-12, and Acts 16:37.

- Reagan, Ronald. Speaking My Mind: Selected Speeches with Personal Reflections. Simon & Schuster Audio, 2004. CD compilation.

About the Author

Elizabeth Maddrey began writing stories as soon as she could form the letters properly and has never looked back. Though her practical nature and love of computers, math, and organization steered her into computer science at Wheaton College, she always had one or more stories in progress to occupy her free time. This continued through a Master's program in Software Engineering, several years in the computer industry, teaching programming at the college level, and a Ph.D. in Computer Technology in Education. When she isn't writing, Elizabeth is a voracious consumer of books and has mastered the art of reading while undertaking just about any other activity.

Elizabeth is the author of more than ten books, both fiction and non-fiction. She lives in the suburbs of Washington, D.C. with her husband and their two incredibly active little boys.

Turn the page for a sneak peek at

A Pinch of Promise

Taste of Romance, Book Two

Rebecca Fisher pulled up her next appointment on her tablet. Her breath caught. Ben Taylor. The image of sandy brown hair and pale blue eyes flashed across her thoughts. Silly. There were probably hundreds—thousands, even—of people in the world with that name. Besides, Ben had never mentioned wanting to live in the D.C. area. And even over the course of a summer, it had been clear that Ben was going to get what he wanted.

Pushing away the ghosts of what might have been, Rebecca strolled through the sprawling therapy room, weaving between weight machines and treadmills before crossing an expanse of floor mats where patients were stretching, some with the assistance of other physical therapists, resistance bands, and medicine balls. Conversations, grunts, groans, and the occasional cry of pain ricocheted off the mirrored walls. She smiled and crossed into the reception area.

"Mr. Taylor?" Rebecca's gaze drifted over the handful of people waiting. Her heart raced as a man about her age, complete with sandy brown hair, wobbled out of a chair.

"That's me." Ben adjusted the position of his crutches and inched his way across the room.

Rebecca pursed her lips, watching his progress. He hadn't been doing the range of motion exercises the surgeon had sent home with him. And he was babying his knee. "When was your surgery?"

"Friday."

Three days. She nodded. Not as bad as she'd thought. "All right. Been doing your exercises?"

Ben hunched his shoulders. "Trying to."

She gestured for him to go ahead of her through the door into the main therapy room. "I know it hurts. But you want to get that full range of motion back, you'll need to do more than try. I'll help. I'm Rebecca, by the way. We'll start with a focus on getting your knee extension back. For now, if you're not here at therapy or doing your exercises, keep the immobilizer on and use your crutches. I'll let you know when you can stop either one."

"Okay. And the swelling?"

"It'll go down, don't worry. I'll send you home with some instructions for that, as well." Rebecca stopped in front of a straight-backed chair positioned against the wall on the far side of the mats. Pale blue eyes met hers and the moisture in her mouth evaporated. "Have a seat."

When Ben was settled, she set his crutches out of reach and helped him remove the immobilizer. "Now what?"

"Now we see how well you can extend your leg. If you want to grab the sides of the chair, that sometimes helps. Straighten your leg as far as you can."

Grimacing, Ben lifted his leg, managing a solid forty-five degree angle.

"How'd you tear your ACL?" Rebecca knelt by Ben's leg and lifted.

Ben sucked in a breath. "Uh. Football with the guys after church. My roommate played semi-pro, so he's always trying to get a game going. I was stupid and caved."

He hadn't been athletic at camp, either. It had to be him. Did he recognize her? He wasn't acting like it. Though it wasn't as if she expected him to be overjoyed anyway. Not after the way she'd vanished after camp. Would he understand if she explained? "Did you at least have fun for a little while?"

"First play."

She winced, biting back a laugh. "Oooh."

He shrugged. "I've never been particularly athletic. I figured I'd get injured one way or another, but I hadn't banked on it being this bad. At least it gets me out of having to play football again. Ever."

"Go ahead and put your foot down. Feeling okay?"

Ben nodded.

"Ok, straighten your leg again, let's see if we can go a little farther this time. While you do, tell me about yourself."

"To help take my mind off the pain?"

"Yeah. Plus we're going to spend a bit of time together while you recuperate. Just pretend I'm your hairdresser."

"Getting my hair cut doesn't hurt like this." Ben ground his teeth together. "Um. Let's see. I work for a hunger relief agency, primarily helping organize money and food drives that churches put together throughout the year."

Maybe not exactly what he'd been planning in college, but definitely close. "That sounds like a worthwhile job. Fulfilling. Go ahead and lower your foot."

"It is. I like knowing that what I do makes a difference for people in countries where food isn't as abundant as it is here."

She nodded. Making a difference had been her dream, once. "Let's go one more time and then we'll spend some time working on that swelling and I'll get you some instructions to supplement what the surgeon probably sent home with you."

"Okay." He cocked his head to the side. "You look familiar. Have we met?

**

Rebecca tossed her keys into the bowl by the front door and dropped her backpack under the small entry-way table. Home. She'd moved to the townhouse in January, but nine months later, she still got a tingle when she walked through the door. Her own space. No neighbors above and below, no roommates. Just the one shared wall, since she'd managed to score an end unit, and the older lady who lived next door was a dear. Maybe it got a little loud when all her grandchildren came to visit, but that wasn't too often, and more often than not, they invited her over anyway. Best of all? She'd done it all on her own. Mom had offered her a loan for a down payment when she'd moved out here... but it was so much better having saved up her own money rather than taking a handout.

Her phone rang. She dragged it out of her pocket and crossed the living room to the kitchen as she answered. "Hey, Mom. How'd you know I was just thinking about you?"

Her mother's laugh made her smile. "Mothers know these things. Plus, it's Monday and you just got home from work, so you knew I'd be calling."

Rebecca took a bottle of sparkling mineral water out of the fridge and twisted off the top. "There's that, too. How are things at home?"

"Oh, you know your father. He's absorbed in his latest book and planning a big speaking tour around its launch. They've asked him to be the keynote at four regional youth rallies this spring as well."

"He must be in heaven." Rebecca took a long drink of water. Why did it still bother her? Especially now, when the stories he used were completely made up?

"Pretty close to it. The first one is in D.C." Her mom's voice lifted at the end, asking an unspoken question.

Rebecca sighed. It had to happen sooner or later. "You know I'd love you to stay here. I have plenty of room."

"Oh. No, that's not it. We'll stay at the hotel they're using for the convention. But... do you think you could squeeze out some time to come down..."

"And let people ogle the bad-girl-turned-good?" Rebecca set the water down on her coffee table. "Mom... I'll come take you sightseeing, have dinner, we can hang out, whatever. But please... please don't ask me to be the poster-child again."

"Ah, Becky, I'm sorry. I promised your father I'd ask. But I also warned him that I didn't think you'd agree."

"How'd he take that?"

"About as well as you'd expect. But he'll get over it."

Probably use it to fabricate some new story about her misspent life. "You sure?"

"Of course. You haven't appeared with him since you left for college. Honestly, I'm not sure why he thought you would just because we were going to be in your new hometown. I think, maybe it's his way of trying to reconnect with you."

Rebecca scoffed. "He has my phone number."

Her mother sighed. "I know, Becky. And you have his. I hate being caught in the middle between you two."

"Mom..."

"Don't get me wrong, I understand why you did what you did. I think, in his heart, he does too, now. But it's too late to undo the damage without ruining all the good he's done—and continues to do. Which isn't fair to you. I'm sorry, Becky."

Heaviness settled on her chest. Had she done the right thing?

"Let's put that aside and talk about something more pleasant. How did your date on Friday go?"

Rebecca gave a mirthless laugh. "I thought you wanted to talk about something more pleasant?"

"No second date in the works, then?"

"He might think so, but no." Ben's face flashed into her thoughts and her heartbeat accelerated. She cleared her throat. "Mom... do you remember when I worked at the camp in Colorado Springs for the summer?"

"Of course. Right after your freshman year. That's when you got the idea to change your name, step away from the notoriety your Dad was forcing on you. Why?"

Rebecca reached for the bottle and took a long swallow of the fizzy water. "Did I ever mention Ben?"

"Hmm. I don't think so. Why?"

She hadn't told her mom about him? She told her mother everything. Now. It hadn't always been that way. She sighed. "Ben Taylor was the counselor for our brother cabin, so he and I ended up doing a lot together over the course of the summer. Even when we had time off, we gravitated toward one another."

"You had feelings for him. I can hear it in your voice. What happened?"

Rebecca squeezed her eyes shut. "I never told him who I was. That summer at camp, I was just Marie Fischer. Not Becky

MacDonald, infamous daughter of the famous pastor-turned-parenting-expert."

"I didn't realize you used your middle name in addition to my maiden name."

"I wanted a clean break, with no way for anyone to connect me to bad-girl-Becky."

"Oh, sweetheart. No one called you that."

Rebecca gave a sardonic laugh. "Mom. They still do. Every time Dad's in the press there's the big 'where is she now' debate about me. Last one had me tucked away in rehab in Switzerland."

"They didn't."

She shook her head. Mom was Dad's biggest supporter, but she stayed out of his business entirely too well. "They did. I think that was about the time you were in Ghana supervising the opening of the new orphanage. I still don't understand how you manage to keep Dad from writing his name across everything the foundation does."

"Give your father a bit of credit, Bec. I know the two of you have your differences, but you know he's a good man."

Rebecca winced at the steel in her mom's voice. "All right, you're right. Sorry. I just wish..."

"I know, honey. Me too. I should have stepped in sooner."

That would've been nice. But at this point there was little point in playing the what-if game. And, all things considered, Rebecca had made a good life for herself. One where Becky MacDonald had no place and cast no shadow.

Her mother cleared her throat. "So...Ben?"

"He's my newest physical therapy patient."

More Books by Elizabeth Maddrey

Contemporary Romance:

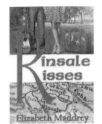

"Kinsale Kisses: An Irish Romance"

She wants stability. He wants spontaneity. What they need is each other.

Colin O'Bryan cashed out of the software company he founded and started a new life in Ireland. Content to wander from town to town as a traveling musician, he had no goals beyond healing from the betrayals that led to his career change, and finding his next gig.

After the death of her parents, Rachel Sullivan hoped her aunt's B&B on the Southern coast of Ireland would be a place for her to settle and start a new life. Though she can't deny the sparks in Colin's touch, his lack of concern for hearth and home leave her torn.

Can this free-spirited minstrel win her heart or will Rachel choose roots and stability over love?

"Wisdom to Know" ('Grant Us Grace' series Book 1)

Is there sin that love can't cover?

Lydia Brown has taken just about every wrong turn she could find. When an abortion leaves her overwhelmed by guilt, she turns to drugs to escape her pain. After a single car accident lands her in the hospital facing DUI charges, Lydia is forced to reevaluate her choices.

Kevin McGregor has been biding his time since high school when he heard God tell him that Lydia Brown was the woman he would marry. In the aftermath of Lydia's accident, Kevin must come to grips with the truth about her secret life.

While Kevin works to convince himself and God that loving Lydia is a mistake, Lydia struggles to accept the feelings she has for Kevin, though she fears her sin may be too much for anyone to forgive.

"Courage to Change" ('Grant Us Grace' series Book 2)

Should you be willing to change for love?

When Phil Reid became a Christian and stopped drinking, his hard-partying wife, Brandi, divorced him. Reeling and betrayed, he becomes convinced Christians should never remarry, and resolves to guard his heart.

Allison Vasak has everything in her life under control, except for one thing. Her heart is irresistibly drawn to fellow attorney and coworker, Phil. Though she knows his history and believes that women should not initiate relationships, she longs to make her feelings known.

As Phil and Allison work closely together to help a pregnant teen, both must re-evaluate their convictions. But when Brandi discovers Phil's new relationship, she decides that though she doesn't want him, no one else can have him either. Can Phil and Allison's love weather the chaos Brandi brings into their lives?

"Serenity to Accept" ('Grant Us Grace' series Book 3)

Is there an exception to every rule? Karin Reid has never had much use for God. There's been too much pain in her life for her to accept that God is anything other than, at best, disinterested or, at worst, sadistic. Until she meets Jason Garcia. After his own mistakes of the past, Jason is committed to dating only Christians. He decides to bend his rule for Karin, as long as she comes to church with him. As their friendship grows, both will have to decide if they'll accept the path God has for them, even if it means losing each other.

"Joint Venture" – A 'Grant Us Grace' Novella

Laura Willis is busy planning her wedding to Ryan when she catches him cheating. Again. This time with her best friend. She throws her fist, and her ring, in his face and immerses herself in work at Brenda's House of Hair. But the salon is awash in drama too as Brenda cuts corners and goes on a rampage.

Laura's coworker hairstylist, Matt Stephenson, is searching for other employment options and a new place to live. Deciding to take a risk, he determines to open his own salon and invites Laura to partner with him.

Can their friendship survive the undertaking or will this joint venture be more than either of them bargained for?

Women's Fiction:

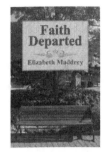

"Faith Departed" ('Remnants' series Book 1)

Starting a family was supposed to be easy.

Twin sisters June and July have never encountered an obstacle they couldn't overcome. Married just after graduating college, the girls and their husbands remained a close-knit group. Now settled and successful, the next logical step is children. But as the couples struggle to conceive, each must reconcile the goodness of God with their present suffering. Will their faith be strong enough to triumph in the midst of trial?

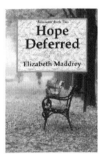

"Hope Deferred" ('Remnants' series Book 2)

Can pursuit of a blessing become a curse?

June and July and their husbands have spent the last year trying to start a family and now they're desperate for answers. As one couple works with specialists to see how medicine can help them conceive, the other must fight to save their marriage. Will their deferred hope leave them heart sick, or start them on the path to the fulfillment of their dreams?

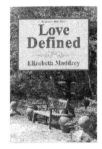

"Love Defined" ('Remnants' series Book 3

Dreams Change. Plans Fail.

July and Gareth have reached the end of their infertility treatment options. With conflicting feelings on adoption, they struggle to discover common ground in their marriage. Meanwhile, July's twin sister, June, and her husband, Toby, are navigating the uncertainties of adoption and the challenges of new parenthood. How much stretching can their relationships endure before they snap?

Non-Fiction

"A Walk in the Valley: Christian Encouragement for Your Journey Through Infertility" by Julie Arduini, Heidi Glick, Elizabeth Maddrey, Kym McNabney, Paula Mowry, and Donna Winters

Everyone's journey through infertility is different. Even women who have the same physical problems will have different courses of treatment, different responses, and different emotional ups and downs as they walk this path. But we also have so much in common: the hurt, anger, frustration, pain, sorrow, hope and joy that we have experienced along the way.

We are women who have experienced infertility. Some of us have gone on to conceive, others have adopted, and others remain childless. All of us have found peace in the loving arms of our Father God at the end of our journey. We want to share our experiences and thoughts with you. It is our hope and prayer that you'll be encouraged.

This devotional workbook starts with how each woman discovered her infertility, then explores the diagnostic testing pursued, how they processed the official diagnosis, what decisions had to be explored regarding treatment, their experiences during infertility treatment (including pregnancy, miscarriage, and childbirth), and finishes with their experiences in remaining childless, adoption, foster care, child sponsorship, and the emotional healing regardless of the outcome of their infertility journey.

Each devotional has a Scripture focus and questions for thought and discussion.